I0627478

Bone DUST

ROCK HILLS BOOK 2

AWARD-WINNING AUTHOR

DD LORENZO

DEDICATION

For my mother,
who always asks me
to tell her a story

NOTE TO READERS

Dear Reader,

Bone Dust touches on sensitive subject matter in the areas of child abuse, rape, and human trafficking. This may be triggering for some. Read with caution.

CHAPTER ONE

Ian

The bar reeks of old smoke, the smell lingering from a time long ago when the promise of wealth lured men away from their homes and loved ones. The scent has penetrated the ancient hardwood, invading every splinter to mix with the aromas of desperation, hopes, and dreams. Dings and scratches mar the unpolished planks and, given the history of the area, old spurs and boot heels seem the most likely culprits for the divots. This building dates back to the 1800's and, as my gaze wanders the room, I take it all in. I can only imagine the goings on here during the gold rush days.

Though this area of the country held the most famous promise of fortune buried within the rocky landscape, it wasn't the first place in the United States that suggested riches to men seeking a better life.

Library shelves now hold dusty books that chronicle tales of those prospectors, some stories taller than the imagination. A few men were lucky, but most lost everything including the families they left behind.

As I cross the room and head toward the bar, my gaze drops to the floor. I'm certain some of the dark and blotchy masses beneath the soles of my boots are bloodstains. A sad remnant of a man's life now permanently etched in validation of his quest. That's what happens when money becomes your god. You find yourself at crossroads that kill friendships and expose a man's rotten core. I feel sorry for the bastards who found themselves on the bullet end of another man's gun.

Love of money is the root of all evil.

Words my momma said drift through my mind. She recited them whenever my daddy left us to travel for work. His job required him to be away more than he was home. Once he was gone Momma played with my emotions, telling me he was absent because he only cared about his money and everything it brought him, while in the next breath, she said he worked so hard because he loved us above everything.

My strongest recollections are of Daddy walking out the door while Momma clung to him. I hid in a corner as she'd plead with him not to leave her, but he always did. Once he left, Momma would sob until she had no more tears, making herself sick. Then, spent and defeated, she'd take my hand and lead me to what she called our 'secret place'. In truth, it was her huge, four-poster bed. She'd put the covers over each one of those posts, constructing a hideaway fortress where she said we'd be safe. The problem, I realized later in life, was really in my mother's imagination and her solution was always a fine whiskey mixed with rock candy at the bottom of her pretty teacups.

The scene consumes my thoughts and I think about how like my father I'd become. How the love of money, and the vices it bought, nearly killed me. I was young when Momma died, but her influence will forever be the words she tattooed on my heart, and they are as real a legacy as the scars my daddy's belt left on my body.

I shake off the memories and, instead, concentrate on the woman performing on the stage. Beneath a lone spotlight, she's perched on a high back barstool, her legs crossed as she plays the weathered wood guitar resting in her lap. A blue and white checked cushion peeks out from beneath her rear end, and a lone microphone mounted on a stand is a breath away from her lips.

An empty seat at the end of the bar beckons me and I lower myself onto it to take everything in. Emblazoned on the wall behind the singer is a logo that I can't quite make out. The bright lights spilling against her distort the image in the shadow her body casts, and yet, that same white light illuminates her. With her head bowed, it showcases slivers of snowy highlights within a curtain of thick blonde hair. The strands fall over her shoulders, cascading like a waterfall, and then disappear as they puddle somewhere on her lap behind the guitar.

"How long's she been playing here?" I pitch the question to the busty strawberry-blonde barmaid, keeping my voice low enough so as not to disturb the patrons at the tables not far from where I'm sitting. She draws closer and I can't help but notice how her ribbed tank top clings to her massive tits.

The size of her bust corrupts the image on the front of her shirt. I make no secret of the fact I'm curious as I stare, which she notes with a sly smile. I can tell she likes the attention. Her emerald-green eyes follow my line of sight. As she looks down, she plucks the bottom of the design with red, dagger-shaped fingernails, and pulls the material away from her skin. Now that I can see it better, I recognize it as the same logo that's on the stage wall; a cigar-smoking bulldog wearing a spiked collar and Aviator sunglasses.

"It's a badass dog, isn't it?" she asks, with a hiked brow and a cheeky smile.

"Sure is."

The smirk that slithers across my lips is because the dog's sunglasses bulge big and round right over the woman's perky nipples. The shirt's tight enough to accentuate her curves and capture the attention of any man in her vicinity. I'm no different. My cock stirs so I divert my attention by glancing over her shoulder to see the wait staff working the floor. All the women are wearing the same top as the barmaid. It's like I'm at the dog version of Hooters. My smile raises half an inch higher. My friend Sam Weston is a wise ass and a smart businessman. He's marketing his *Mad Dog Run* brand brilliantly.

"So, about the singer …" I jut my chin toward the stage.

"Her name's Savannah Grace," she answers.

"She play every night?"

"Just a few nights a week."

The woman leans against the bar top, supporting her ample chest with petite forearms that practically disappear beneath all that boobage. Her stance offers a little peep show and I'm able to see more than a glimpse of cleavage. I'm not new to this game but I haven't played it in a while. When our band, Boundless Hearts, performed, more than enough females flashed their tits from the audience hoping to get a backstage pass, and a chance to meet the band's members.

The woman steals a quick glance between me and the stage, and a knowing, shit-eating grin creeps into her gloss-covered lips.

"You like her." With an eyebrow quirk, she speaks as if she can read my mind.

"Do you?" I toss back.

She straightens up. "Savannah Grace's been here for a few months now, and there isn't anyone who doesn't like her, including me."

"And why is that?" I push.

"Because Savannah is good, and she packs in the place. A packed house means happy customers. Happy customers tip bigger. All of us love that," she says in a matter-of-fact tone. "Besides, Savannah's good people." Distracted by more customers approaching the bar, she tips her head. "What can I get for you?"

"Coke. The bigger the better with lots of ice."

"You got it."

She turns away and I see the back of her is as shapely as the front. Her tight ass sways like a back porch swing in a breeze. I shake my head and chuckle under my breath. She's funny, sweet, and a blatant flirt. *Perfect barmaid.*

I shift my view to the stage. *Savannah Grace, huh?* It hits me that I don't recall Sam saying the singer's name or, for that matter, ever mentioning if it was a girl or a guy. All he said was he wanted me to come to his bar and hear his favorite performer. As I listen to the song, I can see why he likes her so much but am clueless as to why he wants my opinion.

Since I disappeared from the music industry, I'm not sure my thoughts are worth much these days, but she's good. The song she sings is slow and easy and it compliments her tone well. There's a seductive quality to her voice. It's breathy and kind of whispery on this song. She reminds me of Diana Krall or Melody Gardot or even Clare Bowen. The audience is captured. They're quiet; almost reverent. They probably have no idea how much they're into her, but I see it, and I get it. It's all about connecting with those who pay your bills. I know this well from my days with Boundless Hearts.

As lead singer of the hottest band around, and in

typical rockstar fashion, I was as lewd on the stage as I could be without getting arrested. This woman attracts an audience much different than the ones we played to. I got away with almost anything then. Women loved when I shoved my crotch in their faces. I was as vulgar as sin and this woman is the total opposite. She sits so pretty and croons so sweetly. She delivers the melody as if she's giving them a beautifully wrapped gift.

Quietly, I observe the body language of the audience. It speaks volumes. Some people are leaning in toward the stage, while others are so relaxed, they recline easily in their chairs with legs stretched out comfortably in front of them. Whether Savannah Grace realizes it or not, she's working them well, and that means money in the bank for Sam.

"You want to start a tab?" The barmaid suspends my drink in mid-air as she flips a coaster down on the bar. I reach into my front pocket and toss a twenty-dollar bill at her.

"I don't need a tab. Keep the change."

She eyes the bill, then retrieves it. "Thanks."

"No problem," I answer. What's your name?"

The flirty smile is back, and it lights up her eyes. "Jeri."

"Short for Geraldine?"

"Nope." She shakes her head. "Jerilyn—but only my mother and grandmother call me that. What about you?"

"Ian." I stretch out my arm and extend my hand.

"Nice to meet you, Ian." Jeri takes it and gives a

featherlight shake. "Is this your first time at Mad Dog? I don't remember seeing you here before."

I nod. "Yep. I'm supposed to meet Sam."

Jeri glances at the clock on the wall. "He should be here anytime now. Let me know if you need anything." She pauses, leans in, and bats her long, fake lashes at me like they're butterfly wings. "And I won't say anything to anyone that I recognize who you are."

My eyes widen slightly as I search her face. Her expression is playful, as if she enjoys having this little secret between us. "Thanks. I appreciate that."

She gives a quick nod as she moves away from me toward the other customers, and I set my attention elsewhere.

The air is thick, causing a quick melt of the frosted mug. A circle of sweat beads roll to the bottom, and as I lift the glass, it sticks to the cardboard coaster. Almost instantly the coaster falls and rattles against the bar top. I pick it up, hold it, and inspect it. Again, *Mad Dog.*

I couldn't read the writing on Jeri's shirt but can clearly see the bar's tagline on this piece. In a semicircle above the dog's head are the words: *Where the music kicks ass and Mad Dogs Run.*

A smile plays on my lips. This bulldog *is* Sam; tough, cigar-smoking, and sunglass-wearing.

I glance at the clock on the wall then reach into my back pocket. When I pull out my cell phone, I check the screen. No missed calls. *Where the hell is he?*

"You all are familiar with this next song." Savannah's voice diverts my attention. "When I begin, I *dare* you not to think about puppies." She gives a little laugh and a wink.

Puppies?

I'm perplexed and my brows pull together but as soon as she strums the first few chords, I grin. There isn't anyone who hasn't heard Sarah McLachlan's "Angel". The song is played ad nauseam, but the most popular use has been for a public service commercial as an appeal to animal lovers. As pitifully mistreated dogs and cats pull at heartstrings with their sad, silver-dollar-sized eyes, it plays in the background—and it hits the mark for the charity.

"She's something, isn't she?" The deep, coffee-rich baritone hits my ear just as a heavy-handed slap connects with my back. "How you doing, Amigo?"

I lean back. "Where the fuck have you been?"

His eyes snap wide as he pulls back. "Who are you, my mother?" Sam scoffs, then smiles. I draw my spine against the wooden chair back as he leans into me. "So, what do you think? Getting your fill of our Savannah Grace?"

"I am. She's pretty good." I nod.

"Damn straight, she's good. She wouldn't be singing' at my bar if she weren't." He looks over my shoulder. "I see Jerilyn took care of you. Good."

My brow pinches. "She told me only her mother and grandmother call her Jerilyn."

"Do I look like a woman?" He issues a deadpan stare. "By the way, I got to ask; you alright being here? Because, if you aren't comfortable, get on home."

As my AA/NA sponsor, Sam's right to be concerned. No sane, recovering, alcoholic, addict would hang out in a bar but then, I lost my sanity long ago. "I'm good."

My assurance pleases him, and he bobs his head. "Good to hear. I'd never be one to ask a man to put himself in a place where he'd be tempted beyond his limits, and you'd never lead me to believe you could stay here if you couldn't."

"No worries, my friend. I haven't had as much as a sip since the night I OD'd."

"Well then, I'm satisfied. It's been a couple of years for you. I'm sure a near-death experience has made you evaluate how drinking and drugs affected you, but you never know what might trigger a person, and I wouldn't want to chance someone's sobriety for the sake of being in my bar." Confidently, he nods.

"Yeah, though that night scared the shit out of me, I've worked too long and too hard to get to where I am with my life. I'm bull-headed, but I'm not a fool."

"Everybody's different, Ian. I'm the same as you. I haven't had a drink in over fifteen years, and I'm in this bar nearly every night." He clamps his hand on my shoulder and the move reassures me that I always have someone in my corner if I feel I'm going to fall off the wagon. I have no doubt that, if I need him, Sam is there for me.

He looks toward a doorway at the other end of the bar. "I've got to check some things in the kitchen. Keep listening to Savi, and I'll be back in a few minutes."

Savi, huh? He calls Jeri by her given name, and Savannah by a nickname. The man's full of contradictions.

I watch him go. Once he disappears behind the swinging door, I tune back in to Savannah. Somehow, she looks familiar, but I'm thinking it's a coincidence. Looking at her I see a glimpse of my Momma. Her name was Susannah, and her hair was nearly the same length and color.

Momma didn't play an instrument, but she had a soft, lyrical voice, and was a gifted storyteller. She'd regale all kinds of tales, complete with dramatic gestures and voice inflections. She told me stories of the devils who chased her and the angels who saved her. As we hid beneath blankets of makeshift angel wings, she said the canopy "kept the devils away". Every day she reminded me that "we're all sinners" and the enemy was "a lion seeking to devour us". She scared the bejesus out of me with her talk but told me not to be afraid. She said we were protected by invisible warriors; angels carrying swords made of lightning bolts. Unfortunately for both of us, the demons found momma. Years later, they found me.

Applause cuts through my ancient memories with a rusty blade.

"Y'all are great. Thank you so much." Savannah's smile is so wide that I can almost feel her joy. She flips her hair over her shoulder, revealing a slender, swan-like neck. Her movements are graceful, dainty, and sweet. She grips the guitar neck, clutching it in a soft embrace, and as she sings Aerosmith's "Crazy", the knot between my shoulders unravels. I drift into a relaxed state along with the captivated crowd. It's been a long time since I've been out to hear live music. Not only do I like Savannah's voice, but she's also easy on the eyes.

I roll my shoulders as a wave of images carries me. When I first sang this song with the band, we were debuting the group by playing at our high school dance. Eventually, we took the music world by storm, but I still recall the time when we were just kids and not rockstars.

"I go crazy, crazy, crazy for you baby ..."

She's good. *Really* good. Even Steven Tyler would approve.

When Savannah turns her head in my direction, I feel a pinch in my chest and a tightening at my zipper, and I'll not offer one bit of repentance for my depraved thoughts. I'm not sure I've ever seen a woman with a more ethereal quality. Flawless.

"Like an angel, baby ..."

Momma's words once again filter through my thoughts and I shake off a chill from the grave. This much I know for sure; no matter how pretty or sweet I find Savannah Grace to be, she'd do well to keep her distance from me because, while she may be an angel in human form, I'm as damn close to a devil as she'll ever see.

CHAPTER TWO

Savannah

On a wooden stool beside me sits an empty water bottle. My throat is bone dry. The crowd's larger than normal, and it's hot outside. All that body heat, combined with the temperature, is making it unbearable. I'm sticky and gross. Trails of sweat are racing down my spine, and my blouse feels like it's plastered to my back.

"Folks, it's time for me to take a short break. Thank you all for coming out tonight to Mad Dog Run. My name's Savannah Grace. Please, refresh your drinks and be sweet to your servers. I'll be back soon with some more music."

Twisting my arm behind me, I pluck at the fabric to pull it away from my skin. As I stand, I can feel my skirt doing the same to my legs. I need something, more air conditioning, maybe? Or, at least, a fan. I need to talk to Sam. I can't be melting in front of the customers.

As if he reads my thoughts, Sam catches my eye with a wave of his hand. *Good.* Maybe he can get one of the guys to find something in the storeroom that will help, and they can put it on the stage before my break is over. I return his gesture, and he nods.

As I lean my guitar against the chair, I snatch my purse. The underside of my hair feels as gross as my clothes. Reaching inside my bag for the ever-present claw clip, I gather the mass of strands and pull them high on my head. After testing the mess to ensure it's secure, I grab the travel-size body mist I keep in an inside pocket and pump the spray around me for a few light-scented spritzes. Instantly the aroma of vanilla and wildflowers punch the air and, I hope, disguise any perspiration stinkiness.

The space between the bar and the stage isn't a great distance but, it's far enough to hinder my view when I'm performing. There's no mistaking who Sam is but, as I close the gap between us, I make out a new face and my heart stops.

Ian Stanton? What the hell?!

An instantaneous tightening occurs in my chest and invisible bands make it difficult to breathe. After a second or two, I force in some air, sucking in the necessary oxygen to clear my head and keep myself composed.

"Hey, Sam." I quickly plaster on a smile.

His wide grin greets me. He then gestures to the

man sitting beside him with a sweeping wave of his hand. "I got a surprise for ya; Miss Savannah Grace, this here's Ian Stanton."

My body responds on its own by way of quickened breaths and a tripping heart. I don't allow my smile to waver but quickly take control of my mindset and lock down my emotions.

"It's nice to meet you, Mr. Stanton." My tone is pleasant, belying my shock. Other than exchanging pleasantries, I don't feel equipped to hold meaningful conversation. I need an escape to calm my scattered thoughts, so I focus my attention on the Ladies' Room door and issue an apologetic look between the two men. "If y'all will excuse me." I make a quick escape. Oh, how I wish I could sprint away, but that would be much too obvious. After what seems like an eternity, I reach my destination and vanish behind the heavy door.

Jezus. Why is he here?

I snatch a breath to steady my jumbled nerves and close my eyes as I lean my back against the door's faded green paint. *Why now?* It's been four years since I've seen his face and, in a few seconds, my thoughts run amuck. Chastising myself for the uneasiness I feel, I snatch images from my younger years. That time in my life threatens to corrupt my composure and I can't let that happen while I'm singing.

My hands shake. My knees do the same. And to think I was once completely in love with Ian—or so I imagined. He was my rockstar infatuation. My wild dream husband. Though it seems like a lifetime, it wasn't so long ago. Back when my life was still silly and free.

I scrape my nails against the peeling paint as I push away from the door. Slipping inside a vacant stall, I throw the toggle latch and drop down to the seat. A rush of panic hit me like a wet blanket when I realized who he was. With measured breaths, the weight drifts away and I settle back into my skin from what can only be described as an out-of-body experience.

My blurred vision clears and I blankly stare at messages scratched into the stall door and my eyes catch a message that reads "I love Ian." A crystal-clear memory of a Boundless Hearts concert surfaces. A night of birthday craziness with my best friend, Candace, and an unforgettable twenty-four hours later that traded a happy memory for a tragic one.

My breath hitches as I remember the intricate patterns from the blood of my parents forged in our dining room carpet. Sometime, in the hours I was gone celebrating, my childhood home turned into a crime scene. When I returned home from the concert, I found them. News of their murder at the hands of an unknown assailant shared top billing on our local news with a report of Ian's near-fatal overdose. It's a time I hate to remember but am destined to never forget. A shudder ripples through me and my blood chills. If not for Candace booking us a hotel room as a birthday gift, the police might have discovered three bodies instead of two. *Stop!*

I have a few minutes left and need to steady myself before going back out there to sing. Seeing Ian was a sucker punch, but I can't let it affect the rest of my night. Though his presence stirred my memories of a night filled with hopes and dreams, I remind myself that I'm not that innocent lamb from long ago. I've grown in every facet of my life and am a much different person than I was then. I have a show to finish and have no time for indulging old stories.

Taking a moment for nature's call, I rearrange my clothes and unlatch the lock. The cold water keeps me present as I wash my hands and compartmentalize. I imagine my concerns swirling down the drain with the soapy water, then snap off a paper towel as I catch my reflection, and, with a deep breath and tipped-up chin I take my inner frazzle from mountain to molehill. A quick fluff of my hair and a slip of gloss across my lips and I'm almost ready. Checking a near-perfect smile I remind myself again of who I am: a confident woman. *You've got this, girl!*

A deep, smug breath swells my chest as I curl my fingers around the door handle and bid farewell to my reflection. As I pull, the frame and door stick from the humidity before budging open, a reminder that I still never mentioned a word to Sam about the heat.

The scent of beer blends with chattering voices. I zip through the crowd wearing invisible blinders and reach the stage. A surge of pride wells up inside with the knowledge I successfully fought the urge to look in Sam and Ian's direction.

"Did you get a fresh round of drinks?" I ask, pulling the microphone to my lips. I glance over at the barmaid. "Hey Jeri, can you send me over a bottle of water?"

I detect her silhouette and a bob of her head in the dim light, then sit back, adjusting myself in the seat.

"Y'all should be feeling pretty good about now."

They respond with a roar to my softly spoken observation, and I lift my guitar onto my lap. Despite my best efforts to shake off the short-lived panic attack, my fingers still tremble a little bit. I look up, ready to start the next song and see Sam directly in my line of sight in the back of the room. Tall and imposing, he's in a wide-legged stance with his arms folded across his chest. I know that posture and I will not let him make me feel bad or give me a guilt trip because I didn't linger when he wanted me to stay.

A small seed of defiance springs to life inside of me. If he's pissed off that I didn't stick around to chat, so what? I'll be sure to remind him that I was pleasant. I was polite. Nothing more was required.

Meeting his stare with one of my own, I move forward and play the chords of the song's intro.

Screw him.

* * *

AN HOUR WEARS on as I successfully pivot from one song to the next. I play with the idea of sticking to the set list, then decide to sing a song from long ago. One that will resonate with Sam's special guest. I look over at Ian, catching his eyes with mine as best I can.

"Did you know I write many of my songs?" It's a rhetorical question. "I do. I also like to cover songs from famous bands. I hope you enjoy them all."

I boldly pull the pick across the strings, strumming back and forth to set an easy rhythm. The tempo is different than what the crowd will recognize but my pride insists I'm doing this. I open my mouth, take a breath, and close my eyes. *This one's for you, Mr. Rockstar!*

They say makin' mistakes is a part of life
And I say that's good livin'
Sin will stain your mortal soul
And some things ain't forgiven'
How much penance does a person need
Before the whitewash will cover the bleed
How many tears do you cry before you go crazy

Purge my sins, cleanse my soul
Take this heart and make it whole
He-e-e-eal me
Reach inside, take my pain
Can you make me whole again
He-e-e-eal me
Heal me.

Despite my best attempt to remain unnerved, my voice warbles ever so slightly. I croon the song that scored Ian and Boundless Hearts a platinum record. It's a gamble, singing the song in the fashion I wrote it, but it's one I'm willing to take. Their band made millions on a bastardized, heavy-metal version of the song, but I'd signed over the rights for five hundred dollars and VIP tickets to their concert. My parents encouraged me to enter the contest, confident that I had talent. I guess I did because the band made a boatload of money off my song. Now, their lead singer was hearing it the way it was meant to be sung, and not the way they recorded it.

A surge of pleasure rushes through me like a rebel ghost swelling through the mist, and the memory of the brave girl I used to be rises like a phantom. The rush of confidence thickens my blood bringing back a memory of a fearless girl inside her bedroom. She penned those words keeping time with her heartbeat while the lyrics poured out like a waterfall. When I last heard Ian sing them, he was wasted. His garbled version tripped over words that came from my soul. The sloppy slurring disappointed me and others that night, making me cringe when some in the audience booed him. That whole night I straddled a razor's edge of excitement and devotion and walked away disappointed and confused. At the VIP Meet and Greet, I made a fool of myself, starstruck and love-drunk as I fawned over my crush. I tripped over my words and fumbled my questions, just as he had done on the stage. When we were made to move along so that others could meet the band, my ever-loving friend, Candace, walked me to our hotel room in silence. With her comforting arm around my shoulder, we stumbled and tripped our way down the hall. When she fell asleep my mind raced and thoughts stewed. My hopes sunk beneath unanswered questions, so I went to the vending machine to drown my feelings with junk food. It was there I found Ian.

I opened my mouth to thrash him with bitter words, but I couldn't. The man before me wasn't the cocky singer I'd seen hours before. This was a sad man. A broken man. He couldn't get the machine to take his money and was totally defeated. The sight was unexpected. Instead of anger, I pitied him. He asked me to help him to his room and, in doing so, I also helped myself.

I revisited my irresponsible behavior from the night before in the morning and, when a hung-over Candace and I stood at the front desk checking out, we were quickly distracted by a rush of reporters. Outside the lobby doors were several police cars and an ambulance. Candace pressed for information and got it from the gossipy desk clerk. Ian had overdosed. Fear consumed me. *Was I the last person with him?*

I walked away from the desk, desperate to breathe as anxiety consumed me. All I wanted to do was go home, talk to my mom, and wash traces of the night before down the drain. In our Uber Candace reported that housekeeping found Ian, barely breathing. There was an empty bottle of Jack Daniels beside him marred with fingerprint traces of white powder on it, and on top of the nightstand.

Scattered images flash through my mind and prick my heart as I struggle to sing.

Shattered glass.

Crimson dots on a new pair of Vans.

A lake of blood.

The next thing I remember is Sam holding me, telling me it would all be okay as I cried.

For all my life, Sam filled many roles, including surrogate father. He and my dad served together in the military but in this battle, he had my back. There was no other family and, when Sam arrived, he took over. My childhood home was a crime scene and had now become the source of a nightmare from which I'd never escape. Now the house held nothing for me and going back inside the building was an act I couldn't fathom. Sam arranged for me to stay with Candace until he tied up loose ends. She had gotten a job right out of college and moved into a condo. I was staying with my parents until I could figure out what I would do to pay the bills and continue with my music, which they encouraged. But life has a way of changing your best-laid plans. Instead of the future I envisioned, I spent days curled up in a ball on her couch, using the television for background noise while she was at work. Sam checked in on me and did so often. I half-listened when he said an investor had made an offer for the house, and absent-mindedly signed the papers to transfer ownership. I didn't care about anything for a while and, as I teetered between reality and madness, Ian lost his appeal to me. The last I heard of him; they'd moved him from the hospital to a rehab center.

Oooo, I did my best
But failed the tests
Danced a bit with my demons
Reaper stood beside, to hitch a ride
He does that with us heathens
Oh, I lost it all
and ate my pride
Dug a grave,
'cause I almost died
Your road is always one of your own makin'

Purge my sins, cleanse my soul
Take this heart and make it whole
He-e-eal me
Reach inside, take my pain
Can you make me whole again?
He-e-eal me
Heal me.

At the start,
A woman stole my heart,
She said she'd stay
But lied and ran away

I messed with the law,
And found the devil's claw,

Thought I was done,
Down the end of
some man's gun

Purge my sins, cleanse my soul
Take this heart and make it whole
He-e-eal me
Reach inside, take my pain
Can you make me whole again?
He-e-eal me
Heal me.

They say makin' mistakes is a part of life ...

Peace settles over me as I strum the last chord and hold out the last note. I tuck my memories away. Beneath my closed lids, I imagine kissing my parents goodbye. A second later, I open them, and I freeze.

No one is moving.

Did I screw up the words?

A thunderclap of applause hits the air like lightning, and the jolt pops me out of my seat. One by one people rise until everyone in the room is standing.

Tears sting my eyes. My heart fists. Warmth flushes my cheeks then races over my throat and chest.

"Wow." Shock slips through my lips into the microphone, but they can't hear me. It's what my dad called *ne plus ultra*—the moment you reach your highest success. My whispered word floats away, lost in the roar of the crowd.

* * *

I FLOATED on a cloud the remainder of the evening but now, I'm done for the night, and I'm glad because I'm tired. The adrenaline that surged through me from the audience's reaction to *Heal Me* took me high but, now the flow's returned to normal, and I'm spent.

"I'd like to thank you all for a night I'll never forget. Again, I'm Savannah Grace and I'll be back at Mad Dog next week. Enjoy the rest of your night."

My limbs protest as I quickly pack up. I'm stiff from sitting. My bed will feel good tonight and I can't wait to get home.

As I kneel and place my guitar inside its case, the worn, blue velvet lining captures my attention. I didn't keep many things from my house when I moved but I wouldn't dare leave this behind. It's a sweet connection to my parents and something all three of us have touched.

I let my gaze linger on it for a moment. Inside, the creamy, worn fabric begs for my attention, so I slide my fingertips over the cloth. A hint of a smile tugs at my lips. Its deep cobalt color has dulled with age but is now washed-out just enough that it's near the shade of my mother's eyes.

Instantly, a flash of her face sweetly assaults me, and the memory of her beauty trembles my lips.

"I hope you're proud of me, Momma," I whisper to the presence I feel, but can't see.

Emerging tears sting my eyes. I clear my throat to

shake off the threatening emotions. I've got no time for reminiscing. I've dawdled long enough. If I want some quiet time at home to soak in my first standing ovation, I need to get moving.

Quickly, I secure my guitar. As I pull my hand away to close the lid, the garnet ring my parents gifted me for my sixteenth birthday snags a scrap of the material. I toss a look side to side. *Was that you who made my ring catch?*

The thought that my mother could influence such an act runs a smile from my heart to my lips while I contemplate the possibility that her spirit is somewhere nearby. I dislodge the cloth and fondle it between my thumb and fingers, noting to myself that, if she could be close to me in spirit form, she would be. The thought warms me inside as I tuck my new talisman into my pocket.

"Savannah?"

I turn toward the voice at the end of the stage. "Yes?"

A gentleman who appears to be about fortyish looks between himself and the pretty woman whose hand he's holding. Their affection is transparent as they share a loving look between them.

"We just wanted to say, we really felt your song tonight. The way you sang *Heal Me* hit us in a different way than the Boundless Hearts' version. The way you performed it made us like it better than the original."

The original huh? I smother a snicker. "Thanks. That means a lot to me."

"We'll be back next week and hope you'll do it again," the woman adds.

My brow quirks high. "I just might."

They depart and I grab the guitar and my purse to make a quick exit.

"Savi!" Sam's voice booms across the thinned-out crowd.

Shit.

My head falls back, and I close my eyes, feeling defeated. I'm never going to get out of here.

Irritation bristles my temper, yet I tamp down the slow-simmering anger within as I take the necessary steps to approach him. "Yes?"

My feelings must be showing because Sam's jolly expression fades. "I thought you might take a minute for my friend."

And there goes my plan to get out of here fast.

"Oh, I'm sorry. I thought I'd done that during my break." The strain in my voice is apparent.

I exaggerate a slow turn and am instantly sucked in by Ian's beautiful amber eyes. Over the years I've convinced myself that my infatuation with this man has waned, but I can't deny the fact that he's still hotter than hell as I'm pulled into the warm, smokey color.

"I'm sorry, Mr. Stanton. Forgive me. I'm Savannah. It's nice to meet you—*again.*"

Ian's expression goes blank with my cocky attitude. Perfecting my resting bitch face I, ever-so-slowly, turn back to Sam.

"Will there be anything else?"

CHAPTER THREE

Ian

Sam's brows pinch tight. "I'll see you at dinner. Sunday. We'll talk then." His words are flat and measured.

"Is that an invitation?" She perks, flippantly. "I thought you gave that up?"

The curl of his lip is barely visible beneath his thick mustache. "I like my Sundays off, Savannah. It's a good day for reflection, don't you think? For some of us, it helps to plan our week. You know; to do a better job and be a better person than we were the week before— as the good Lord intended."

The verbal sparring is intense and her forehead wrinkles. She levels him with the smile of an evil queen.

"Far be it from me to *ever* strive to disappoint the Lord."

My brow quirks. The effect she has on him with her sugar-sweet, sing-song tone and her wise-ass attitude is pissing me off.

I look from her to him and see a tick of Sam's jaw. I could swear he's grinding his teeth. The look in his eyes could flatten her right now. It's like one a father gives a disobedient child. I note he's dropped her nick-name and, instead, is using her formal name like a whip.

I want to say something, but I bite my tongue. I don't like her attitude and can feel the small hairs on the back of my neck bristle. Since I'm ignorant of their relationship dynamic, I back off.

"My, my. That's good to hear, Savannah, seeing how the Lord knows your heart and all." A twitch curdles the corner of his eye, tainting the remainder of the conversation. "I'll see you on Sunday."

"You absolutely will." Her tone is as mockingly bright as his is sour. Dismissing him, she turns to me and extends her arm to shake my hand. "Mr. Stanton, it's been a pleasure. Safe travels."

Her smug expression makes me angry, but I take her hand with a firm grip. Her fingers are as cold as her attitude and I'm not fond of bourgeois bitches.

"Oh, Ian's not going anywhere. He lives here." Sam interjects.

Wide-eyed, she snaps her icy blue eyes back to him. "Excuse me?"

She tries to pull her hand from mine, but I maintain

my grip. It has a rebound effect and her gaze pops back to me. "Let go."

I don't budge. "Before I do, I've got a question: have we met?"

"What?" She answers, clearly annoyed.

"You look slightly familiar but then, there are too many blondes in my past to remember them all." I reluctantly let go but can't hide the satisfied grin sneaking up the corners of my mouth. I'm pissing her off. *Good.*

Her spine stiffens with an artic intensity, and, with narrowed eyes, her blue orbs throw icicle daggers.

"We have." She punches the words like a death blow.

"I don't remember you. Want to throw me a bone?"

She instantly attempts to school her expression and I'm amused at her effort. It's for sure I've hit a nerve—which only makes this that much more fun.

She doesn't answer me. Sam watches the exchange, and the curl of his lip reveals he's entertained. I'm not sure I have to, but I rein myself in.

"Ms. Grace, I get the feeling you don't like me very much."

"Really?" She hikes up a perfectly shaped brow. "Why would you say that?"

"Well, I'm no Sherlock Holmes, but I detect those knives you're throwing at me have a story behind them."

She pauses, studies me, and, with a slight turn of her head, gives me a sanctimonious look. "We met after a concert. The last one you performed."

"The last one, huh?" I purse my lips and bob my head. "Not one I like to remember but I'll bet I was a real charmer."

"You absolutely were." She deadpans.

"I'm guessing you had a VIP ticket?"

"I did." A painfully slow tip of her chin affirms her words.

I throw up my hands. "Well, there you go. Mystery solved. Guess I do have a bit of Sherlock in me." I turn my back to her.

"That's it? Nothing more to say?"

Her self-righteousness is showing. Little does she know I'm done being judged for the man I used to be. The seat of the barstool swivels as I turn back in her direction and lock down her eyes with my own.

"In case you missed it, I was shit-faced that night. But let me take a stab at what happened: you were excited, and I was rude. You got offended, so I ruined your night. End of story. That about right?"

"Slightly." She shrugs off my snarky response like she's swatting off a bug.

"*Slightly*, huh? I can't imagine why so little. From what I heard, I *totally* ruined everybody's night. Was it a special occasion?"

"My birthday."

"Did you go to the concert to celebrate?"

"I did."

"Give me a minute to think." I study her face, this time in earnest. I should remember a woman so beautiful, but nothing comes to me. "Sorry. I don't remember you."

The flinch she tries to hide is proof my words sting, and she strikes back. "Here's a clue; that song I played tonight, *Heal Me?*"

"Yep. Nice cover. It didn't resemble our version, but I liked it."

"You *liked* it, huh?" Venom drips through her tone and feeds her scowl. "It's my song."

"Excuse me?" I blink, sincerely confused.

"*It's. My. Song.*" She practically snarls the clipped words.

I'm baffled.

"Look, you aren't the first woman who's ever said, 'Oh, my god! This is my song'. I'm happy you made a personal connection; it's a great song. But my fucking up your birthday is no reason to be rude to my friend. Sorry you had a shitty night—but I'm glad you like the song."

Her chin drops and her head tips to the side. Just like before, she peers up at me with malice in her eyes. She mutters an evil chuckle as her eyes take on a devilish glow, and a knowing grin slinks through her lips.

"*Noooo.* I'm glad *you* like it. The song is mine. I wrote it."

This chick is crazy.

Perplexed, I look between her and Sam. He leans back against the bar with his arms folded across his chest. I have no idea what's going on and he isn't giving me any clues.

"What are you talking about?"

"I'm the songwriter—though technically, it belongs to you and Boundless Hearts." She musters a hint of resignation to accompany her eye roll.

"Interesting." I shrug, pressing my lips together. "Good for you."

She props a hand on her hip. "You guys recorded it but, the way I sang it tonight, is the way it was originally conceived."

I surrender another shrug. "I get it. Your song. Our music. Money in both our pockets."

I swallow a painful lump as memories rush at me. We made a lot of money with that song. Dash took care of the business side of the band. All of it. He was wicked smart and took care of me and the guys in every way. He not only wrote songs but acquired others. The contests were to engage fans. I trusted Dash with everything, including my life. Unfortunately, his didn't have a happy ending.

Remembering Dash's death hits me with a sucker punch and my mouth has gone dry. I gulp down the remaining contents of my drink. The effort to fight my hands from shaking suddenly seems Herculean. Jeri, like Sam, has been watching and listening. Noting my uneasiness, Jeri taps my hand and points to my glass. I nod, desperate for a refill.

"So, I guess that's it." The twitch in Savannah's full,

pink lips slams hard and I revert to the defensive prick I used to be.

"That song—*your* song—was the last song I recorded with my best friend before he died. You're pissed I didn't bow at your feet on your birthday. I get that, but big fucking deal. I didn't know it was your birthday or many other things that night. I went to my room and took so much shit I nearly died."

Her face goes pale. "I—"

I cut her off. "See, for you, that's where that night ends. That isn't where it ends for me. Every day I remember that it was *that* song we were singing when he went blank and forgot the words. Words you now inform me *you* wrote. I wish I could forget some of the bad shit that happened to Dash but I can't. He forgot how to play guitar. Forgot he'd earned Grammys. Forgot the guys, his wife … me. There's only three people who ever gave a shit about me and two of them are dead. I fucked things up for a lot of people. After tonight, I'll remember I fucked it up for you, too."

Savannah's expression goes blank and, when I look at Sam and Jeri, I see sorrow in theirs.

"I—"

"Spare me." I cut her off. "I danced with my demons that night. Thanks for the little walk down memory lane."

Savannah blinks back in shock and her tone softens. "It was a bad night for us both."

"Are you serious? After what I just told you?" I look

from her to Sam. I want to say more but I see pain in his eyes.

I take a couple of deep breaths and stuff down the hurtful words I want to hurl at her. She's someone to him and, because of that, I tread lighter.

"Look—Savannah—in my mind we've just met. Tonight, I had no intentions of being a dick but you're making it really hard."

A tremble snags her bottom lip as a shadow falls over her expression. I feel like there's something more here but speaking of Dash's last days has left a deathly tang on my tongue. Sam or no Sam, I'm done.

Savannah grabs her stuff. "I gotta go."

CHAPTER FOUR

Savannah

I bolt out the door. A few steps into the parking lot, I double over, desperately needing fresh air.

After pulling a few deep breaths into my lungs, I stomp across the parking lot, shoulders slumped and mind still spinning. I'm no better than a child having a temper tantrum. *What was Sam thinking?*

Ian unleashed on me, saying his piece with a tone that was much harsher than the sexy one I remember. The buttery edge of Boundless Hearts' lead singer's earliest recordings. I used to crave listening to his voice and, tonight, he used it to cut me down. My pissy attitude made him hostile, and he made sure every word he spoke was so deliberate I wouldn't mistake his feelings. I thought I had complete control, but his rage left me second-guessing myself. *Who was that woman in there?*

My emotions are pricked and bloodied. I mourned his pain and, when he recalled how he wanted to die, something inside me broke. I wanted to say more but I had to get out of there before I gave myself away and revealed things I'd rather forget.

Disbelief shakes my head. I'm not that woman. I'm not a bitch who stabs and hurts. I'm more a woman who cares and comforts—and now I feel like crap. I had a chance to express my condolences and say how sorry I was for his loss but didn't. Now, my brain hurts. My head throbs. My stomach churns with a mix of anger and sorrow. I was riding a high tonight, and what should have been a night I'll always remember will be tainted forever by Ian's pained expression. The scene between us snuffed out my joy and, I'm sure, will haunt me forever.

Exhausted and angry more with myself than anyone else, I yank open the car door and drop like a stone into the seat. My throat clamps down as I choke on my behavior. I only thought of myself, and I'm mortified.

Damn! Damn! Damn!

I hit the steering wheel with both fists in a futile attempt to release some frustration. Why did I let him get to me?

I take a few more breaths as I lay my head down on the wheel. It's a poor substitute for a pillow but I need a moment to find some calm in this chaos. Two encounters with Ian at different times in my life. Both have been a mess.

Sam said Ian lives in Rock Hills. If that's so, when did that happen, and why here? I want to know. Until tonight when he blurted it out Sam's never mentioned a word—and he knows everything about my life. He knows about the song and the contest and everything else.

My dad and Sam were brothers in arms and that made them as close as if they shared a bloodline. He was, and is, part of our family. Dad and Sam talked on the phone once or twice a week. He stayed with us during the summers and most holidays. He never married. Never had kids. I was his substitute child. He even teased how he liked having a kid with none of the hassle. Whenever Dad needed him, he was always there. Just as he's been for me.

What I remember of the night I found my parents are my screams. They started before Candace doubled back in the Uber. I was in a hurry to get in the house and talk to my mom about the concert and my phone fell out of my pocket. What I remember are fragments.

The police.

A photographer.

Body bags.

When something pricked my arm, I barely flinched. Everything went dark and when I opened my eyes hours later Sam was there, and he stayed because I needed him.

No one warns you about grief. How everything

hurts. How the pain goes so deep and raw it feels like flesh ripping from a bone. I found no relief in my tears and my heart hurt so badly I prayed I'd drown in them. My eyes burned. I barely slept and, when I did, nightmares waited.

Time passed.

Why is it that death is the one thing we all know is coming but is the one thing for which we're prepared?

2Acceptance came and, instead of screaming, I began to breathe.

Sam did everything. As he shared my grief, he held my hand and dried my tears. He's stood by me as the pain of losing my parents became bittersweet memories.

"Love does that," I say the words out loud. Conviction pinches my conscience. I owe Sam an apology.

Drawing my back into the seat, I pull myself erect, start the engine, and lower the windows. As I pull out of the parking lot and onto the main road, I push the button on the radio and note the slight of my hand as I lower the volume. It's a pretty ride home. Hopefully, I'll mellow out as I drive.

There's something special about Rock Hills. I'm glad Sam convinced me to move here. The air is warm and the breeze rushing through plays with my hair. There's a scent to Bristlecone pine that's clean and fresh. The night's dark denim canopy is dotted with stars that play peek-a-boo with drifting clouds. This beautiful expanse is Mother Nature's medicine and has played an instrumental part in my healing.

A familiar tune steals my attention away. I huff a laugh at the irony of a Boundless Hearts love song. I'd roll my eyes but it's sweet. Dash Barrows said he wrote it the night he met his wife.

THE FIRST TIME I saw you, girl, I knew my life had changed
My lonely heart beat faster, my life you rearranged
You're the very reason I love to sleep at night
In my arms forever, our future burning bright

IAN'S WORDS play through my head. He's right; it was such a tragic end for such a beautiful soul. Before it was just a sad story but seeing the pain of his loss written all over his face, I'm empathetic. *Death and demons.* It's a wonder he survived.

Thoughts of Ian return and, this time, instead of fighting, I go with them. He looks so damn good. He's gained weight and put on muscle. His face has filled out where he used to look gaunt. There's a scar I remember that runs through his eyebrow. The story goes that he put a metal bucket on his head when he was a kid to make other kids laugh. If the story is true, it only makes the mark more appealing. His hair is shorter and looks nothing like the bed-head mess he used to wear. It's long enough that it brushes his shoulder and falls just below his strong and chiseled jaw. His eyes are most definitely brighter. They aren't bloodshot and glazed like the last time I saw him. There's a danger in those eyes; a delicious mix of amber with flecks of gold. Like the woods in autumn, the brown reminds me of a warm campfire with a mug of hot cider. *And he smells so good.* A crisp, clean, salt air scent wave drifted in the distance between us—or did it come from the black tee-shirt that showcased the muscle he'd gained since I last saw him? No doubt he's been working out. Ian was sexy when he was skinny but, now that there's so much more of him, he looks even sexier. I'll never forget that night in the elevator. It stopped between floors, and we were stuck inside. He tasted like whiskey and called me his angel.

Stop.

Straddling my thoughts, I lock them down and focus on the present instead of the past. There's someone at home waiting for me.

CHAPTER FIVE

Ian

"I don't think she likes you very much." Sam's half-cocked smile mocks me, but his words ring true.

"What gave it away," I snark back.

"That ain't important." He changes the subject. "Anyway, how'd you like her singing?"

My brow hitches. "She's okay."

"O-KAY?" Sam's posture springs up, accompanying an indignant look.

I pop back, raising my hands in surrender. "All right. Calm down. I'll be honest, she's good. Real good."

"Well, thanks. That's just what I needed to hear." A satisfied expression settles over his face.

Adopting a more relaxed posture, he leans on the bar. Sam's tall. His body hits the counter at his waist. He's a bit older than me but middle age hasn't settled on him. His broad chest and muscular arms give him an overwhelming presence. I have no doubt he can take care of himself against anyone who pisses him off.

I bide my time as I sip my drink and give him a minute to recalibrate. "I can tell you really like that girl."

"Maybe I do. Maybe I don't." He shrugs. "You don't need to pay that no never mind. She's pretty and she's smart. She's got one of them voices that can set fire to the rain."

I raise an eyebrow. "You, referencing Adele? Are you kidding me?"

"Yep. She's exactly like that, but better. Softer. More real." He nods as a dreamy look captures his eyes.

I chuckle beneath my breath, disbelief shaking my head. "I never took you for such a romantic."

"Nah," he waves me off. "It ain't got nothing to do with romance. I just know what I like."

Suddenly, one of the wooden double doors not far from the bar bursts open and a group of rowdy men stomp in, capturing our attention. Their footsteps echo near the near-empty bar. One of them, a tall, muscle-cut specimen sets his sights on me. Thick, untrimmed, stubble covers his chin and jawline. Arrogance pours off him sending an unspoken warning like an incoming storm. His lips curve in a snarl. He closes the distance between us until he's only a few feet away.

"Well, well, well," he drawls, his breath reeking of whiskey. "If it ain't Ian Stanton."

Sam tenses and slides through the opening, moving

behind the bar. In a quiet way, he sets the tone by placing a Louisville Slugger on the counter. I slip my hand on top of it to stop any angry impulse he might be entertaining.

"Do I know you?" I ask, calmly.

The man smirks, his eyes flicking over to Sam and then back to me. "I doubt that, but I know people who know you. I'm sure they'd love to know where you are. A lot of people got screwed over when you disappeared. I'm sure they'd like it if you got back into the business."

"Not interested." I turn away from him. Sam flicks a glance from the man to me. I see what he's saying in an unspoken exchange; he's got my back.

"What a dump!" The man sucks back and spits a wad of phlegm on the floor.

"This 'dump' is my place of business," Sam lifts the bat and snaps it in his palm.

The man snickers and puts up his hand. "Relax, man. Just want to talk to Ian."

How the hell did he know I'd be here? I raise an eyebrow. "I guess you didn't hear me. I'm not interested." I turn away again. He's undeterred. I can see his shark-like grin and tobacco-stained teeth in the mirror behind the bar.

"Some people would pay big to get you back on stage."

"No thanks."

His grin fades as he comes up alongside me. He

lowers his voice. "You sure about that, Ian? You had a pretty good life. You could have it back."

"I said no," I repeat firmly.

He turns away and walks back to his three friends, but not before giving me a final temptation.

"You might not think so but there are some very powerful people who'd spend a shitload of money to get you. You could be a solo act. Tell me your price and they'll book you all over the world." He strides back to me and Sam tenses. He slams a business card down on the bar top. "If I were you, I'd think about it. You won't get a better offer."

He and his entourage slink toward the door. Impressing some of their physical features to memory, I count them. Four in total. Four men who look like trouble and who, to my knowledge, I've never seen before. Once they're out the door Sam picks up the card.

"You know them?"

I shake my head. "Don't think so but can't say for sure."

"Whaddya mean?"

I shrug. "I didn't remember Savannah. I was wasted most of the time I was with the band and even more so after Dash died."

He gets it and nods as he picks up the card. "It's a record company. Black Shadow."

"I don't remember that name, but that doesn't mean anything."

Sam's raised brows beg a question. "If they're legit,

maybe they'd want to talk to Savi." He lays the card back down. Perplexed as to why he would even suggest such a thing, shock sends a rod down my back.

"You're kidding, right? That guy was a dick and, I could almost bet he's nothing but trouble. Why would you want him around her?"

He silently pours himself a Coke and slides a new one to me. "Maybe not him, but there might be some record executives on the other end of this phone number."

I slowly take a sip, buying myself a minute to put my mind in gear before I put my mouth in motion. I picked up that Sam and Savannah are close. What I don't know is how close. "You didn't tell me you know her."

Sam's brow quirks. A smug expression settles into his features as he folds his arms across his chest.

"No. I didn't. Mainly, because that don't factor into what I'm asking you. I told you she's a singer at my bar. That's what you needed to know. As far as your opinion goes, you got a set of ears don'tcha?"

His smart-ass attitude draws me back. "Need to know? That *is* all I know. You never told me if I was coming to hear a man or a woman. You gave me nothing."

"And why would I? It ain't like you need to know her life story to tell me if you think she's got talent. You don't need no more information. Tell you the truth, after the exchange I saw tonight, I'm not sure I want you to know her."

He leans back and locks down his cocky bearing with a solid folding of his arms across his broad chest. Though he's got a point, I'm taken back. Of all people, I thought Sam would have a different opinion of me than the rest of the world. He's watched the transformation in me over the past couple of years, but I guess opinions are slow to change. I can't fault him for being cautious with someone he obviously cares about. No matter if they're related or not, no decent uncle, surrogate father, friend—whatever—would want a girl like her around me. I guess it's true when they say your reputation precedes you. In most people's minds, mine is lit with neon lights.

"I'll keep my distance. Got it." I press my lips tight and nod.

"I ain't telling you what to do but, you're right; she is special to me—and Savi don't usually act like that. Tell the truth, I ain't never seen her behave like that before."

I should have seen that chip on her shoulder as soon as recognition dawned in her eyes. An opinion was formed by an earlier run-in, putting me, and all the work I've done to better myself, at a disadvantage. To her, I'm a pariah—but Sam? His comments sting. Because of all the help he's given me, I owe him. My loyalty to him is bigger than my ego.

"You don't want Savannah to deal with that company. Trust me."

He scoffs. "Yeah, they'd had some to drink, but they

might not be like that when they're at work. Most people that come to a bar leave a little tipsy."

"That wasn't 'tipsy'. If you give Savannah that card, you might as well throw her to the wolves. I know. People like that only have money on their minds. I know first-hand. If you have reservations about me getting to know Savannah, you sure as hell don't want them around her."

Sam's eyes narrow and his gaze intensifies. He leans in and props his chin on his hand. "You aren't so bad and make no mistake; I'm not trying to hook you up with that girl. Truth be told, I'd prefer you don't get no ideas like that, but I need you to be straight with me first before I ever present the idea of helpin' her get a record deal. Tell me, Ian—no bullshittin'—she got what it takes?"

His voice descends and his tone is more serious than I've heard in a long time. I study his face. Honesty is all Sam and I have ever exchanged but, he should know, my opinion isn't worth shit. The last thing he should ever do is put faith in the view of a junkie—*former* junkie.

"I don't know." I shake my head and shrug.

His eyes narrow. "Why the hell not? You got ears and experience. Your opinion means something to me. She's got the voice of a got' damn angel."

"Well, my judgment might not be what you're looking for, so I can't give you an answer. The music industry can be unkind. It's a different kind of devil."

"Dammit!" He shouts.

"Stop. Take a breath, will you?" I raise my hands in surrender. "All I can say is I liked what I heard."

"If you'd a come here more, you woulda' heard more. It ain't like I haven't been invitin' you for over a month."

I watch him as he slips off the barstool and stomps away, putting some distance between us. A few seconds later he turns and eyeballs me with an agitated stare while I measure the rise and fall of his chest in huffed breaths.

"Ian, I know that guy looked like a sleazebag but, if he really does know people, and I don't give Savi his card …"

He stops talking mid-thought. Somehow, I feel I'm in an alternate reality. Maybe he didn't see what I saw, but I'd think that years spent as a sponsor would have exposed him to some of the worst people. It's a few minutes before his irritability deflates.

Finally, a sigh escapes on a rush of air. His shoulders slump. He drags a hand through his thick mop of gunmetal-colored hair and pulls the bar towel off his shoulder, carelessly tossing it onto the counter before dropping into a seat beside me. A sense of defeat wraps around him.

"I don't know anything about those guys. That's the honest-to-God truth. But, for you, I'll check around."

He lifts his chin. "I want her to get a break, Ian."

"It isn't the end of the world if she doesn't. It doesn't always work out the best for people, Sam. You know how it fucked me up."

"Yeah, but she ain't you. She's got her feet on the ground." He looks up with pleading eyes.

"Nobody's me at first but, given unfamiliar circumstances, the worst things happen to the best people."

"She deserves a break. You don't know … I just want her to find success."

"Let me rephrase then; I was a *successful* fuck-up. But, in the end, I almost lost everything."

He rubs the back of his neck. "I didn't mean to be an asshole."

I smile. "It happens to the best of us."

THE MOTORCYCLE RIDE to my house helps to clear my head and, once there, I throw a few logs in the fireplace and light it up.

My body aches. I'm physically and emotionally worn out from a day of working on the ranch and verbal sparring with Sam.

Mesmerizing bright tangerine and buttercup-colored flames ease my weary mind while the tango of colors seduces me into a more relaxed state and sleep entices me.

I stretch out my legs in front of me as warmth spreads through the night's biting chill. Fire has its own music filled with pops and crackles. I listen as I stare at the blaze, following the sparks as I sink deep into my favorite worn leather chair. An image of Savannah comes to mind.

I've shied away from the social aspects of life. Sam's visits to the ranch and an occasional trip into town for mail, groceries, and supplies are enough for me. But there's something about her that hooks me, and I'm not sure if I like that or not.

The night is cool and the breeze drifting through the open windows brings traces of evergreen and pine from the surrounding trees. They've left indelible scents in the walls of this old house along with other scents I can't yet identify. Over time I've gotten used to the fresh smells. I enjoy them. After years of concert venues thick with pot smoke, and hotel rooms saturated with mixed aromas of cleaning supplies and air freshener, the spicy mix of smoking wood and cool pine draws me in as they complement the peace and quiet I crave. Since moving to the ranch, I've discovered many things about myself. Contentment comes along with the haunting of my former existence. I have little memory of what I've done or who I hurt, and I need this life I'm making to bind up the wounds hidden on the inside of me.

I close my eyes, trudging through mental images of empty bottles, nameless women, and broken dreams. That fateful night when it all almost ended, my angel came to me. Though I remember seeing her, I still question her existence. Was it just wishful thinking, or did I really experience something supernatural? The mental picture is never clear. What is embedded like concrete in my mind is I was given another chance at life. The problem is I don't what to do with it.

I lean forward and run my hand through my hair. Most men wish for a wife and family, but I've resigned myself to knowing those are things I'll never have. This is the best I can hope for. My place in the world is working this ranch. It's the only thing that's ever provided a sense of simplicity and peace. Here, I don't need to rehash all the bullshit. It isn't useful. Neither are regrets, especially when you've buried the man you used to be.

I shift my body as my eyelids grow heavy and fall into sleep as I throw more dirt on the grave of my misdeeds.

CHAPTER SIX

Savannah

"Momma!"

I sink to the floor, my arms opening wide. This little human with the big, cerulean blue eyes refreshes my soul like a cool drink of water. She leaps into my chest, and I pull her close. We meld into an embrace, my arms tightening around her slight frame. I snuggle against her until the top of her head fits into the hollow space at the base of my throat and in return, she presses harder against me. The smell and feel of her soothes me like nothing else in the world.

"I missed you so much, momma."

"I missed you more, baby love."

I never, ever get tired of this routine. In fact, I treasure it. Despite being away from her for only a few hours, our reunions are always filled with sweetness.

My little Guiliana—called "Gigi" by those who love her —isn't one to linger in sentiments. She quickly severs our embrace. Though she's an old soul she's also a bundle of energy like any other three-year-old.

Gigi pushes away and takes a moment to study me. She knows things, this little one, and sizes me up quickly.

"You not have a good night, Momma?"

"I'm good, baby. Just had my feathers ruffled a bit."

She takes a second look, and when she feels confident that I'm okay, her smile widens.

"I got 'choo."

"You know how much I love you?"

Her head bobs. "A bushel and a peck and a hug around the neck."

"Yes ma'am!"

"Guess what? I drew a pitchur, and took a walk, and danced to some music, and made puddin' pops, and helped cook, and washed my hands, and drew a pitchur' …" She swiftly changes topics.

"You're repeating yourself, baby."

Propping her hands on her hips, she issues a serious look. "I know dat, Momma. I wanted to see if youse payin' attention." She lifts her gaze to her babysitter. "Right, Ms. Cora? I was a good girl today, right?"

"Absolutely. You also helped me to make a cake. You licked the chocolate icing clean off the spoon."

Gigi's nose scrunches as she smiles. "I did, Momma, and the chocolate was weally good."

"Chocolate, huh?" I feign surprise. "I'll bet you liked that. After all, chocolate is your absolute favorite."

Again, she throws her arms around my neck, displaying her affection. "It is! It's so yummy—and you can have some cake, Momma! All you want!" She glances at Cora. "Momma can have some, Ms. Cora?"

"Yep. Momma can have some."

Cora Brooks looks at my little one with love in her eyes. "*Ms.* Cora", as she's affectionately known to Gigi, is in her late forties, but you'd never know it. Her toned figure and vibrant aura make her seem younger than her years. With fiery red hair and an infectious laugh, she puts me in mind of an actress in an old Elvis Presley movie. Ann Margaret and Cora could be sisters and the likeness had me doing a double take the first time I saw her.

I had strolled by her house with Gigi in tow, enjoying the reprieve that only comes when a teething child is fast asleep. The sweet scent of roses lured me toward her garden. It was in full bloom with flowers so big and fragrant that I smelled them before I saw them. I stopped, taking in the heady fragrance that cleared away remnants of Gigi's earlier diaper blowout. Cora's back was to me as she worked diligently in the flower bed. She paused when I complimented her work, and laughed off the praise, pushing damp, coppery strands from her forehead with the back of her gloved hand.

"I have no idea what I'm doing." She confessed. "But I'll take the compliment."

She approached me. "May I?"

I nodded and she peeked in on a peaceful Gigi, gushing over my little girl's perfection. Of course, I agreed with her, like any new mom would. After chatting for quite a while, I invited her to come visit us, and a few days later, Cora arrived on my doorstep with homemade biscotti and a bottle of wine.

"You looked like you needed a break when I saw you last." I opened the door wide for her to enter while placing a finger to my lips in a silent message.

"The baby's asleep."

"Then, it's a perfect time for wine."

"I can't," I protested. "She'll be up soon."

"You can. That's why I'm here. I can help."

I was a leary. After all, we'd just met, but after half of a glass Gigi woke up and true to her word, she helped me, rocking Gigi in her arms as I rinsed off some dishes and put them in the dishwasher. Our friendship grew deep roots, and three years later, I count Cora as close as family. It was she who encouraged me to get out of the house and when Sam offered me a spot to sing at Mad Dog, she volunteered to babysit Gigi.

Not all family are blood ties.

Gigi lifts her hands and places them on my face. "Momma, you cheeks is red—and they's hot." Her brows crunch with concern.

"Your cheeks *are* red, sweet girl." I correct her and press the back of my hand against my face.

"No, Momma. It's *youse* cheeks. Not mine." She pulls

back, ignoring the grammar correction. A second later, she splays her fingers against me to test the temperature of my skin. "Is you sick?" She cocks her head to the side like a curious puppy, her eyes filled with concern.

"No, baby doll. I'm okay. Just tired." I push against my knees to stand, and Gigi remains near me, slipping her hand into mine. "Good day today?" I ask Cora.

"How could I have a bad day with this perfect angel," Cora answers, and Gigi's expression brightens like the sun. "She's always a good girl for me, Savi. No trouble at all. Her vocabulary is really expanding. Today she informed me that the pudding was *scrumptious.*" Gigi's ears perk up.

Cora always knows how to send me an unspoken message. While I fret over things like correcting my child's grammar, she makes a comment that turns my focus to something positive I've done. Gigi does have a big vocabulary for someone her age, but I didn't linger with a lot of baby talk when teaching Gigi how to speak.

I look down at my baby's face. She's glowing with pride. "You're such an intelligent little girl, you know that? I hook my hands under her arms and smoothly glide her onto my hip. "You are absolutely, positively, the best little girl in the whole wide world," I say as I nuzzle her, planting tickling kisses on her neck until she giggles.

"I don't know what we'd do without Ms. Cora."

Cora joins our love huddle. "And you won't ever

find out. You're my girls! I love you—especially this little munchkin." Cora lovingly caresses Gigi's silky, blonde curls. "Why don't you stay for dinner?"

You've had Gigi all day. That's the last thing you should worry about."

"Stop. It isn't a big deal. Gigi's already eaten. I made beef stew and rolls, and Gigi helped. It was good. All I have to do is warm it up."

Gigi glides her fingers into my hand. "I did, Momma. It's yummy."

The two of them have already made my decision for me, it seems. I give her hand a slight squeeze. "If you're sure it's no trouble—but I'll do the cleanup."

"And I'll have a puddin' pop, 'k Momma?"

I nod and Gigi goes over to Cora. She takes her hand and pulls her toward the kitchen. "C'mon."

Cora obeys and glances over her shoulder while dragging behind Gigi. "Go lay down on the sofa. You look tired. I'll get you when it's ready.

"I don't ne—"

"A fifteen-minute power nap," she insists.

I can't resist but watch as they vanish down the hallway. With just a few steps I'm near the sofa and lower myself down. I'm drained. Seeing Ian churned up all sorts of emotions, as did the standing ovation, and the overstuffed, flowery-print cushions are calling to me.

I stretch out and pull a crocheted afghan from the back to cover me. "Just a power nap," I mutter to myself, just before closing my eyes.

* * *

"Momma ..."

"Momma."

"MOMMA!"

My eyes pop wide. I'm instantly awakened by the jolting tone of my daughter's call. My hands fly protectively to my chest to protect my racing heart.

"Gigi! Don't do that!" My words soar on anxious wings.

"Do what, Momma?" Gigi's scrunched expression begs an explanation. With her hand on her hip, she waits for an answer. "Whatsamatter?"

"You called me like there's an emergency." I draw myself to an upright position.

Gigi's mouth pinches. "Oh, nufing's a 'ergency. It's just—DINNER'S WEADY!" She throws her arms up in the air as she bounces up and down.

I roll my eyes and wrestle with uncooperative limbs. It takes a minute before I finally stand and Gigi bolts out of the room. In my groggy state, I battle to synchronize my rapid heartbeat and unwilling body.

"You commin' Momma?" Gigi pokes her head around the corner of the doorway.

"I'll be there in a minute."

"Okay but youse foods getting' cold." She pauses, then gives me a very serious look. "You know, Momma, youse gotta eat. They's children starvin' for food like 'dis."

I freeze as Gigi echoes something my mother used

to say. I don't believe I've ever uttered that sentiment to her. Maybe she learned it from Cora. Nonetheless, she sounded just like my mother. *She would have loved her granddaughter.*

Gigi sails back to me, taking me from a melancholy path.

"I telled you dinner's weady, Momma."

"Yes, you did."

"But youse not weady."

"Yes, I am."

Her expression brightens. "Okay! Let's go!" She grabs my hand and tugs on my arm.

"I have to wash my hands."

She nods. "Okay."

"You go ahead to the kitchen. I'll be right there."

Ugh. I catch my reflection in the mirror after flipping on the light switch. Mascara's left smudges beneath my eyes. I rub at the dark crescents and then wash my hands. A quick fluff of my hair and I drift back a few years to note the difference in my appearance. I used to look so fresh. Now, I've got a few wrinkles at the corners of my eyes, and I look like I could use a vacation. The girl I was back then is no more. She was quite the dreamer and I'm so much more a realist. *Because, that night, everything changed.*

I shake off the introspection and head to the kitchen.

"Did you get a little rest?" Cora places a bowl of stew in front of me.

"I did. I think power naps have become my new way of operating."

"Why? Are you having trouble sleeping?" Cora's tone is one of concern.

I shrug. "I haven't slept well since my parents died."

"Death robs you of a lot of things," she says, with a sad tone. She places a comforting hand on mine.

CHAPTER SEVEN

Ian

A few weeks have passed, and I find myself heading to Mad Dog Run once again.

"You're becoming a regular, ain't you, Ian? Is it the food or my winnin' personality?" Sam's smirk is laughable.

"I wouldn't exactly say I'm a regular." I chuckle.

"The hell you ain't! You been here nearly every night for the last month."

"Not true." I roll my eyes.

Sam pops from the barstool and leans forward onto the counter, his bushy eyebrows forming a knot between them before hitching up. "You callin' me a liar?"

"Never," I assure him. "So, stop raggin' on me. I'd think you'd appreciate paying customers."

"I do, and you're a regular good one."

Disbelief shakes my head. "You don't give up, do you, old man?"

"Never," he assures with a triumphant smug.

The stage lights cast long shadows over Savannah's high cheekbones and long, smooth hair. She packs up her equipment with her back to the tables, oblivious to the way my eyes follow her every move.

We both watch as she steps off the stage, crosses the room, and waves to Sam before exiting. He returns the gesture, then turns to me. "She still ain't wantin' no part of you." He says under his breath.

"I don't expect her to." I shrug off the comment, unfazed. "She's got a right to her opinion."

"I don't like it. She's acting like a child," he states, emphasizing the sentiment.

"Maybe, but it's her prerogative. I'm not everybody's cup of tea."

"I don't like it. You're good people—both of you—but you're both hardheaded too." He straightens up. "Be back in a minute. I gotta take care of something."

I'm grateful for the reprieve. I haven't been coming to Mad Dog as much as Sam implies but it's more than I planned to be. As much as I hate to admit it, I've developed a taste for seeing Savannah perform. I like her soothing sound, so much so that it's grown like a cancer. The more I see her the more she's in my head. I see her in my fantasies, and, like any man, I like the relief I feel after I imagine the things I'd do to her.

When I was a teenager, I chalked up my insatiable sex drive to being a growing boy with active glands. Drinking, getting high, and screwing any girl who'd let me felt good. It felt even better when the band was on the road. I didn't have to look for it. Somehow, memories of those days don't compare to the unadulterated physical sensations that course through me when pleasuring myself to mental pictures of Savannah—and that's a problem.

I shake my head. If Sam knew how much I've been thinking of his 'niece' he'd kick my ass. Maybe it's wrong but I'm not hurting anyone, and I'm not ashamed. She's a gorgeous woman. The woman barely tolerates me but my attraction to her is undeniable. So, I appease the urge, stroking the beast inside until I'm spent.

I take in the crowd, my gaze drifting from face to face. Although another performer is setting up, the place has thinned out now that Savannah has finished. The scent of alcohol lingers in the air, the heady aromas mixing with the familiar smell of sweat that always comes to a crowded bar. She's got some pipes and, the more I listen, the more I think Sam is right; her voice is perfection. She hits every single note with precision. Savannah could get a music deal if she met the right people and though I do know exactly who the right ones would be to talk to, I'm not sure they'd welcome my presence, much less my recommendation.

I've followed my bandmates, Charlie, and Tom.

Both are still playing but with different groups. I haven't spoken to them in years, but I would for her sake. They might have a better insight on who's looking for what in the business and that knowledge might prove valuable to Savannah *if* she's looking for a contract.

The creaky kitchen door springs open, revealing Sam pushing through with four buckets of ice; two in each hand.

"Need some help?" I rise from the barstool I just claimed and approach to assist. As I do I take a quick look around for the bar back. "Where's Mac?"

"Mac done quit on me. He's following true love and moving across the country with his girlfriend."

My brows knit together. "You gonna hire someone new?"

"I guess. That's the only thing I hate about owning my own place. It's a pain in the ass sifting through bull-shitters to find someone reliable but, I can't do it all myself." He glances over his shoulder. "As you can see, I'm the only one behind the bar tonight."

He dumps the contents of the ice buckets into the stainless steel cooler. It's always hotter in Mad Dog than it should be, and sweat beads quickly sprout on the metal sides.

Sam brushes his hands together then swipes them down the side of his jeans. "Mine ain't the only place where good help is a priority. Rock Hills is growin' but it ain't Nashville." He pauses, cocks his head, and his eyes meet mine. A sly grin creeps into his lips. "Not yet anyway." He juts his chin. "What about you? You wanna make some extra money till I find some muscle-bound kid for the job."

"You can keep your money," I scoff, "but I'll help you out 'till you find somebody. I owe you."

He waves off my comment. "You don't owe me shit. I'd be glad for the help, though, and you'll take the money. If you don't want it, give it away—or use it to hire somebody to help at your place. You did great on the inside but you've a shitload of work on the grounds."

I look down at the cooler and the sinks. "I never worked in a bar. You'll have to show me what to do."

He grabs some glasses from one basin of water and dips them in another. "It ain't rocket science but it's hard work. A lotta lifting. It's a good workout, though. Keeps my ass in shape." He flexes both arms to show off his guns.

Amused, I roll my eyes. "I'll take it. Hard work keeps me out of trouble."

Sam acknowledges with a nod. "Start tomorrow?"

"Give me a time and I'll be here."

His lips curve into a smile. "Thanks, Ian. I appreciate it."

As Sam goes into the back once more, I go back to my seat. Savannah's noticed my frequent visits here and she's been civil to me. I can't help but wonder how she's going to take me working here. Somehow, I've got to find a way to forge a truce. It's possible, though it might be uncomfortable, but I think she and I can get along for Sam's sake. We've moved from open hostility to polite tolerance. I get the feeling it isn't the level of friendship Sam would like us to have, but I think we can make it work so it's easier on us all.

CHAPTER EIGHT

Savannah

When Sam told me Ian would temporarily be working at the bar, I bit my tongue. It isn't like I hate the man. I don't. I just have too little in common with him to forge a friendship. He's single and handsome. I'm a working mom. His life revolves around him, and Gigi is the center of my world. I think Sam's noted the tension. He waited to tell me till the end of my night. It just so happened I had a few days off and those days away from Mad Dog gave me some time to think and clear my head. Once you've lived through burying someone you love, there isn't much that'll rattle you.

"Momma, I help you knock?" Gigi's question catches me with my knuckles about to kiss the wood of Sam's front door. I give her a nod of approval as my hand drifts down to my side but, instead of her copying my gingerly touch, she pounds on the wood with a tiny, mallet-like fist.

The door opens, the entrance barely breached, and my daughter summons all her strength to rush through it. Sam jumps back but is completely unfazed. This is a natural occurrence for Gigi. She launches herself at him, throwing her arms around his legs in a vice grip as her head drops back. "I missed you soooo much!"

"I missed you, too, Chickadee!"

My heart melts at the sight of the two of them together. She scrunches her nose and her eyes pinch as she hugs him, while his eyes crinkle at the corners from a face-splitting smile.

Gigi's face lights up as Sam reaches down, hooks both hands under her arms, and swings her high in the air. He lets go and, once she's airborne, she squeals. Gravity finds her back in his arms and the result is gut-busting giggles. He repeats the aerobatics a few times then lowers her onto his hip. Now at his eye level, she busses his cheek and makes a disapproving face.

"You's got sticky whispers."

"Whiskers, honey," I softly interject.

"Yeah, Momma." She rubs her face. "Dem whispers is really pokey."

Sam's lip puckers. "I'm sorry, sweetie. I don't normally shave on the weekend but, for you, I'll go right in there and take them off." He lowers her to the floor. "Be right back. You go get something to drink for both of you," he says to me and then winks at Gigi. "I gotta make myself pretty for my best girl."

It's obvious Sam adores her and delights in the simplicity she brings to his life. Everything they do together is an adventure. It's like, through her eyes, Sam sees everything for the first time.

"Bandit's lying in the family room," he calls out. I'm surprised she didn't mosey in when she heard your voice."

"Bye, Momma."

All Sam had to say was Bandit's name and Gigi tears off. Sam's old Retriever is half-deaf and doesn't see as well as she used to, but she has a gentle soul, and Gigi's love for her surpasses almost everything else. The two of them return together, Bandit's toenails making clickity-clack sounds on the floor as she walks beside her girl. Gigi hooks her fingers beneath the dog's frayed, nylon collar, holding onto it like it's a bridle. I watch as they go over to, what's affectionately known as "Gigi's Corner". Once there, my daughter plops down on her butt, and the dog lowers herself to the floor beside her.

I turn and shout to Sam down the hallway. "I brought wine. I'm putting it in the freezer to chill."

He pokes his head out of the bathroom doorway, wiping his hands on a fuchsia towel. "I saw it in your hand when you two walked in."

"I felt like chilling out with a glass or two today. It's been a long week. Gigi got a booster shot the other day and was up all night complaining about her arm. Then there was laundry to do, and bills to pay ... you know what I mean. I just want to relax a little."

"Then put it in there. Just remember it's there or you'll have a wine slushy."

A mental picture of a huge slushy cup of wine makes an entrance into my thoughts. It's an idea I'll bet lots of moms would enjoy. As I close the freezer door, I sense Sam behind me and tip up my chin The mixed scent of spice and wood swirls in the air. I peck a kiss on his freshly shaven face. "You smell nice."

"Thanks." We move in opposite directions, him toward the stove and me toward the table and chairs where I pull one out and take a seat.

"What have you been up to?"

His brow quirks. "Savi, it's only been three days that you ain't seen me, so not a whole helluva lot." He takes a wooden spoon from the counter to the pot and stirs the contents. "What about you? Did you enjoy your days off?"

"Kind of," I shrug. "I caught up on a lot of stuff. Cora took Gigi for a day while I cleaned the house. It looked so nice and orderly until hurricane Gigi ran through. Honestly, I thought you might stop by. I can't remember when you've gone longer than a day or two without seeing your princess."

"Yeah. I would've but I've been more busy than usual with Mac quitting on me and interviewing for his replacement."

"Why *did* Mac quit? I thought he loved it at Mad Dog."

"Yeah, well … let's just say he loves his fiancé more. She lives over on the East Coast."

"So, he left for her?"

He nods. "Yup."

"And Ian's taking his place?"

"Yep. You're right on both counts. Mac's leavin'. Ian's stayin'. He offered to help. I lucked out. It would've been just me and Jeri. That bar gets too crowded for one person to cover a shift. I'm gonna hire two people to take Mac's place: one bartender and one bar back, and cross-train them both. It's not rocket science. It shouldn't take long to bring them up to speed once I pick who I'm going to hire."

I'm quiet, taking in every word. He eyeballs me, studying my reaction. I catch a curl of his lip before he turns his back to me and tends to his cooking.

"Sam?"

"Yes, Savannah."

"How long will Ian be working there?"

He turns. "Why don't you just spit it out, Savi? You don't like him, and you don't want him there."

"I don't, and I don't. How long do you plan to keep him there?"

"As long as I need him, I suppose." He shrugs, matter-of-factly.

"Any idea how long that will be?" Exasperation shades my tone.

"I don't know yet." His eyes catch mine. "Maybe long enough to address the elephant in the room."

My spine stiffens. "And that is?"

Gigi runs into the room, interrupting our conversation. "A ELEPHANT? Where's a elephant?" Her voice is a high-pitched squeal. She runs over to me bouncing up and down. "Where's a elephant, Momma? I wanna see. I wanna see!"

"It's you, Chickadee!" Sam sets the spoon down and hunches over. An observant Gigi watches as he buries his nose into his armpit and sways his arm loosely back and forth to mimic an elephant walk. "C'mon, Gigi. Let's pretend we're elephants."

Gigi squeals again then wiggles out from between my knees, impatient to follow Sam's lead. The mounting tension I felt a moment before dissipates as I, too, surrender to the silliness and assume the same posture. We drop heavy footsteps, swaying back and forth as the three of us take our best shots at being pachyderms. We keep up the act for several minutes until Sam, feigning exhaustion, falls to the floor. A horrified Gigi runs to him.

"Is you okay?" Gigi grabs his hand and pulls, as I quietly move back into a chair and watch their exchange.

"I'm fine, Chickadee. This is how elephants rest. They fall to their sides."

"Oh. Okay." Gigi, now having lost interest turns away and heads toward the family room once again.

"I wish I had her energy."

"Me, too." Sam pushes up off the floor and brushes off his pants.

"If I haven't said so lately, I love you. I'm so glad we have you in our lives."

"The feelin's mutual. I love you both like you're my own."

I wipe away unexpected tears.

"Are you crying?"

I look away, embarrassed, and dismiss the emotion as fluctuating hormones.

"You're turning into an old fart, Savi," he laughs.

"Stop. I can't help it. I, honestly don't know where Gigi and I would be without you." He hands me a napkin.

"I'm gonna make a salad. Stir that sauce for me, will ya? I don't want it to burn on the bottom of the pot."

I do as he asks, stealing glimpses of him over my shoulder. He's texting someone. Sufficiently stirred, I set the utensil down and go back to my seat.

His brow lifts. "Why are you lookin' at me like that?"

"What are you doing?"

His forehead wrinkles. "Texting on my phone, nosey. You writin' a book?"

I dismiss the comment and roll my eyes. He's impossible.

"Savannah, let's talk about somethin' more important, like, what's up between you and Ian?"

I look away. "There's nothing between me and Ian."

His expression turns to stone. "Uh-huh. Right."

We're interrupted by a knock on the door and I'm grateful for the interruption. "You expecting somebody?"

"Yep." A sly smile slides across his lips. "Savi, why don't you go let Ian in and I'll set the table."

CHAPTER NINE

Ian

I press the Velcro wrist catch of my riding gloves against the inside of the helmet, then place them in the trunk of my Harley. Not wanting to come to dinner empty-handed, I stopped at Sweetcakes Bake Shop for a full box of fresh pastries. I hook my fingers in the red cord securing the white cardboard box and walk toward the front door, glancing over at the driveway.

Two cars? Shit!

A quick refresh of my memory and I recall Sam and Savannah's talk about Sunday dinners.

My mood plummets. Once she sees me, it'll take more than pastries to sweeten the room.

I knock on the door and a few seconds later it opens. Savannah backs up. "He's in the kitchen," she says, her tone clipped.

"Can you show me the way? It's my first time here."

She rolls her eyes but reluctantly steps aside. It's apparent she's not happy to see me. I follow her through a hallway lined with landscape paintings. "Just so you know, I didn't know you'd be here."

"That makes two of us." Her tone is thick with tension.

"Hey, I brought dessert," I say lightheartedly. I hope there isn't anything lemon-flavored in there because her mood is sour enough.

I flick my tongue over dry lips, tasting a remnant of my morning coffee. *This'll be fun.*

I lift the box and muster a smile, trying to make light of the situation. My fingers, still hooked through the red cotton cord, are turning blue beneath my tight grip. She glances over her shoulder as we walk but doesn't miss a step.

"When Sam invited me, he said he looks forward to Sunday dinners."

"Of course he did." Her tone is flat, her disgust undeniable. There's no mistaking I've become an interloper and have crossed some imaginary line. Her cool response affects me, and though I don't like it, I feel the arctic air she casts.

"The kitchen is there." She points ahead of her using an unnecessary flat tone. If the rest of the day's going to be like this, I'll make up an excuse to leave.

"Your guest is here." Her voice is tense with an uncomfortable edge. When she veers in a different direction, I follow the sound of clanking dishes, looking between her and Sam for a reaction. Although her chill pricks me, Sam is unaffected. He smiles and offers his hand.

"Hey, Ian. So glad you could make it," he says with his usual charm. I can't help but notice the contrast between the two of them.

I take his hand and lower my voice, snatching a glance at Savannah. "That makes one of you but thanks for the invite."

"Don't pay her no mind," he scoffs, his tone equally low.

I lift the box so he can see. "I remembered your sweet tooth."

His eyes light up. "Sweetcakes?"

"Yep."

"Well, damn! Thank ya. We can dig in after dinner." He carries the box over to the countertop. "I can smell them through the box." He glances over at Savannah. "Ian brought dessert. Isn't that nice?"

She gives a slight nod, but her expression is still dark and unyielding like a storm cloud ready to burst.

"I got some fresh tea in the fridge." Sam walks over to the countertop and pulls open the wooden cabinet door. After grabbing a glass, he fills it with ice and tea and points to the table. "Have a seat and take a load off."

I do as Savannah disappears into another room. "Are you sure I should be here?"

"It's my house. I invite who I want. If she doesn't like it, she can go home." The confidence in his tone belies any hesitation or worry. He quickly changes the subject and drops the stern attitude. "Dinner'll be ready soon but it ain't nothin' fancy. Just spaghetti and meat sauce. I'm no chef, but I ain't too bad on the grill. Next time we'll do burgers and dogs."

Next time? What an ambitious thought.

"Heww-o."

A little voice comes from behind me and when I turn, I see a set of big blue eyes belonging to a miniature version of Savannah. Loops of blonde curls frame her innocent features.

"Who is you?" She asks, her words muddled but endearing.

"*Are* you, baby … Who *are* you?" Savannah instructs from a short distance away.

The little girl looks confused. "*I* is Gigi."

"No, sweetie. The way you ask the question is 'who are you'."

"Oh! Okay, Momma." Her head bobs. She pauses. Who ar-rr you?" she asks, placing extra emphasis as she exaggerates the word, attempting to copy her mother.

"My name's Ian. What's yours?"

"I's Gigi! I'm free." She answers exuberantly and holds up three fingers. She points towards a dozing dog nearby. "I gotto go. I's babysittin'."

"Babysitting, huh? Looks more like dog sitting." I comment with a chuckle, noting the way the child has taken on the responsibility of caring for the dog.

She cocks her head like a little puppy as she considers what I've said to her. Then bobs her head.

"Youse wight!" A mischievous sparkle lights up her eyes. "I's dogsittin'."

I can't help but raise an eyebrow at her youthful innocence. "Aren't you a little young for all that responsibility?" I ask, not really expecting an answer. I'm attempting to fill the awkward silence.

Gigi's delicate nose scrunches into a tight little snout, her blonde eyebrows furrowing as she squeezes her eyes shut. A small chuckle escapes me at the clear expression of disdain on her face. It seems I have the same effect on the child as I do on the mother, who often wears a similar look whenever she's near me.

"I is a big girl. I can," Gigi declares confidently. Her frown lasts but a few seconds, then she opens her eyes. "I gotta go. Bye." Her words are accompanied by a quick skip and hop toward the dog.

Through the doorway, I catch a glimpse of Savannah. Her eyes are fixed on the little girl as she watches her drop to the floor and tenderly cradle the dog's head in her lap. Our eyes meet.

"That's your daughter?"

"Yes." There's a hint of pride in her voice.

"How old is she?"

"Three."

"She looks just like you."

"So, I've been told," she says with a smile.

Savannah turns up the television, possibly to drown out any conversation between Sam and me. I take a moment to watch her and Gigi as they exchange something humorous.

I turn to Sam. "I've said it before, but it bears repeating; she's not happy and I seem to be the cause. Maybe it's best if I leave."

"You ain't going nowhere. I want you here." His commanding tone holds me in place, and I realize leaving isn't an option.

"I've apologized for being an ass when she met me but, I'm guessing it wasn't enough."

Sam's expression turns stoic, and his furrowed brow smooths out. "Figuring females out ain't a talent of mine—or any man, for that matter." He brushes off the topic and turns to another one. "I appreciate your help at the bar. Dinner is my way of saying thanks." He wanders over to the refrigerator. "Can I get you some iced tea?"

"Sure. Thanks." I reply, grateful for the kind gesture during an awkward situation.

My attention shifts to Savannah. Her posture's stiff. Her lips are pressed tight. A clear sign of tension and unease.

As Sam sets the drink down in front of me, he lowers his voice to a hushed tone. "Don't worry about Savannah. She'll come around eventually. Whatever's bothering her, she'll work her way through it."

"Um, 'scuse me." The little girl is back, relentlessly tapping on my knee with her small fingers as she points to the dog with the other. "Pet her," she insists.

I smile but hesitate. "Maybe in a little bit. She's resting right now."

The determined look on the little girl's face tells me

she isn't taking no for an answer. Before I can protest further, she grabs my hand and pulls me toward the dozing dog.

I do as she instructs—*orders*—and catch Savannah watching us again. Even though her face is pointed in the direction of the television I can see her watching us out of the corner of her eye.

"Sit here!" With the command, Gigi unceremoniously drops to the floor and points to a spot right beside her. "I want you to sit with me."

Her authoritative way amuses me, and I note Sam watching as well. It seems both Savannah and Sam are used to the little girl's bossiness.

"Pet her!" She commands.

I snap to attention and salute the miniature general. "Yes, ma'am.

Suppressing a grin, I follow instructions and take a seat next to her. Despite an innocent appearance, there's no doubt this girl has the makings of a leader. She may look all sugar and spice with her curls and innocent face, but it would be interesting to see how her mother handles her teenage years.

I gently place my hand on the animal's soft back and feel the warmth of her fur and steady rise and fall of her breathing. The pooch immediately responds flipping over onto her back in a move of trust. Gigi watches with pride, a smug little smile blooming on her face. I wink at her. "She's a sweet dog. I think she lik—"

"SHH!"

I freeze as Gigi jumps up and clamps a hand over my mouth.

"E-ban you has to be quiet," Gigi scolds in a whisper-shout. "It's time for Bandit to go to seep."

Muffled laughs drift past my ears, proof of Sam and Savannah's amusement. I'm at the mercy of Gigi's piercing lapis-colored eyes. They're filled with a mix of admonishment and affection as she pulls her hand away from my mouth. A peaceful hush settles in the room, enveloping us as we watch Bandit's chest rise and fall. The dog drifts off to sleep with an occasional snore.

As quickly as Gigi stood, she returns to sitting, this time scooting closer to me. She rests her small, delicate hand atop mine, the warmth of her palm seeping through my skin and into my veins. Leaning her head back against the wall, she lowers her eyelids in a peaceful way. Memories of my own insecure childhood flood my mind as I gaze down at our intertwined fingers. Her simple, sweet gesture causes an unexpected swell in my chest. I'm not sure exactly what I'm feeling in this moment. Her trust is both surprising and overwhelming. She knows nothing of me or my past but appears to accept me without judgment and I feel something unfamiliar squeeze my heart. I don't know if I should fight it or embrace it.

The answer eludes me, and I take this moment to enjoy the simple pleasure of holding a child's hand.

CHAPTER TEN

Savannah

"Gigi, please don't fiddle with your food," I plead with a soft sigh, trying to maintain a calm tone.

"I don't want a 'poon, Momma. I want a folk like you."

Gigi pouts and pushes her plate away refusing to use the spoon I've given her. Her cheeks are rosy with defiance, but her eyes hold a touch of mischief. Her relentless energy and current antics aren't making it any better. Despite my frustration, a smile tugs at my lips as I listen with smothered amusement to the way my daughter mispronounces "fork" as "folk."

"Why can't I hab a folk, Momma? I wanna folk!"

Gigi's independent streak is on full display today. She pokes her fingers in the spaghetti as I bite back a "because I said so" response. Lately, I feel she wants me to provide a dissertation to reason everything I tell her to do. The use of a utensil shouldn't be a battle. I'd give in but the idea of cleaning tomato stains off her new outfit chafes me. I exhale an exasperated sigh.

In moments like these, I desperately crave a glass of wine.

"Spaghetti's messy, baby. Just use the spoon." I guide the tip of the utensil down into the bottom of the bowl and slide my fingers to pinch the middle of the metal handle so I can give her a full spoonful. In a surprise move, before she can take it from me, she smacks it out of my hand. The sauce goes flying but my reflexes are quick. I duck. The spoon hits the table, and the bright red sauce goes flying, landing all over the front of Ian. My jaw drops.

"Gigi!" I scold as my temper flares. "That is not nice!"

Sam's eyes widen at the outburst.

I turn to Ian. "I'm so sorry. Let me get something to clean up your shirt."

I make a mad dash to the sink for something to help with the mess, wetting a few paper towels and adding some drops of soap. I rush back to the table and hand them to Ian with some quick instructions, so the stain doesn't set.

"Dab the spots and let it sit for a few minutes." I turn to Gigi with a hard look. She's looking at me with tear-filled eyes. "Tell Ian you're sorry."

"Sowwy, E-ban." The slight tremble in her bottom

lip warns me tears are about to fall. She senses the weight of what she's done.

"It's okay," Ian reassures. "It'll wash out."

I meet his dismissal with a stern expression. "She knows better," I say firmly, turning to my daughter with narrowed eyes. "Don't you, Gigi?"

As if on cue a loud wail escapes her lips, starting out low and building to a full-blown bawl. Gigi's hands fly to her face. She's embarrassed, but as I look closer, I can see there's more going on; sauce has gotten into her eyes and is causing them to burn. I send a pleading look across the table. "Sam?"

"I'm on it." He sees what I see and rushes to the sink, quickly returning with a wet cloth. "Here you go."

I reach behind me and blindly take it while simultaneously capturing both of her wrists.

"Don't touch your face," I remind her gently as I wipe the goop from her eyes and cheeks. Sam hands me a second cloth, and I repeat the process until her face is clean again. When I release her hands, I ask, "Does it still burn?" Gigi shakes her head, her bottom lip puckered in a pout.

I look over at Ian. "I apologize."

"I'm good. I mean, she's only three," he shrugs off any concern. "You do what you need to do for your daughter. I'm fine."

I study his expression, meeting his eyes. There's no trace of annoyance on his face, only an understanding expression.

I lift Gigi from the booster seat and sit her on my

lap. Her crying has reduced to hiccups and, embarrassed and seeking comfort, she hides her face in my chest. Her unexpected move turned a civil dinner into chaos, but she's repentant and, like Ian said, she's only three. I tighten my arms around her. Like any mother, I'm not immune to my child's cries.

"Momma, I sorry," she mumbles through her sobs.

"Shh." I console. "It's okay, sweetie. I'm sure it won't happen again—right?"

"No, Momma." She promises shakily.

Planting a soft kiss on top of her head, I hold her close as she shyly peeks out from behind her fingers to steal glances at Ian.

He smiles warmly at her. "It's alright, kiddo. I'm not mad."

Our eyes meet, and I can feel something's changed. An unexplainable connection between us has occurred. It's as if the barrier around my heart begins to crack. Gigi removes her hand from her face and spreads her fingers so she can see Ian through the gaps. My gaze follows him as he stands up and, with my guard slowly falling, my shoulders relax. Ian smiles at me before making his way to the bathroom—most likely to clean off the goop—but surprises us all by stopping in front of Gigi and me.

"BOO!"

Gigi jumps then giggles as Ian acts playful. Just as quickly she shyly buries her face back into my chest.

With a sudden movement, Ian straightens up and turns away, appearing to go about his task, but with a swift motion, he snaps back on the other side of me, crouching down at Gigi's eye level.

"BOO!" he exclaims again, causing Gigi to burst into a fit of delighted laughter. The tension in the air dissipates like a puff of smoke and I can't help but smile at the sight as her delight gains traction and a giggle blooms into a belly laugh.

"Youse silly, E-ban," Gigi says, sitting up to beam at him.

"You're not the first person who's told me that," he responds with a grin. As he looks over at me, his posture straightens, and he speaks again. "Looks like she still has some sauce on her fingers. You might want to wash her hands at the sink."

I take Gigi's hand in mine for inspection and notice the traces of sticky sauce that still linger. "It's under your nails, Gigi. Let's go wash up." I scoop my arm under her bottom and lift her as I stand. She wraps her arms around my neck but tries to break away so she can walk.

"Momma, I want E-ban to take me," she insists, looking up at Ian with pleading eyes. I bend over and she scrambles away until she's beside him. She takes his hand, looking up at him. "You take me, E-ban?"

By his reaction, he seems momentarily caught off guard and looks from her to me. "Is this okay with you?"

I nod in approval and watch as they walk down the hallway towards the bathroom. Once they've disappeared, I turn to Sam, completely stunned.

"What just happened?"

"What do you mean?" Sam asks innocently.

"She never acts like that—I don't understand."

"She's just a kid, Savi," he reassures me.

"But ... she's never done anything like this before."

"Ian seems fine and no worse for wear. I wouldn't worry about it," he says with a shrug of his shoulders.

A whirlwind of emotions crashes into me, demanding clarity.

"Why is he here? Why did you bring him to Mad Dog?" My voice trembles. "You know about his struggles with drugs and alcohol."

Sam's response is calm and confident, "I do know about it, and it used to be a problem. But trust me, because there ain't much I don't know about Ian; he's not the same person he was when he overdosed. He's been in recovery for nearly four years now."

My eyebrows shoot up in disbelief. "And you think it's a good idea for him to be in a bar?"

Sam doesn't flinch. "I'm in a bar too, Savi, and I'm a drunk. But I'm clean."

He holds my gaze firmly, but I can't help feeling hesitant. "And Ian? Are you positive he's really sober?"

Sam nods without hesitation. "He's a changed man because of what he's been through. You have my word —and I don't give that lightly."

Despite his reassurances, I still feel unsure. "But—"

His palm snaps up between us. "We can discuss Ian another time, Savannah."

His tone goes low, so Ian doesn't hear us. I know if I

pose any more questions, I won't get any more answers. Not today.

Although I trust Sam's opinion, my mind is plagued by a separate persistent niggle. "On a different topic: I don't feel like the epitome of motherhood right now. I teach her 'stranger danger' and all of that, and yet, though she doesn't know him, she goes with him without a second thought."

Sam waves me off. "You worry too much, Savi. She's got good instincts, and Ian may be more decent than he lets on. Kids are like dogs, you know? They have a keen sense for telling if someone's good or bad."

I consider his comment with a subtle toss of my head. "You always manage to find the silver lining. In people and in situations. I honestly don't know how you do it."

He smiles, cocking a brow and giving me a reassuring look. "Well, darlin', bright spots are easy to find. There's nothing else worth seeing, in my opinion—and it sure as hell beats lookin' for the bad in people."

ON THE RIDE HOME, Gigi's chatter slowly fades into a peaceful slumber. Once home I carry her into the house. It's way past her bedtime and as I carefully navigate the stairs, I watch the gentle rise and fall of her chest. It's mesmerizing. Her small body is a solid thirty-three pounds of weight in my arms. With each step, I feel exhaustion creep into my bones, but am filled with love and contentment as I gaze at her sleeping face.

I lay her down on her bed and she stirs. I move back slightly and watch as she settles into a deep sleep. My heart swells with adoration as I watch her, taking in every perfect detail. Her thumb finds its way to her mouth, a comforting ritual that she still holds onto at night. She curls up into a cozy ball, and I reach for the beloved blue and white striped blanket that has been washed countless times since she was born. As I gently unfold it over her, she sighs in contentment and a soft snore escapes her lips.

I slowly back out of her room, I take those moments to admire the peaceful scene before me. The room is adorned with pictures and toys, all carefully chosen with love. The air is filled with the scent of baby powder and lavender from her nightly baths. Closing the door softly behind me, I tiptoe away, not wanting to disturb her peaceful slumber.

I inhale deeply with a sense of quiet satisfaction. My next stop is to the kitchen for a cup of herbal tea before heading to bed myself. The day may have been busy and tiring, but the tranquil moments that follow make it all worth it in the end.

With each step, the stairs quietly creak beneath my weight. The house is still and calm as I make my way down to the first floor. Just as I reach the bottom step, my phone begins to ring. My heart sinks as I remember I had promised to call Sam as soon as I got home. Fumbling through my purse, I finally locate my phone.

"Sorry, Sam," I whisper into the receiver, trying not to wake Gigi sleeping soundly above me.

"Hello, Savannah."

My blood runs cold at the sound of his voice. Drake. How did he find me? Panic sets in as I struggle to keep my composure.

"I know you're there," he taunts, his voice dripping with malice.

"Why are you calling, Drake? I have nothing to say to you."

"Aww, now my feelings are hurt. Did you think changing your name would make you invisible?"

He chuckles, a sound that sends shivers down my spine. His mocking tone cuts through me like a knife. "You have ten seconds, then I'm hanging up."

"Nice family you've got there. It would be a shame if something were to happen to it."

His words linger in the air like a heavy fog, and something snaps inside of me. *Did he dare threaten my child?*

My blood boils with anger as Drake's true nature reveals itself once again. I'd forgotten how evil he is.

"You're a psychopath," I spit out. "I changed my name for reasons that have nothing to do with you," I lie. "And don't threaten me or my family."

"Just saying … he sneers. "Your little girl is lovely."

His direct reference to my daughter makes bile rise in my throat. Memories flood back of how he went from being a loving boyfriend to a monster.

"It's been four years, Savannah. You'd think you'd

have forgiven me by now." His tone turns venomous. "And wouldn't that be around the time you got pregnant?"

His words strike a nerve, dredging up painful memories of the night he took everything from me. "You're disgusting," I manage to choke out.

"Just doing the math. I believe her conception might be around the time when we last made love."

"Made love?" A maniacal laugh escapes and then I turn deadly serious. "It was rape."

"You say tomato ..." He trails off, enjoying my discomfort. "By the way, did they ever find who was responsible for your parents' murder?"

The casual way he says that stops me in my tracks. My mind goes blank as I stand in stunned silence, then hang up and chuck the phone across the room.

CHAPTER ELEVEN

Ian

I should hate myself, but I don't. The woman in my head is the surrogate daughter of my only friend and my thoughts are far from chaste.

I go down a mental list that reminds me of all the reasons I should stay away from Savannah. She's bitchy. Passive-aggressive, even. Her attitude could use a little work but, damn, she's a good mom. The way she comforted Gigi after letting her know what she did wrong ... man, it tugged at my heart. Who knew you could discipline with love and not a fist. That shit's real, and I'd never seen it before tonight. Savannah has the balance perfected. Maybe I'm a pussy but, *shit* ... this was normal. I never knew *normal*.

I don't know what to think, but I know how I feel. My worldview has been through a lens that's different than most people's. Parenting? Mine was shit. The right girl? Well, Dash got Skylar, so there's that. Me? Up to now, my normal experiences have been few. But tonight … I liked it.

Seeing Savannah and Gigi together makes me wonder what it would be like to have a family. For a little while tonight I felt that I might want something I've never, and that scares the hell out of me.

Before sobriety, I would never have desired something that would have tied me down. I've never had more than a casual relationship. The longest was three months and, when it ended, the only reason I felt bad was because she was a good lay. But something happened today with Savannah. I can't get it out of my head, and I can't explain it. It was some weird cosmic connection when our eyes met. Ten seconds at most but, in that time, everything but the two of us faded away.

I close my eyes and indulge the forbidden mental picture; Savannah beneath me in my bed.

I want to make love to her. Feel her skin against mine. Take her all through the night and make her breakfast in the morning. The thought of myself buried deep inside of her has me hard as stone.

Sam would kill me if he knew what I was thinking. He should never have asked me to dinner and given me my first glimpse of normal life since Dash was alive. I'd be good being by myself. But every man has needs.

Since I got sober, I told myself I didn't need a relationship. Women complicate things, or so I used to think. Now, I wonder what it would be like to have a white picket fence and all that goes with it.

I need to stop. Savannah's a mother, for God's sake, and all I can think about is how I want to bend her over and sink my cock deep. I want to smother myself in her tits, tease until she's drenched with desire, and hold her captive to every depraved thought while taking us to an undiscovered level of pleasure. *And that would screw up everything.*

"Jesus, fuckin' christ."

I vomit the words out loud as I adjust my swollen dick. Thoughts of Savannah playing through my mind have me painfully hard. It was dinner. Just a damn dinner, but it turned into something more. I'd never have guessed that getting smacked with a spoonful of spaghetti by an ill-tempered imp would be the highlight of my day but that unexpected hit gave me a hint of what's escaped me nearly my whole life, normalcy. There were no food fights in my growing years. No laughter at the table. No children to take me at face value.

Savannah only knows me through my former life and, though more reserved than not, tolerated my presence at dinner. She, Gigi, and Sam define what a family is, unconditional love at its worst and best. The coming together of the best and worst. A gathering of sinners and saints who understand the meaning of love.

That little Gigi is an awesome kid who, apparently, has an aversion to orders. I identify with that. My father barked orders at me like I was his dog. There was no affection in my growing years. No relationship. Gigi is secure in her love with her mother, whereas I had none from my father. Seeing them together made me feel the absence of that kind of relationship. I've never thought myself particularly fond of kids, but this little girl ... she's special. So is her mom.

I need something. Something to make me feel good. Something to satisfy this craving inside of me.

I stride to the bedroom and strip off my clothes, leaving them in a heap on the floor. Too many thoughts are going through my head. I haven't felt like this in a long time. I need to rid myself of road grit but, more than that, I need to tend to my throbbing dick.

My cock chafes. Thoughts of Savannah have sustained a painful erection and the entire ride home it rubbed the inside of my jeans. I turn on the hot water and brush my teeth as the room fills with steam. Once I rinse my mouth I look down. Nearly purple and painfully engorged I step into the shower and use Savannah as fodder for my fantasies.

The pulsating shaft throbs, a steady reminder that I haven't done this as often as I should. As the water cascades over me I imagine the soft feel of her skin. The taste of her lips. The pointed tips of her breasts as lust fills her, and the sound of my name falling from her lips. *Ian.*

I reach for the soap, turning it over and over until a frothy lather coats my hands. When I fist my cock, I'm rocked by a shudder of pleasure, so I close my eyes and think of her.

Droplets of water trail over my skin as the inside of my lids become an impromptu movie screen where Savannah is the star. Scenes play as I look into her ocean-hued eyes. She's naked except for the thick cover of her hair. It falls like a sunshine-colored curtain over her breasts and back, and nearly kisses her sweet, tight ass.

I imagine her long, slender body against mine. Our limbs tangle, the heat between us palpable, as we begin a wonton dance of desire. I envision kissing her with a connection forged by lust and desire. Our tongues explore each other's mouths. I can almost feel her fingernails raking down my back, setting off shivers that course through my body. I stroke my soap-coated erection and tease the engorged head, feeling the exquisite sensation I imagine loving her to be. My fantasy wraps around me as my fist quickens its pace.

Thoughts of our lovemaking intensify. Thoughts of her fingers grazing the underside of my shaft cause me to tremble and my balls grow heavy, begging for release.

I'm close, I can feel it. My heart pounds in my chest and my body shakes with the intensity of the moment. I pick up the pace to an unrelenting rhythm and groan as I imagine my name, once again, tumbling out on her breath.

The first jet of hot white seed hits the tiles and a

roar tears from my throat. I throttle my dick, arcing high as I imagine her moans of pleasure. My legs shake as I picture myself capturing her mouth and swallowing the sweet sounds until the lightning strike ripping through me begins to subside, and my knees buckle as I fall onto the tiled seat.

After a few minutes, I stand up and shower off the remains of my release.

Structure.

It's what works best for me.

I exit the shower and as I towel myself dry, I think about the things I've lacked for most of my life and the things I value most. I'd never considered anyone but me in the carefully configured framework of my days. The intentional linear regimen has worked for me thus far. No one else entered the mix.

Until Savannah.

Wrestling with my thoughts, I toss the towel in the hamper and lie naked on my bed, staring at the ceiling. My endorphin-soaked brain is sated, and the evidence of my imaginary fuck session's been swallowed down the drain. I wish I could scrub my thoughts as well as I wash the dirt off my body, but mental images of Savannah jumpstart my emotions, and make me want things I've never had. Maybe, just once, I could ask her out for coffee—*No.*

No!

Instantly, I strangle the thought, suffocating it before it takes another breath. I know what's good for me. She defines the word "normal" and that word fits nowhere in my life. So, no matter how I feel, or what I want to do with her, the answer is a hard *fuck no*.

CHAPTER TWELVE

Savannah

Though I've tried not to let it affect me, Drake's call still has me slightly unnerved. A few times I've looked over my shoulder because the lingering sound of his snide tone put me on edge. I shouldn't allow him rent-free space in my head but I'm only human and I have someone else to consider I hold dear enough to die for—Gigi.

A lump forms in my throat as I think of her. The mere thought of something happening to Gigi chokes me up. No matter what I have to do, I'll keep her safe from him. He's a chameleon, a master of manipulation, and he has a knack for reading the room so he can fit in. His words are sweet, but his actions sour any relationship that's more than superficial. He was sweet. He was kind. He said he loved me.

He lied.

I'll never forget the night we broke up. Tired of being caught in a cycle of vicious emotions, I'd had enough. I told him we were through, and he smiled. It wasn't a warm smile, more like the leer of a shark. He asked me if he could give me a kiss goodbye. I'd kissed him a hundred times and, since I'd lost any emotional connection to him, I agreed. It started sweet but soon grew forceful. He pinned me, yanked up my skirt, and held me captive, ripping my hair as he brutally forced himself inside of me. The more I tried to fight him, the more violent he became, tearing tender flesh as he drilled himself inside of me. I fought. I begged. He ignored me. But instead of crying, rage festered inside of me. I told him I was going to go to the police. He said "Go ahead. They won't do anything."

I went home and cleaned myself up. I lay in bed. The rape was horrible, but the implication that he could get away with it left me curled up in my bed, numb, and confused. Was he right?

He continued to call me repeatedly and my father grew suspicious. Dad knew something happened, so I told him Drake threatened to hurt me. He took me to the police and insisted on a restraining order. I blink back tears remembering that time in my life, now thankful that I never told him the truth. Two weeks later, my parents were dead.

The pain and trauma from that time haunts me but the strain in my voice fits the song. As I finish Roy Orbison's "Crying", tears blur my vision, but I'm met with a round of applause. As I catch my breath, I address the audience one final time before ending the evening.

"Thanks for coming out tonight. My name's Savannah Grace and I'll be back next week."

As the bar fills with chatter and laughter, I begin the familiar task of gathering my purse and guitar. I'm not afraid of him but am mentally preparing for the possibility of an encounter and, though my thoughts are scattered, I need some sort of strategy. Should I tell Sam or play the waiting game?

For now, I shake off troublesome thoughts as I toss my hair back and head to the exit leading to the parking lot.

"Night, Sam. I'll see you tomorrow," I call over to him.

He nods. "Give my girl a kiss for me."

"Will do."

I toss a wave as I exit the building. Once outside, I smile. The parking lot is nearly full, and I pause to take in the scene. As much as Sam's helped me achieve a dream, I've also helped him achieve his. A warm, satisfied feeling wraps around me. This is his vision and it's coming true.

"Cough."

The sound makes me snap to attention, and anxiety pools within me, instantly capturing my thoughts. I stop, listen, and place my finger in position on the container of pepper spray on my key ring until I'm confident in continuing to my car.

Every step I take leaves an imprint in the digital

world and as I look at the security camera overlooking the lot, I remember how adept Drake Caruso is at navigating the dark corners of the internet. I can't help but wonder what he's learned about me. His reputation for stalking isn't unfounded—he's well-connected and has access to resources most people can only dream of. Drake's father is a powerful figure, with a seemingly reputable commercial sanitation business as a front. Rumors swirl about a nefarious shadow operation and Drake hinted at his involvement in clandestine dealings. His sanitation business looks legitimate enough. He boasted of lunches and dinners with prominent, affluent individuals, solidifying his walk from college graduation to a position as his dad's right-hand man and eventual successor. My heart races at the thought of him spying on me.

Snatching a look over my shoulder, I continue to my car. For peace of mind tonight I need the comfort of home, a big bowl of freshly popped popcorn, and singing every word of "Under the Sea" with my best little girlfriend as we watch The Little Mermaid for, what seems like, the millionth time.

As I press the key fob, the horn honks, and the doors unlock with a satisfying click. I barely have time to wrap my fingers around the handle when a sudden noise, once again, pierces the quiet night.

The sound is a gunshot to my rattled nerves. My body tenses as if preparing for attack. Survival instincts kick into gear and I scramble to get in the car.

Fumbling for the door handle, I finally manage to

pull it open and slide inside the car. My hand automatically reaches for the steering wheel, using it as an anchor as I sink into the seat. Just as I'm about to slam the door shut and speed away from, what in my mind could be a potentially dangerous situation, the sound again catches my attention. It's faint at first, but then it grows louder and more urgent. Is that … a moan?

It sounds like someone is hurt.

Curiosity wins over fear. I stick my head back out of the car, my ears acting as a satellite to pinpoint where the sound is coming from. Cautious concern and empathy for whoever may be hurt or in need of help outweighs any thoughts of danger. I step out of the car slowly, keeping my hand on the door handle as I listen.

It's not a moan I hear. It's a grunt.

I exit the car and take a few steps. Barely making it ten feet away, I see someone lying on the ground by a motorcycle, their bent, jean-clad legs blocking a full view.

"Hello? Are you hurt?"

My words come out on a shaky whisper, caution evident in my tone. I take one step back as the person stirs. Peering, I get a clearer picture of scattered tools nearby.

"I'm not hurt, but I can't say the same for my bike." Ian leans up, his eyes widening with recognition.

"Hey, Savannah. Is your show over? It's kind of early."

"I'm on a different schedule today." I had no desire

to elaborate on my personal life but, after working around him for a few weeks, our initial animosity has faded to a more civil level. I gesture to the sleek machine. "You have a nice bike there."

"Thanks. I like it but I'm still getting used to being my own mechanic." He stands and brushes off his jeans which reveal smudges of oil and grease.

"I'm guessing you didn't get that around here." I tip my chin toward the bike. "Would a Harley dealership pick it up and take it to a shop?"

"There's no Harley dealership around here. The closest one is in Melody Lake. That's a four-hour drive. Discord Flats has a bike repair place. That's about a hundred miles away."

"Discord Flats?" I feel a sudden chill. "Isn't that the town with that motorcycle gang, Sinful Sons?"

"Yeah. I've been there once. Just in and out of town. I picked up a part for the bike. It was a nice ride, but I should've just had them ship it to me."

"I'd think, if you bought the bike there, they'd want to keep their customer happy."

"I didn't—buy it there, I mean. The bike was a gift from a friend."

"Oh, wow! That's some friend." The words fly out of my mouth, and I instantly regret the tone. I wish I could bite them back but it's too late. "I'm sorry. I didn't mean to sound snarky."

He doesn't seem offended. In fact, his words are touched with sadness.

"It's okay. You're right. She is quite a friend. One of the few I've got. Dash Barrows' widow gave it to me."

"Oh, I remember. The writer. What's her name? Sky something?"

"Eden Skye's her pen name. Her real name is Skylar —or Sky. That's what everybody calls her." He thumbs over his shoulder. "He loved that bike. I'm trying to keep it nice. She also gave me one of his guitars."

Sadness drapes his eyes, and sorrow etches his features. There's no mistaking the heartbreak in his voice and it hits me with more of a punch than a prick. For a moment we share the deep pain of love and loss. Battered hearts have a language of their own.

"I'm sorry for your loss."

My words hang in the air as his expression softens, revealing a vulnerability that tugs at my heartstrings. The mention of Dash's passing brings a somber heaviness to the conversation. I know I should end it here and make my exit, but I can't resist staying a little longer.

Ian's expression softens. "I appreciate that. Dash was a hell of a guy."

"Can you fix it?" I look over his shoulder toward the motorcycle.

"I don't know. I don't think so. Not now, anyway. I don't have the right tools with me."

How are you getting home?"

My question is met with a shrug and a defeated tone. "Uber, I guess, or I can go back into the bar. Sam'll give me a ride when the bar closes."

"But that's not 'till later. A couple more hours, at least."

His palms turn up as he shrugs. "I don't see as I have a lot of options."

I tell myself I'm not his rescuer. *I'm not. I'm not his resc—* "I can drive you home."

My words take flight despite my intentions. He gives me a tentative look.

"I can't let you do that," he says with a hint of hesitation. "Besides, I'm kinda dirty." He looks down at his jeans.

I brush off the concern with a sigh. "It's only a ride, and I have something you can sit on. You'd do the same if the situation was reversed, I'm sure."

"Maybe." A coy smile appears and awakens a playful twinkle in his eyes. "You sure about offering me a ride, Savannah?"

His sexy smile reawakens old feelings. It's been a long time since I thought someone sexy, and his scampish look nudges my dormant libido. I press my lips together and bite the inside of my cheek, the pinch a reminder to stay focused.

* * *

As the engine comes to life, I drift from the parking lot to the road. "I have to pick up Gigi first, but then I can take you home.

"I'll pay for gas."

His offer catches me off guard and I shake my head. "That's not necessary."

"Stop, Savannah. You're doing me a favor. The least I can do is pay for it." His tone incites an internal shiver.

"We're good, Ian. Unless you live on the outskirts of Melody Lake or Harmony, we're good. I've got a full tank." The ring of my cell phone interrupts our conversation and I answer it through the car's speakers. "Hello?"

"Where is you, Momma?"

I'm on my way, sweetie. I'll be there soon."

"Okay. Love you, Momma. Bye." Gigi's voice echoes through the car before she hangs up.

Ian turns to me with a smile on his face. "Someone misses you. She's pretty clever to know how to call you."

"It's easy for her. All she has to do is push a button. Her babysitter has me on speed dial. Gigi knows how to press the number one but doesn't understand the concept of time yet. She likes to keep tabs on me."

"I think it's sweet. She's a good kid."

I chuckle as I steal a glance at him. "I'm surprised to hear you say that, considering you were a victim of her temper."

"It's no big deal and it's done and over with. My shirt washed out just fine." He pauses. "So, back to what we were talking about—me compensating you for giving me a ride."

I shift my eyes and shoot him a disapproving look before turning my eyes back to the road.

"I mean it, Savannah. I want to give you some money."

"Nope—and I don't want to hear any more about it."

"In that case, I'll wash your car for you." He takes a deep breath and sniffs the air. "*And* detail it. What is that disgusting smell?"

A laugh escapes me. "That's the smell of spilled milk that's soured. It'll never come out." I sneak a peek at him. Confusion wrinkles his brow. "I drive with the windows down a lot."

"What about—"

I hold up my hand, effectively cutting him off. "Stop, Ian. It's just a freakin' ride. Can't you just accept a simple act of kindness?" Exasperation is evident in my tone.

"No."

No? I snap my head toward him and see he's serious.

"I'm not good at that; accepting favors. I prefer to pay my way. Maybe it's kindness. Maybe it's pride. I haven't figured that out yet."

His humble reply catches me off guard and the sound weighs heavy on my heart. I shake my head in disbelief.

"Not everybody expects something from you, you know? Sometimes, people do something nice without expectation of payback. They do it just because they want to."

CHAPTER THIRTEEN

Ian

Savannah exits the car and I follow in her footsteps, keeping with her pace. As we approach the home of Gigi's caregiver, the door swings open wide, revealing the little girl eagerly waiting inside.

"MOMMA!" The high-pitched squeal cuts through the air like a knife.

"Baby love!" Savannah responds with equal enthusiasm, her arms outstretched for her daughter. Gigi runs into them and melts into her chest.

"I missed you, Momma. You's late again." Gigi pouts.

"*You're* late, Gigi," Savannah gently corrects.

"No, I not."

"*I'm* not."

"Yes, you are, Momma. You. Is. Late."

"You *are* late."

"No, I not, Momma!" Gigi stomps her foot in frustration and steels her gaze as she locks eyes with her mother. "You is! You is!"

She buries her face against Savannah's body, her tiny shoulders shaking with angry tears.

"Gigi …" Savannah's gentle, coaxing tone is filled with love and understanding. She lifts the girl onto her hip. I spy her quivering bottom lip and it tugs my heart. "Gigi, it's okay. It's not important."

She pushes herself back to see Savannah's face. "But it is impo-tant. Momma. I wanna be a big gal. I not—don't—wanna talk like a baby."

I chime in, the empathetic squeeze inside my ribs compelling me to interject. "Kiddo, I don't think you talk like a baby at all. You just corrected yourself. Just like a big girl."

Savannah turns to look at me over her shoulder. "Sorry. Maybe you should've waited in the car."

Gigi wriggles out of her mother's arms and skips to me. Her bright smile replaces her distress from a moment ago. I can't help feeling shocked at how quickly she bounces from one emotion to the other and the emotional whiplash leaves me dumbfounded.

She looks up at me with wide eyes, her head falling so far back she reminds me of a Pez dispenser. She takes my hand firmly in hers and, suddenly, I'm putty in her grasp.

"Hi E-ban, you's not a stwanger no more. I can say hi."

"I guess I'm not," I reply, a lopsided grin forming on my face. "How are you, kiddo?" I sneak a look at Savannah, certain my smile has turned into a lopsided grin. "Bet she gets away with a lot, huh?"

"She sure tries, and most of the time, she succeeds." She glances down at Gigi. "Don't let that cute little face fool you. There's definitely a mischievous gremlin hiding inside all that adorableness."

"You're doing great as a mom, Savannah."

"I try." Defeat creeps into her tone. "But she gets her way a lot."

Gigi raises her arms toward me. "Pick me up, E-ban!"

I shoot a quick glance at Savannah for permission, and she nods with a small smile.

"Yes, ma'am." I bend down to lift Gigi into my arms. She's barely the weight of the buckets of ice I lift at the bar. It dawns on me that I've never held a child, but she wiggles in my arms until she fits against me. Savannah's eyes meet mine and her expression softens.

"She may only be three, but she knows what she wants and how to get it," she says with a mix of exhaustion and pride. "I just hope I can make it through her teenage years."

"Excuse me." As I stand by Savannah, a woman with gentle brown eyes approaches us. Her voice is a melodious blend that sounds somewhere between a purr and a coo. Although she appears older than Savannah, she's fit and stunning. Cascading down her shoulder are soft curls of copper-colored hair that only adds to her allure. With a warm smile, she extends her hand. "I don't believe we've met."

I take her outstretched hand. "Ian. It's a pleasure."

"Cora. Cora Brooks—and I believe the pleasure is mine." She gives Savannah a coy look. "I don't believe you've ever mentioned Ian, Savi."

"Dis is E-ban!" Gigi announces.

"I heard." Cora chuckles with a sweet smile at Gigi, then turns back to me with an inviting look.

"Can I get you something to drink, Ian?"

"Thank you, ma'am—but no."

"Ma'am?" she chuckles. "I think I'm insulted," She turns to Savannah. "I'll get Gigi's things." With a playful glance towards me, she adds, "Ian, it was very nice meeting you."

"Likewise, ma'am."

She raises an eyebrow. "Now, Ian," she says playfully, "if you call me ma'am again, I may have to persuade Savi not to bring you back." As she walks away, she looks over her shoulder and her suggestive expression lingers. "And that would be a shame."

A bewildered Savannah looks between Cora and me, and I struggle to suppress a chuckle. It seems like the woman had been flirting with me.

"I'm not sure what all that was about." Bewildered, her lips purse and pull to the side. "And you ... *ma'am?*"

"What? You're surprised I have manners?"

"I don't know what I think—of you *or* her."

I study her closely as I hold onto Gigi. What stories

has she heard about me? Hopefully, she sees me as a better man than the one she thought she knew. I can't deny my past mistakes, whether it's the full front-page photo on The Buzz when I mooned the audience at a concert, or the incident where I got a citation for public urination. But I've worked hard to turn my life around since then, and it's important to me that Savannah knows that.

"I know you've heard a lot about me," I say, meeting her gaze. "But whether you believe it or not, that guy's gone."

She seems hesitant, as if she's struggling with some inner conflict. I don't blame her. If our roles were reversed, I'd be cautious about me too but, the truth is, getting sober revealed many sides to me. The introvert who brooded over his past mistakes. The friend grieving the loss of another friend, dealing with buried anger issues. And, yes, the cocky bastard who despised mind games.

"Mmm-Mm!" Suddenly, Gigi wraps her arms around my neck and hugs me. The faint scent of lavender and fresh laundry clings to her clothes. It's soothing and comforting and her actions take me by surprise. Her grip is strong, a sharp contrast to her delicate stature. I freeze for a moment. Her open display of trust and innocence hits my emotions like a blowtorch, melting away the icy walls around my heart with the beauty and purity of unconditional acceptance, and making my insides melt.

Cora returns to the room with a pink and white

striped bag. A brown teddy bear's head peeks out from the top.

"Here you go. You're all set," she says with a smile.

"Thanks, Cora." Savannah takes the bag and loops the straps over her arm.

Cora turns to me. "It was nice meeting you, Ian."

"Same here, Ma—Cora." I quickly correct myself.

"Good catch," she says with a kittenish smile then looks from me to Savannah. "You'll have to bring Ian around again, Savi. He's cute."

Savannah's expression goes blank while I stifle a twitch to laugh.

I HOLD the car door open as Savannah safely secures her daughter into her car seat. The little one fidgets and kicks her legs, eager to start her journey. I watch as Savannah carefully snaps the buckle, making sure not to pinch her daughter's delicate skin. When I hear the telltale click assuring she's secured, I note Savannah covering Gigi's legs with a partially folded blanket. She plants a light kiss on her head before closing the door. "This is in case you get cold."

Gigi gazes out the window, suddenly indifferent. As Savannah backs out of the car, she bumps into me and pops back up, falling back against the car's frame. "What are you doing?"

"Trying to be a gentleman," I say with a small smile.

She walks around the back door as I open the front.

Gracefully dipping low into the driver's seat, she keeps watch as I close both doors, and stroll around to the passenger side of the car, and get inside. With the press of a button, she starts the car then turns to me.

"I'm sorry about Cora," she says with sincerity.

"No need to be. She seems nice." I pause for a moment before adding, "I'll show you the way."

"What?" Savannah gives me a confused look.

"To my house. You don't know where I live. I can guide you there—unless you want to use your GPS." As we approach a stop sign at the intersection, I recite directions. "Make a left here and go straight. It's about ten miles, then you'll take a right." Despite following my directions, Savannah remains suspiciously quiet throughout the drive. It's uncomfortable, so I break the silence. "Why don't you say what's on your mind, Savannah."

She glances at me, then finally speaks up. "How do you know Sam?"

The question takes me by surprise. "What do you mean?" I know they're close but have no idea what information he might have shared with her about me.

"You two seem to know each other pretty well. I've known Sam all my life, and he's never mentioned you to me. So, how do you know him? How did you meet? And seeing you two that night at the bar, and how friendly you seemed to be, I'm confused. He's never mentioned you. He only knew of Boundless Hearts because of my winning the contest, so ..." Her words trail off.

"If you've known him all your life, then you should also know he wouldn't betray a confidence. Sam's my sponsor." The words may be simple, but they hold a deeper meaning. One of trust that we both should understand.

With a sudden, sharp movement, she turns her head to look at me, her eyes wide with surprise. Then, just as quickly, she returns her gaze to the road ahead. "So that's what he meant," she murmurs, her shoulders relaxing, as if releasing a burden. "He mentioned something, but never directly, so I didn't pry." A sense of vulnerability radiates from her words, and I feel a pang of sympathy. "You don't have to tell me anything you're not comfortable with," she gently assures me. "But, since my daughter's taken a liking to you, if you're willing to share, I'm all ears."

"I have nothing to hide. I met Sam when I was in rehab. The media made sure that everyone knew I was there, but my relationship with Sam is private. It isn't information I feel I need to offer to strangers but, since you aren't one, ask away."

She reaches up to the nape of her neck and gathers the thick cascade of hair with one hand. With a graceful gesture, she drapes it over her shoulder, revealing smooth skin and delicate features. The fading sunlight catches in her hair, giving it an ethereal glow as it tumbles over her front like a golden waterfall. I'm mesmerized. Does she know how beautiful she is? A sense of vulnerability radiates from her as she fiddles with the gold chain around her neck.

My cell buzzes in my pocket, breaking the flow of our conversation. Reluctantly, I pull it out and glance at the screen. The name appearing on the screen is none other than the subject of our conversation. I quickly type out a short message to let him know I left the bike in the parking lot before tucking my phone away again.

Turning back to Savannah, the brief interruption has given me a moment to catch my breath. She looks over at me, curiosity sparkling in her eyes. "It was Sam. I sent him a message telling him about the motorcycle. I'll call him back later."

"Oh." She nods.

"So, tell me," I prompt, "what else do you want to know?"

"I guess about the relationship between the two of you."

"If memory serves me correctly, he was in town taking care of something for a friend. He mentioned reading about me and when he discovered I was undergoing treatment just twenty minutes away, he reached out to the facility staff."

"I didn't know."

"Why would you? Sponsors are entrusted with confidential information. It's not their place to betray someone's trust. The pastor of your downtown church could be struggling with addiction and be in recovery themselves. People don't reach out unless they need help. If sponsors or therapists or even just people in a support group can't be trusted to keep a confidence, it can ruin someone's life."

"You only know about me because I was a public figure, and you were a fan of the band. All sorts of rumors circulated since the day they carried me out of that hotel room. Some rag magazines even reported my death, which they then had to retract. Of course, they put it on the back page. They said all sorts of shit about me."

Savannah flashes me a disapproving look. "Ian! Little ears."

"Youse said a naughty word!" Gigi chimes in.

"Sorry." I grimace at Savannah, then glance over my shoulder at Gigi. "Sorry, munchkin."

"Is okay, E-ban," Gigi reassures sleepily.

"Go on with your story," Savannah says.

I take a deep breath, my finger tapping furiously on my thigh. This is the part I don't like to revisit. "There really isn't much more to say. I'd hit rock bottom—lower than ever before. I did whatever they told me to do. When they put me in that sterile room in a white gown with bright white lights, I felt like I was going crazy." A shiver runs down my spine. "I played the perfect patient, nodding and smiling at all the right moments just so I could get out of there and do it again."

"Do what again? Overdose?" The shock makes her voice go shrill. She quickly catches herself and steals a look in the rearview mirror. I mimic her actions and turn to look over my shoulder. Taking in the peaceful sight of my little friend fast asleep.

When Savannah's gaze returns to me, it's only for a fleeting moment as she turns her attention to the road. a brief look. She turns her attention back to the road and shakes her head.

"Why in god's name would you want to do something that reckless, Ian? Can't you see how much pain it would cause to the people who care about you?" Her tone is laced with pain and confusion, mirroring the furrowed lines on her forehead.

I pause, allowing the weight of her question to burrow in. My eyes roam over her silhouette, taking in every delicate curve of her face and flutter of her lashes. Even in the dim light, I can see how they feather out, casting a slight shadow above her nose and chin. How can I explain to someone so effortlessly perfect that I have always been anything but? That I've struggled with feelings of self-doubt and worthlessness for as long as I can remember? I'm not sure I can find the right words to convey my despair. That I felt I had nothing to offer the world and that, in that mental state, I believed I was better off dead? That I was only worth something when Dash was alive because he made me feel I had some small contribution and my existence in the world was valid. Is it any wonder that at one point, death seemed a better option than living in a world where I never felt I fit in?

As I stare out the window, words catch in my throat. There is no adequate way to articulate how a person feels when they lose the only person who ever made them feel like they mattered, but, for her, I'll try.

"Growing up, I was nothing to my father. My worth was dependent on what I could do for him. He was cruel, but now I see it was his pain that made him mean. We both lost my mother and, instead of leaning on each other for strength, he used me as his whipping boy, so to speak. There were times when he would say 'I wish you were—" I pause. "I knew what he meant, Savannah because he made me feel as if I was breathing oxygen that would be better spent on someone else. But everything changed when I met Dash and the band found fame. Green became his favorite color, and suddenly I had value. My dad died of a faulty liver, and I didn't know how to feel about his passing. Dash was the brother I never had. He made me believe there was hope for me despite the crappy thoughts my father drilled into me. When Dash died ..." I take a breath and clear my throat.

"Dash's death hit me with a wave of sorrow that took me to an unbearable level of pain. That grief affected everything, especially performances. I spent thousands of dollars to numb the pain. My drinking problem and drug use spiraled out of control. Ticket sales declined. The guys in the band tolerated me, but everyone has their limits—especially when it hits them in the wallet. I was nothing but a burden, or so I believed. I'm sure you can figure out the rest."

She looks at me with sadness in her eyes and I manage a weak smile as I struggle in the emotional undertow. "Grief isn't always visible, you know? It really fucked me up." I flinch, noting the curse word that slipped out of my mouth, and shoot a glance at the back seat. Gigi's out cold in the back seat. "Sorry. She didn't hear me."

"Ian, I'm so sorry."

Her voice is thick with genuine emotion. I can't help the small smile that presses at my lips at the realization that she cares. "Thanks."

"You don't have to thank me for being human. You've been through a lot."

"Apart from Sam, I'm not used to anyone caring about me. I'm okay now. I've rebuilt myself from the inside. I went to counseling; moved to Rock Hills. The ranch has been a place of healing and growth for me. It takes time, for sure, but I'm better. Now, I'm happier Dash lived than sad that he died."

A sense of peace washes over me when I realize just how far I've come. Then I hear a sniffle.

"Are you crying?" We stop for a red light, and I see her swipe at her face.

"It's just … you had everything." Her voice strains with emotion.

"I did. Then it was gone. But now, I feel like I have it again, though in a different way. Most people wouldn't understand unless they've been through it …"

"But I have," she interrupts softly, her eyes filled with empathy. "My parents were murdered."

My eyes widen with shock and my heart sinks with

pity. "Damn." My stomach twists with sympathy. "I'm so sorry, Savi. That's tough."

She nods, her expression pained but resolute. "It is but counseling helped.

Though I'm curious to know more, I go with the switched topic. "Yeah. It does. At first, I thought I looked weak and pathetic, but I needed to deal with the pain." A wistful smile comes to my lips as a memory rises to the surface. "Then someone wrote me a letter, and it changed things."

"A letter?" She steals another glance before the light changes.

"Yeah. Someone *saw* me. Really saw me. It helped me navigate my next steps. I carry it in my wallet."

"You've piqued my interest."

"It was from Dash's widow. She reminded me I was loved, and it broke me—in a good way."

"And now?"

I shrug indifferently. "I work on it every day. Sam helps."

Savannah's tone softens, and she sweetly smiles. "That sounds like him."

I shake my head in amazement. "I have no idea how I lucked out getting Sam for a sponsor. He's the reason I'm here. He's become a good friend."

"And now you have even more friends. Me, Gigi, and, maybe, even Cora." Her expression turns cheeky and her lips purse. "No, definitely Cora," she laughs. "There's no doubt she's taken a liking to you."

Savannah

"How far out is your house?"

Ian lets out a deep, throaty chuckle. "When I said it was in the next town, I meant on the outskirts. That's why I offered you gas money."

"I'll definitely be relying on the GPS to get me home."

"It isn't too far now."

I switch on the radio and my Bluetooth connects, filling the car with soft jazz.

"Miles Davis?" Ian asks, surprise evident in his tone.

I nod with a smile. "Yeah. He's one of my favorites. Whenever Gigi's in the car, I have to play him." I jut my thumb toward the backseat and glance in the rearview mirror. "She's out right now but, you know what they say about music soothing savage beasts? It works on my little girl."

He laughs, his deep voice mingling with the smooth sounds of a saxophone. "I hardly think she's a savage."

I furrow my brow and feel the familiar pinch that forms ruts across my forehead. "You might have a different opinion if you knew her better. Her temper tantrums are beastly." I laugh.

"Seriously?" The humor in his tone is unmistakable.

"When a temperamental three-year-old's unpredictable moods take you hostage in the middle of a crowded grocery store you fervently pray for survival until you can escape and get home with your sanity."

"Was that what happened at Cora's house?"

I jab an accusing finger toward him. "See? She's got you fooled. That wasn't even a bad one. There's a reason why they say 'sugar and spice' when describing little girls but don't be fooled, that 'spice' part is cayenne pepper. And, as far as the music, it chills her out."

"It does for most people."

"When she was a baby, and had a crying jag, there were few things that soothed her. Rides in the car and, you know that acapella group, Pentatonix? When Gigi started pulling herself up, she would hold onto the coffee table and wiggle to the music."

Ian looks over his shoulder and smiles. "She's completely out, isn't she? —and she's sucking her thumb. Cute. And Miles Davis does all that, huh?"

"Works like a charm. Miles Davis. John Coltrane. Lee Morgan. They all work."

"She's got good taste."

I toss him a skeptical glance. "I would have pegged you more for a Nine Inch Nails or Dream Theatre fan."

"I like them too. I guess I have a pretty eclectic taste in music."

"I think I'm guilty of pigeonholing you. I would have thought all heavy metal."

He shrugs. "Most people thought that about Dash, too but his parents had an amazing vinyl collection and a kick-ass stereo system. They all played instruments too. His dad the guitar, his mom the keyboard, and his two sisters played too. I loved being around them. I ate so good when I was over at his house. His mom was Italian and the food ... man, I miss it. They always included me. Game nights. Holidays. Would you believe they even gave me Christmas presents? I wasn't a relative and they gave me presents." His voice trembles. "They didn't love me, but it felt like they did."

"Oh, I beg to differ. It sounds to me like they love you." I insist.

"Nah. I'm not blood."

"Not all family is blood, Ian."

A comfortable silence settles in as we continue down the highway, buildings and cars becoming scarcer the farther we go. I look at the clock. It's been nearly half an hour since we left Cora's house.

"We're almost there. Sorry. Maybe you should have looked at your GPS. You might have changed your mind."

"I wouldn't have. I've not been this far out in the country. The drive's been nice, though." I glance at him.

He gives me a sideways appraising glance as a sly smile plays at the corners of his lips. "Yeah, you look pretty chill." His tone changes to a more serious one. "Savannah, I know you don't have a high opinion of me, so I don't blame you for being skeptical, but I have no reason not to be transparent. It's just, judge me for who I am, and not who I used to be," he says softly, his voice laced with sincerity. He points to a spot ahead of us and I follow with my eyes. "See that red mailbox? That's the driveway. Turn right there."

I make the turn and am met with an expanse of darkness that seems to swallow everything in its path. "Wow, it's dark. How far back is your house?"

"Not far. It's in the middle of the property. Once we're close a motion light should trigger."

The trek through the pitch-black night has all the remnants of a horror movie and, when the first light pops on, I jump.

"You okay?" Ian laughs. "It's just two of them."

"I'm okay," I respond with a shaky laugh. "Just got spooked for a second."

The hard asphalt beneath the tires graduates to rough gravel adding a crunchy sound to the already eerie atmosphere.

"We're here," he announces.

As I bring the car to a stop another light comes on combining with my headlights. It's as if we've stepped into another world. "Wow." My eyes widen and my mouth falls open with amazement. Like Dorothy's travel from the dull monotony of Kansas to the technicolor Oz, multi-hued gardens showcase the area surrounding a charming and rustic stone and log cabin. I lift my gaze from the colorful gardens to take in the wrap-around porch, and just as I spy an enticing porch swing, the light disappears.

"Did you landscape all of this?" I ask, breathless with wonder.

"I did." His voice is confident and full of pride.

"It's magnificent."

"Thank you." His tone drops to a humbler one, though pride still shines in his eyes. Moonlight, like a gentle hand, caresses his face with soft illumination. A glimmer of self-assurance reflects in his expression, and I'm humbled to witness its sweetness.

Ian reaches for the door handle and then turns to me. "Thanks again for the ride."

I stop him by placing my hand on his arm. "Before you go, can I ask you a question?"

He nods, granting me permission to do so.

"What kept you from going back to your old life?"

"Love."

"I don't understand," I'm genuinely curious, but still am slightly confused.

"And that's okay. I don't understand it all myself, so I don't expect you to. I'm still learning to love myself, this life, and the things I like to do that make me happy. I may not be where I want to be, yet, but I'm not where I used to be." His head turns left and right as he takes in the breathtaking moonscape scene shadowing the property. "Four years ago ..." He pauses, damming threatening emotions, and clears his throat before continuing. "Let's just say I traded that life for this one and I'm finally finding myself."

It's a moment of growth and vulnerability that I'm humbled to witness. I sit, in awe, watching as this tough-as-nails, macho, heavy metal-loving, former rock star's eyes shimmer.

Ian

"I shouldn't have pried." Regret seeps into her voice, illuminating the silver flecks that bring light to her sapphire eyes. Suddenly, I fall under a spell.

My body floods with desire, drowning me in a sea of euphoria. It's been nearly four years since drugs or alcohol have entered my system but, this feeling, rocks me. I'm unsteady. There's something unspoken in her eyes, a tenderness that wasn't there before that's new and unfamiliar. I drift forward, overwhelmed by an invisible force and a dangerous, consuming urge to kiss her.

"Momma."

We snap back, our lips doomed not to meet, as a small, sleepy voice breaks the enchantment.

"Hi E-ban." Gigi's voice is quiet and groggy as she

rubs her eyes with her fists. When she puts her hands down, her eyes go wide while her body springs to life. She points out the windshield. "What's dat?"

I've not seen such a curious expression. Her dark, thick lashes nearly kiss her brows as her eyes widen further. I follow her line of sight, a smile blooming inside of me.

"Savannah," I murmur, my voice low and excited. "Turn off your headlights and watch Gigi's reaction."

Slightly confused, she does as I instruct, twisting the toggle switch as she steals a glance in the rear-view mirror.

"Wow."

In unison, Mother and Daughter breathlessly voice the word as the sky surrounding us combusts. Unhindered by light pollution, the dark canvas ignites with a kaleidoscope of stars. They mimic the beauty of diamonds resting on a bed of black velvet, sparkling, and twinkling as they dance against the dark expanse. Constellations come into view with each star having its own unique glow. Savannah's gaze hops back and forth between the wondrous gaze before her and the one behind. My smile widens at the sight as I'm taken back to my first night in Rock Hills. Rediscovering that same sense of awe with the two of them is a new kind of happiness for me, one I never knew existed.

"This is amazing!" Savannah breathes out, fixing her eyes on the sky above.

"I think so. My first night here I had the same reaction as you. I snatched a blanket off the bed and slept outside. The cool breeze and the starry sky completely mesmerized me. After a life of confinement in my bedroom, and then tour buses, hotel rooms, and hospitals, I craved fresh air more than anything. That night was the first time I truly felt I could breathe. It's still hard for me to believe this place is mine."

"It's breathtakingly beautiful. If I lived here I'd want to be outside every night."

"Most nights, I am. I even built a fire pit so I can sit out here after working on the ranch. This is my first real home and I have a feeling it will be my last."

"Does it ever get old? It seems so magical. I can't imagine it would."

"You know, I thought I might get used to it but it never grows old and, just now, watching your expression and Gigi's, it's like I'm seeing it for the first time."

She nods in agreement. "As with everything a child does, it's as if you're seeing it for the first time. The taste of ice cream. Walking on a sandy beach. A spider's web—not that I like spiders, but watching as one spins a web outside our window is something that kept our attention for days. When it rained, Gigi wouldn't leave her perch because she was so worried about the spider." A gentle laugh escapes her.

"Savannah, look." I point up to the sky.

"Oh, my gosh! Gigi, look," Savannah exclaims. "A shooting star!" Her tone fills with wonder.

I turn and hear Gigi suck in an astonished breath as she peers from the back seat with a pure, wonder-filled look. Gone is any remnant of the sleepy demeanor she possessed when we arrived.

Something happens inside of me as I gaze at her wonder-filled expression. A fissure. A crack, maybe. I can't define it but seeing her filled with such pure joy brings something inside me to life. I catch the emotion as the feeling expands and forms a lump in my throat.

"There's magic here, Ian." Savannah's whispery tone holds reverence.

"Yep. Do you see da magic, E-ban?" Gigi asks.

"I think I do, kiddo." My chest tightens. Unlike me at her age, Gigi has a world of possibilities ahead of her and is unencumbered by the kind of limitations that plagued me as a child.

"In rehab, one counselor told me that everything has a purpose, even the devastating events that brought us there. Though I carried a darkness that sent me to that place, when I moved here, a different kind of darkness healed me. Under the night's spell, I found solace and peace. It may sound strange but I'm grateful for what happened to me because it brought me to this place. Without that, I wouldn't have this."

Suddenly, Gigi lunges forward with her legs and arms outstretched. She's restrained by the safety straps but her excitement is palpable. "What's dem? See it? SEE IT?"

"What?" My eyes follow her gaze and I can't help but let out a light chuckle. "Oh, those? They're fireflies."

Gigi's expression turns to one of horror. "Fire? Do dems burn?"

"*They* burn, Gigi." Savannah corrects.

"Dems do?" Instantly her brows shoot up with worry and lines form a pattern on her forehead.

Savannah emits a sigh and rolls her eyes. I stifle my laughter and bite the inside of my lip as I begin to understand the exasperating challenge of teaching a child how to speak properly. I place my hand on her arm. "Want to let me take this?"

She throws up her hands in defeat. "Be my guest."

"Don't worry, kiddo. They don't actually burn. It's just their name. Some people call them lightning bugs and others call them fireflies. Haven't you ever seen them before?"

"I don't think we have," Savannah interjects. "There's a lot of light pollution where we live and not many trees."

I turn my attention back to Gigi. "Well, they're nature's nightlight, and they don't burn. You can touch them *if* you can catch one."

"I can?" Gigi's body snaps forward, eager for escape as she grabs at the straps. Excitement consumes her and her enthusiasm electrifies the air. "Git me out! Git me out!"

Savannah hurries to the backseat to free her from the restraints. As soon as the belt is unbuckled Gigi catapults herself out of the seat and pushes past her mother to get outside of the car. She kicks off her shoes the minute her feet hit the earth and, suddenly, it's as if she's sprouted wings. She flies toward the tree line as air catches her curls and she sprints barefoot across the cool grass.

Savannah chases after her while I quickly duck into the car and snatch the soft, woolen blanket that was earlier draped across Gigi's lap. They may not be aware of the temperature drop as we draw closer to the trees, but I'm well acquainted with the chill.

They run, their laughter carrying through the dark while having no idea where they're going. With only the moon and stars to guide us, I follow, tasting the clean air as it fills my lungs, and only stop when I see Gigi come to an abrupt halt. Her head falls back, her eyes filled with wonder and her mouth takes the shape of an 'O', as the expanse of the night sky consumes her.

"Dis is a mazen, Momma," she whispers, her voice barely audible over the stillness.

Tranquility stills me. There's harmony between us. It's as if their pleasure is also my own. I watch in awe as the trees sway in unison, their branches coming together to sing their own kind of music. Above us, time suspends beneath a deep indigo sky graced with shimmering jewels carelessly strewn across the heavens. A breeze picks up and a celestial hand takes charge, orchestrating a natural symphony in harmony with a magical universe.

"Look up there." I break the spell in a quiet voice, pointing my finger to a constellation. The Milky Way stretches across the sky like a glittering silver belt. I steal a glance at Savannah, her face turned upward in awe. There's something so right about the informality of this moment. Sharing the simple pleasure of stargazing with her is such a sweet, but foreign, feeling.

"Ian, look! Another shooting star!"

Savannah goes up on her tiptoes as she points at the sky. The awe in her voice strokes the child within me that's long been buried. I follow the diamond hurling across the sky as it tosses a glittery trail of stardust indulging in the pleasure of watching Gigi come close to her mother's side. Warmth spreads within me and unexpected tears sting my eyes.

I watch the two of them, etching to memory this magical moment. Savannah tosses a look over her shoulder and I feel a squeeze in my chest, savoring my first taste of appreciation as she catches my eyes and mouths the words "thank you."

CHAPTER SIXTEEN

Savannah

"Wook, Momma. You see dat bug?"

I nod. A small, knowing smile teases my lips as I look down at my daughter. Gigi pulls her petite hand from mine and, with a gleeful giggle and arms outstretched, she dashes off and runs wild and free. The night breeze tousles her hair as she dances with the fireflies. She plucks at the air with eager hands, hoping to catch a beckoning bug. As she twirls, the moonlight catches glittery polka dots on her snowy white dress turning them into crystalline stars.

As I watch her, a fresh memory of me and my mother surfaces. I remember doing this same thing when I was a child. Seeing my Gigi completely immersed in nature, unhindered and uninhibited, brings a rush of emotions and I feel my heart swell. Gigi's never known freedom like this in our busy neighborhood. There are too many people and too many houses to let a child run with abandon. Whether we were more naïve back then or if the world has gotten more dangerous, I can't say for sure. I just won't take any chances with her safety because, as much as I hate the memory of Drake or how I found my parents, those experiences taught me bad things happen to good people.

I cross my arms over my chest and briskly rub my hands over my skin to ward away the chill. The temperature seems to have dropped from when we left Cora's house.

"Here. This might help. It's always a little chillier near the trees." Ian notes my slight shivering and comes behind me, covering my shoulders.

"Thanks."

"I grabbed Gigi's blanket when you were following her out into the field. I thought she might need it. She doesn't seem to be bothered at all, but she's running around. Seems you can better use it."

The gesture is thoughtful, as is his tone, and I pinch the soft material between my fingers, pulling it around me like a shawl. The moonlight slants across his face, accentuating the contrast between his strong jawline and tender expression.

I look out into the field where Gigi's darting about with boundless energy in her eager attempts to capture a lightning bug, and I stand, breathless, as I take in the sight before me. It's like looking into a magical wonderland. The air is alive with flickering light dancing among the tall grasses and wildflowers. Each flash illuminates an airborne creature and my sweet girl follows their flights.

"This is beautiful, Ian. I've never seen anything like it." My voice is a reverent whisper filled with gratitude. "There are so many lightning bugs. It looks like a forest of Christmas trees."

The lightning bugs congregate near the line of Jeffrey pines. It truly seems as if they've been lit with thousands of twinkling lights. The evergreens flash in patterns with no rhyme or reason. They're sweet victims of nature's timing and the winged creatures who saturate their branches. I can't help but wonder if Ian realized he was doing Mother Nature a service by not clearing them from his property. I'd recently read lightning bugs are endangered and now, seeing this, I'm happy he left the trees in place. How wonderful a place to be to witness this exchange between bugs and trees and a clear night sky glistening with stars. Gigi's laughter echoes through the night as she twirls endlessly among the trees and fireflies, the joyful sound rising to the heavens.

I look over at Ian, who seems lost in the moment, as he tries to blink away an unexpected mist of tears. His reaction tugs at my heartstrings, affecting me in a way I couldn't have imagined. I've long known Ian is Gigi's father and, as I look from him to her, emerging tears sting my eyes as I solidify that knowledge. Their profiles are nearly identical. Same nose. Same chin.

Fear and doubt, and a hefty dose of pride formed

my decision not to tell him. I'd always believed I would raise her alone and cared not one bit about leaning on anyone for additional support. But seeing this ... feeling this ... questions swirl in my mind. If he knew, would he want her? Love her? Deny her?

I swallow an emotional lump as the biggest fear of all invades all the other thoughts; would he try to take her away from me?

As Ian fixes his eyes on her, I push the tortured thoughts aside. Though my guard will always be up when it comes to my daughter, my gut feeling is that, though he may not know it, he already loves her.

"This is overwhelming. I feel like words are inadequate to describe this sensory experience.

"What you're feeling is what sold me on this place," he explains, his expression soft as he swipes the back of his hand over his cheeks. "It was abandoned and long forgotten and, somehow, silly as it might sound, we shared that connection. While sober and in recovery I realized I never felt seen, both growing up and when on the stage and in front of thousands. No one was living here, like it had been waiting for me. The old man who owned it had passed away and had no family to inherit the house and possessions. The taxes were in arrears, so it was cheap and was offered for sale with all the furniture and tools. But it was this field—this magic—that sold me. I had one request; would they allow me to spend one night before my final decision. Though I felt a connection when I walked through the door, it was this that made me never want to leave." He waves outstretched arms, then jabs the air with a pointed finger. "Look, Savannah. There's another shooting star."

Catching a glance at Gigi to ensure she's okay, I then turn my eyes to the sky. "There are so many out here."

His smile widens. "Every clear night you see many of them. I'd never seen a shooting star until the night I stayed here. I bought the place the next day."

"Momma, wook!" Gigi runs toward us lightning fast then stops, her toes digging into the grass. She barely moves as excitement shines in her bright blue eyes, and she struggles to contain her enthusiasm. Then, painfully slow, she extends her clasped hands. Ian and I both bend down, pulling close, looking to see what she's hiding. Slowly, ever so slowly, she slides her thumbs aside to show the small object nestled in her hands. When the opening is wide enough to form a tiny opening in her cupped hands, she peeks inside with one eye at what's hiding inside and then holds her hands up for us to see. "It's a wightning bug," she whispers.

I mold my hands around hers, feeling her grip, and hook my thumbs over hers. I ease the tension in her hold, so the grasp doesn't squish her prisoner. I calm her zeal with a soothing tone. "Easy, sweetie. You don't want to hurt him."

With eyes as wide and blue as a sapphire sky, she looks up at me with pleasure. "Isn't he just so 'dorable and cute, Momma?"

"So cute," I agree.

"I crouch down to get beside her, momentarily stealing her attention away from the bug. "There are hundreds of them, maybe even thousands, that live in these woods. This is where they live; all among the trees."

Ian looks over to spy what's inside, then talks to Gigi with an almost equally breathless expectation. "There's a miniature world inside this big, grassy patch. Every night they come out and put on a show. Maybe you and your mom can come here again while it's still light out. The three of us can come to the field and watch as they appear." There's a childlike tone to his excitement and a sense of wonder which almost matches Gigi's.

"Can we, Momma? Peeeeeease?"

Her plea is so sweet and hopeful that I feel my heart puddling. I release her hands and crouch down to her level. "We can, but for now, you have to let this little guy go. He has to fly back to his family."

Her brows pinch and her smile flips upside down. "No, momma," she protests. "I don't want to."

I look into her eyes, almost feeling the heartbreak I see there. "Gigi, you have to let him fly, baby. That's what he was born to do. He works with his friends to light up the night. You don't want to stop him, do you?"

Ian, sensing the sensitivity of the moment, meanders away from us, affording me a bit of privacy with my girl. I watch him, the distance great enough to fade him into a shadow, and then, once again, I cover Gigi's hands with my own. "You like Dominoes, right? The ones we stand up, then tip over?"

She answers me with a nod and a pout.

"Every living thing has a connection, just like the Dominoes. When one falls, it affects all the others. Somewhere, this little bug has a family and they help him light up the sky. When you take one away, a light goes out. I promise, if we let him go, his family will be happy to see him—just like you are to see me when I pick you up from Cora's. If you don't release him, they'll be sad. So, it's your choice, baby. I'm going to let you decide. Which do you pick? Keep him, or let him go?"

The gentle hum of crickets fills the air as Gigi's chin drops to her chest. She mulls over her decision for a bit, then mumbles sadly. "Let him go."

I kiss the top of her head as I stand. "You have a good heart, my sweet girl." With my thumbs on top of hers, I gently press and enlarge the gap. "We can let him go together."

The scene becomes dramatic as Gigi's bottom lip quivers. Her tears glisten amidst a sea of blue and my heart aches for the loss she feels. With a sad expression, she looks down to the place where our hands are joined and her body shudders as she heaves a sorrowful sigh. "No, Momma. I do it myself."

Oh, my heart. I take a step back, watching as she ever so slowly opens her hands. The bug's head pops out.

Gigi gives him a sad smile. "Fie away, buggie. Go back home."

The back end of the bug in her palm, its delicate body now visible as it creeps up and over her fingers, steadily blinks its light as it cautiously moves about. The fragile creature navigates the treacherous world of a tiny tot's fingers and, as it does, Gigi goes completely still. I know her heart. It's tender. The last thing she would want to do is to cause any living creature harm. The descent from Gigi's palm to her fingers is tentative, but the slight wind around us sifts through her hand and, when it reaches the tip of her thumb, its wings fully extend. It flutters, as if testing the appendages to assure a successful flight, and then, with a puff of breeze, it turns, catches the air, and is gone.

Gigi's head drops back, and I spy a duet of tears trailing over her cheeks as she follows the bug's flight into the sky. The instant loss of a newfound friend gives her a stab of pain and she throws herself at my belly and hides her face in my skirt. Ian appears behind her, closing the distance he placed between us. My heart pinches as I take in his expression. He looks as sad as Gigi.

"It's okay, baby. You did the right thing and I'm proud of you." I rub soothing circles on her back, as she quietly cries. "It's time to go home. It's past your bedtime."

She leans back and looks up, sniffing back her sadness. "A few more minutes, Momma, peease?"

I can't deny her. At the age of three, given a choice

to make her own decision, instead of my telling her what to do, is a big deal—and she made the right decision, which is huge to me. "One more minute while I talk to Ian—but when I call you, we have to go, got it?"

She nods, then spies another amber bug. "Wook, Momma! It's Blinky's fwiend." *Blinky?* Skipping away, she follows its light.

Ian watches her. "I hope she's had fun, despite having to let the bug go."

"She definitely has." I nod.

"That was big of you. Giving her a choice and all."

"She has to learn. If I give her room to make decisions while she's little, hopefully, she'll make decent choices when she's older."

"I've never thought about it. I did what I was told. Then I screwed up my life."

"Even if you'd had choices, there's no guarantee you would have made ones different than you did when you got older."

"I'd like to think I would have, but then, maybe not." He reasons. "I don't know why I made it through the overdose. Buying this place was the first, decent, decision I ever made. It was a good one. At least, I'm sure of that."

His sincerity and transparency moves me. "Everything happens for a reason. I truly believe that. You've made other decisions—BIG decisions. You could have checked yourself out of rehab. You didn't, and you got clean. You stepped away from the spotlight, knowing you'd fall back into unhealthy patterns.

That's a big deal. You bought this place, true, but you could have hired people to take on this place. Instead, you worked it. That garden is amazing. I'm sure I could find some other examples but, what I'm getting at is, that your decisions, past and present, brought you here. To this moment." I look in the distance at the massive space. "And, *here,* doesn't look so bad to me." I drop the subject and glimpse over at Gigi who is sweetly sitting on the grass, staring up at the sky. Emotion hits me. The way the moonlight hits her serene expression is a picture I'll never forget. "Thank you, Ian."

His forehead wrinkles. "For?"

"For this." I nod toward Gigi. "For sharing this with us. For giving my daughter an experience she'll never forget. I mean, look at her. This is a side of Gigi I've not seen. She's so full of wonder. A few minutes ago, she was a little wildling running about, and now she's the picture of serenity. There's so much light pollution in our development and very few trees. All of this is new to her. And, in case you have any doubt because of her crying over the bug, she loves it. So, thank you."

A gentle smile fills his lips as a tender look reflects in his eyes. "You're welcome. You can bring Gigi any time. You're always welcome. There's a horse in the barn. I got her from a rescue. I also rescued a cat not long ago. I didn't know it at the time but she was pregnant so, now, I've got a bunch of kittens."

"Oh, she would love that." I pause, feeling a sudden wave of vulnerability. "You know, I get so caught up in all the mothering stuff— making sure she has healthy food, gets enough sleep, correcting her grammar ... all of that kind of stuff ... but, seeing her like this is new. It takes me back to when my mom did things like this with me. It's so different when you have a kid. You see things again for the first time. Seriously, look at her. She looks like one of the little woodland fairies."

A hearty laugh escapes him. "I'm not sure I'd know a woodland fairy if it bit me on the ass."

"My mom used to read me bedtime stories about them." A wistful feeling tugs my heart. "I haven't thought about that in years."

"You miss her."

"I do." I go to Ian's side and thread my arm through his and the unexpected move widens his eyes. "You did a good thing here, Ian. You gave a child a memory. She'll be talking about stars and bugs for days."

Ian

We stand quietly as I digest the tranquility of the moment. Not wanting the emotion I'm feeling to make me look like a weak little bitch, I glance down at the spot where Savannah and I are linked. That unfamiliar pinch in my chest is becoming a regular visitor. "I thought you didn't like me."

"I don't," she shrugs, "but it's dark and I don't want to risk breaking my neck while walking back to the car."

The humor in her voice is unmistakable, and the lighthearted tone is cute. I took so many things for granted when I saw them with bloodshot eyes. My perception of the world has shifted from what it used to be. I am satisfied with the quietness shared between

Savannah and me. As we watch Gigi chasing bugs and tiring herself out, it gives me a satisfaction I've not known. I'm learning to appreciate the little things and spending time with these two taps on a softer side of me.

A smile teases Savannah's lips as she gazes into my eyes. Her face, so beautiful and perfect, is bathed with an ethereal glow.

"I know I said Gigi won't be forgetting this night. Neither will I."

I respond instinctively, barely giving myself a moment to think or breathe. That same night magic casting its spell on them is now bewitching me. With little regard for consequences, I hook her waist and pull her into me. Her full, pink lips are begging to be kissed. I crash my lips to hers, and a moan escapes. Savannah's mouth was made for kissing and damn me, forbidden fruit never tasted so sweet. Her body melds into mine and the heat between us ignites. Passion rises, fueling my need. Lust careens through me with a dizzying rush more powerful than any drug that entered my veins. I want her. I crave her. There's a need in me I've never felt before. She's a sin I want to commit. A prayer I beg. Heaven couldn't be any sweeter than the thought of being inside her. Addict that I am, I can't get my fill.

Our tongues twist together as my lungs with the scent of lavender and vanilla. Something inside me fractures and a rush of blood hardens my cock. How can one damn kiss be more potent than whiskey or blow? I don't have the answer and, despite what logic tells me, for her, I'd want something more than cheap fuckery.

"Momma?"

One word and a pint-sized girl stop us dead in our tracks. Instantly, we separate. The spell suddenly broken and so is the kiss.

"Oh, my god."

Breathless, Savannah pushes me away, her fingers flying up to her lips. A smiling Gigi props her hands on her hips and I chuckle. She looks like she's ready to scold us. Savannah hits me with a flash of anger in her eyes, and I smother a laugh. It seems my finding humor in this situation is not well received.

Savannah rushes over to Gigi and grabs her hand. "It's time to go home."

"Savannah." Her name rides on a plea but hits deaf ears. Instead, she ignores me and goes faster.

"Savannah." Again, no response as she continues toward her car tugging Gigi as she goes. I note that my chasing, coaxing, pleading have caused her to quicken her steps even more and an alarm bell goes off as the little girl struggles to keep up.

"Savannah, stop. You're practically dragging your daughter. She's going to trip."

Like a viper, she spins, her expression venomous and, in a lightning-fast move she hoists Gigi onto her hip. "I am NOT dragging my daughter." She points at me and wags her finger as she goes around in circles. "You. You!"

"Me, what? Are you pissed off because I kissed you?" She freezes and stares at me, making a sound like some feral animal, then stomps away.

"Did you just growl at me?" I snicker but stop before it morphs into a full-fledged laugh, and continue to follow behind her. "Really, Savannah? It was just a fucking kiss."

"Youse said a bad word again, E-ban!"

"Great. Just, great." We reach the car and she yanks the door open, bending to place Gigi inside.

"Bye E-ban," she waves to me, her cheeks raised by a cheerful smile.

"Later, kiddo." I stand by, refusing to budge and block her as she moves side to side, both of us dodging back and forth like an awkward dance. "Why are you acting like this?" My tone is calm but is met with a vicious narrowing of her eyes. She darts, slipping her arm by me enough to grab the handle on the driver's side door. I grab it too, momentarily cementing it in place, but she persists with the makeshift tug of war. When she doesn't achieve her goal, she stops and hits me with an icy blue stare.

"Let go, Ian."

"No. You're making this into a big deal. It was noth-ing, so stop acting like this."

"Nothing?" She stuns me, her tone deadly, enunciating the word slowly like a stake through my heart. "Get your hands off my goddamn car."

I pop my hands off the metal, obeying her command like I've been burned. Her chest heaves. Her complexion darkens as the angry red creeps from her neck to her cheeks and I suddenly have a better understanding of that saying that goes something like women and 'hell hath no fury'."

I feel like, somehow, I have to de-escalate this situation so she doesn't leave here like a bat out of hell. Unleashing my old rockstar charm, I wink at her as I move aside to let her get into the car. "You know, you're really cute when you're angry."

She shakes her head as she secures the seatbelt, then looks at me as she closes the door. "Screw you, Ian."

I watch, confused as she flies down the driveway, and stay there until the glow of the white headlights disappears.

* * *

LIKE A CHILD, I throw myself down into the worn, leather chair and a rush of air hisses as my ass hits the seat. Normal, I don't mind the emitting faint scents of cedar and tobacco but at the moment it makes me feel sick. The room is as dark as my mood. Shadows dance on the walls as a storm of accusations, condemnations, and pompous opinions weasel their way into my head. Feelings I'd hoped were buried rise from the dead, their stagnant stench seeping into my pores. Hurtful memories tug at me, combining with a fresh sense of disgust to pull me into a dark abyss. The convicting thought chain is broken only by the jangling ring of my phone. I pull it out of my pocket, tempted to chuck it at the wall. *Sky Barrows.* Dash's widow. If it were anyone else, I would have dismissed the call.

"Hey." My tone is flat.

"What's wrong?" She instantly picks up on my mood.

"Just stupid shit. Just me being me."

"You want to talk? I might be able to help."

I roll my eyes. "It's stupid. I kissed a woman. Apparently, I shouldn't have."

"Oh yeah?" She chirps. "Is she cute? Is it promising?"

"Well, yes, but, hell, no."

"Stop it." She scolds. "Did she kiss you back?"

"I think so—thought so. How the fuck do I know? I caught her off guard. There's another thing; it might screw up my friendship with Sam."

"How so?"

"They're close. Real close. Like family."

"Oh." She pauses.

"He loves her."

"He loves you too."

"I'm nobody to love."

"I do. Sam does. You know it. This woman might too."

"Yeah, right. I don't know how to do the love thing. She'd be better off staying away from me."

"Ian, you are not as expendable as you think."

"I might have crossed a line with this one."

"What's her name?"

"Savannah."

"Pretty."

"Sky, her little girl saw me kiss her. I made a major mistake, and she was pissed. I saw what I wanted and took it—like I always do. I didn't even think of the kid seeing us. She's three years old and Savannah has every right to never speak to me again." I pause to take a breath.

"Oh, Ian. Please don't think like that. Dash wouldn't want you to. Neither do I," she says.

The sorrowful weight in her tone makes me slump over, and I catch my head with my hand. "Right now I feel like I'm a waste of oxygen. It started out well and went from really, really good, to shit—because of me."

"You're your own worst critic. So, what's your plan to fix this?"

"I don't know if I can," I say truthfully. "There's something about her Sky. I can't put my finger on it. I just … she matters. I feel like she's always mattered, but I don't know how to explain that."

"You don't have to explain it. I don't quite know how to explain me and Dash, but I've told you our story. You even heard him call me a different name. Maybe there is something to reincarnation and time-line jumps. I can't explain it, and many would dismiss it, but not me. I only know what happened with him. How I saw the whole thing, and how it could have been in another lifetime. If it's as real as I felt it was then, I can only hope we'll find each other again."

"He really loved you, Sky." Tears blind my vision.

"And he really loved you, too. Think positively. You can do this." She encourages. "You're stronger and wiser than you know. I believe in you."

"Yeah? Well, you might be the only one."

CHAPTER EIGHTEEN

Savannah

I glance in the rear-view mirror to see Gigi's fallen fast asleep. Relief swiftly unravels my thoughts. My tense shoulders descend from their earlobe-high perch as soft music drifts through the car speakers. It's apparent that the soft jazz sound has the same relaxing effect on me as it does my daughter.

I breathe in a full, expansive breath and, as I exhale, conversation from earlier this evening floods my mind. I told Ian that the events of tonight would imprint on my daughter's memories. My kissing Ian would be part of those as well.

The ride home from Ian's is sufficient time for my nerves to unjumble and soothe like rainwater over stones but, I can't forget his kiss.

I barely had time to catch my breath when he moved on me. The effect of the impact was mind-blowing. Instantaneously, my thoughts scattered. Sparks turned to flames as an exciting and unexpected fire careened through my system. The intensity of the kiss sucked me into the flashback. Due to my pitiful lack of self-control, the kiss would have led me straight into his bed. I wanted him with an intensity that left my will as cinder, the ash skittering away in the night breeze. I was mere seconds away from melding into him fully when the sound of my sweet little girl's voice hit me like a cold dose of water.

I hadn't realized until that moment how starved I was for a connection. I craved his immoral lips. Our comingled tongues danced a sordid tempo. For a careless moment, the world fell away. I loved it. *Gah!*

The red light brings me to a frustrating stop. *Damn it, Ian. Why the hell did you have to come back into my life?*

My thoughts continue to linger over tonight's events and, though I'd prefer to only recall the sweet memories made with Gigi, it's Ian who corrupts my musings. While the car idles at a standstill, reality slowly drips in. Pleasurable thoughts crash over me as I recall the scene. How quickly Ian bewitched me. The spell made its way to my core. His body, so different than I remembered, enchanted me with firm, thick ropey arms, and well-honed biceps. My breast crashed against his chest, the wall of muscle assaulting tender flesh while his kiss awakened it, and the pleasure that followed soothed the hurt.

I glance at my fingers gripping the steering wheel to see white knuckles. How is it possible that he can have this effect on me, especially after so many years? But he's here now and he's so much more real to me now than then. His lips on mine induced the same shivers I felt so long ago, but with even more intensity than I remember. I'm such a different person than I was then —so is he—but in my wildest imagination, I never dreamed I'd again be in a heated moment with Ian Stanton. Not again. My thoughts are muddled because I'm not sure I would have stopped myself. Instead, it was the sweet voice of the little person who always saves me from the worst parts of myself.

I try to tune out the warring sexy thoughts and self-incrimination the remainder of the drive and notably exhale when I press the control for the garage door. Inch by inch it lifts until it's open wide and revealing evidence of the perfectionism that occurred after my parent's death. I suppose my obsessive compulsiveness could be worse than arranging a variety of garden tools on a pegboard-covered wall. A container of baby clothes triggers images of an infant Gigi in my arms. Like any nervous new mother, I'm always worried about making mistakes. But then, am I doing a disservice to my daughter by not letting her see the vulnerable parts of me?

I close my eyes and take a deep breath, collecting my thoughts. Am I capable of a relationship? I thought I was until Drake became violent and I reasoned that what happened with Ian was because I was drunk.

Once Gigi was born I resigned myself to raising her alone and then convinced myself that a relationship with anyone was something I neither needed nor wanted but something happened tonight. Something equally freeing and frightening. There is more substance to Ian than the man I remember.

I savor a quiet moment as the garage door drifts closed. Maybe to Ian it was 'just a kiss' but the way he looks at me with those piercing eyes makes me feel as if he can see right through me. With one touch, he reminded me I'm a woman and not simply someone's mom, and I'm not sure how I feel about that.

I unbuckle Gigi without waking her and she easily positions herself as I carefully carry her from the car into the house. An emerging headache is tapping an annoying beat against the back side of my eyeballs and I'm anxious to lay her down and swallow some pain relievers. Thank god she's out as I navigate through the house, balancing her so as not to disturb her. I tiptoe up the steps and make it to her room without waking her. Moms don't get enough credit. Balancing babies, groceries, and laundry baskets may not seem like a magnificent feat, but doing our part to keep our acts up and running makes us seem like circus folk, yet we never take a bow.

As I lay Gigi down, her breath brushes against my neck and my heart swells. She's my reason. My everything. As I kiss her rosy cheek I imagine her dreams tonight will be quite full. Stars, fireflies, and wide-open spaces will emerge once again. When—if—a man enters our lives, her needs will come before my own.

"I love you, my angel." I lightly pet her head. "You are the most perfect thing I've ever done." Whispering the words, I steal one more kiss, and then tuck her in.

ONCE GIGI'S bedroom door closes, exhaustion hits me. The pounding in my head is relentless and has increased in intensity. I slip down the stairs quietly and quickly to find a remedy to take away the ache and, as I enter the kitchen, my phone rings. The display flashes an unknown number but I answer anyway.

"Hello."

"Savannah, it's Ian—and before you hang up on me —I'm sorry."

I hit the speaker button and grab two headache pills and a glass of water. I pop them in my mouth and gulp down a couple of swallows. Now is not the time I want to talk. "Ian, I don't want to—"

"I know you don't but just listen." He pauses. "Please, just listen to me for a minute; it was an impulsive move and I'm sorry. I took something from you that you weren't willing to give. I'm not good at this. You might not believe it, but you are my first sober kiss."

My forehead pinches. "You're kidding, right? You mean, I'm the first woman you've kissed since moving to Rock Hills."

"No. I mean, you're the first girl I've ever kissed—like, seriously kissed."

"No way." I spout.

"Yeah, It's true."

"Not even when you were a kid?"

"Nope."

"Spin the bottle? Truth or dare? Any of those games?"

"I started drinking when I was seven years old, so no. You're the first. I shouldn't have moved on you like that—especially in front of Gigi—but, I'm not gonna lie; I liked it but it wasn't right to steal it."

I sit quietly, dumbfounded. I don't know how to respond.

"Are you there?" he asks, breaking the silence.

"I'm here. A little shocked, is all."

"Yeah, well … sometimes truth's stranger than fiction." He exhales a vast sigh. "Anyway, I called to apologize. You're a beautiful woman. I saw what I wanted, and I took it. I'm sorry."

I breathe in deep and sheepishly roll my eyes "You think I'm beautiful?"

"Don't you?"

"No. Not always."

"Take a look in the mirror, Savannah. You're gorgeous." He pauses. "So, you forgive me for kissing you?"

I shrug. "I didn't hate it, Ian."

"So, you liked it?" I can almost hear the lilt in his

voice. His tone pitches to a more upbeat one, and I imagine that sexy lip curl.

"I didn't say that either," I say with a lighter tone.

He laughs. "Honestly, you don't have to say anything."

"I appreciate that you called, and I appreciate the apology." I think of something my mother used to say. *Until the day comes that you don't need forgiveness, you can't not forgive someone else.* Convicted by the memory, my tone softens. "It's water under the bridge, as Sam would say, and let's be real; I can think of scores of women who would have loved a kiss from you." Time passes like the ticking of a clock as I head into the living room with the phone to my ear. "Ian?"

"I get what you're saying but here's the difference: I respect you. I didn't them." His voice fades away.

Any remnant of anger and confusion that lingered from earlier tonight slipped away like a deflating balloon. "Ian?" He doesn't answer. "Ian? Are you still there?"

"Yes."

"Why are you so hard on yourself?"

He pauses. "Because I know what I am; a fuck-up. You're a decent person. I'm not. In fact, the word 'worthless' has pretty much been drummed into my head. I wouldn't blame you if you think so, too."

I suck in an angry breath. "You're not worthless."

"Yeah, well maybe I'm not as much a screw-up now as I was then, but I have my moments."

"Who would say something like that?"

"My father. My mother. They guys in the band." He pauses. "He was never a 'dad,' you know? I was young when my mom died and, after she did, he didn't like me very much. After Dash died, well … I don't need to tell you the rest. The press took care of that."

My heart sinks. "I'm sorry for your pain, Ian, and I don't think you're worthless."

"Thanks. It was a long time ago." There's a slight tremble in his voice.

"If you don't mind me asking, what happened to your mom?"

"Momma had issues. She died by suicide. My father hated her for it. He hated her even more for leaving him with a kid." He paused. "She was a great storyteller, though." His tone pitches, and the lighter, tender one presses a smile to my lips. "That's what I remember most."

"You loved her very much."

"I did. I'm surprised I remember as much about her as I do. She was beautiful and loving. She doled out affection like candy on Halloween. She made me feel special, even if all she was doing was holding my hand. What I remember most are her hugs. They were amazing. I was the sun and her world revolved around me. I can't remember a day when she didn't make me happy. Everything changed when she died."

"How so?" I press.

"Both of my parents were only children, and my grandparents were dead. My dad was it. There was no one else. He told me he couldn't stand to look at me because I looked too much like my mother. He blamed her issues and her death on me. 'She was fine till you came along', was the most frequently used phrase. Now that I'm older, and I've been through some pretty extensive counseling, I believe she might have suffered post-partum depression that lingered. I don't know for sure. In my mother's absence, things with my father got ugly. There was no affection, and he seemed happiest when taking his rage out on me." Sadness lingers at the edge of his voice. "Love is a risk. It can take you from the highest high to the lowest low but it's worth the gamble."

I swallow the lump in my throat. All I'd ever known growing up was security and love. Mine and Ian's upbringings couldn't have been more different. The loneliness in his tone is hard for me to stomach, especially because I'm a mother.

"Anyway, back to tonight," he continues. "This is an apology. We both have a connection with Sam. I wouldn't want to do anything that would jeopardize it. He means a lot to me, and I know you mean a lot to him. I wanted to call and make right my wrong."

"I appreciate that."

"So, are we good? I mean, the night wasn't a total loss; Gigi had a good time and, if we're at odds, it might put a bad spin on how she remembers it." He takes a breath. "I can take pretty much anything, Savannah, but I don't think I could forgive myself if something I did stole a smile from that kid. She's a sweetheart."

The tenderness in his voice brings a sheen of tears to my eyes. "Yes, she is."

"If I'm not overstepping here; she's also pretty independent."

A laugh bursts out. "That's an understatement!"

"She's cool, though. I like her. She's hard on herself when she doesn't get her words right, but other than that, she's a pretty happy kid." He clears his throat. "Now, you? You seem to take everything seriously."

"I do not," I laugh out a protest.

"If you say so, but that's why I called. To apologize and make things right so you wouldn't overthink it. Old habits are hard to break. I don't really think of myself as 'asshole Ian' anymore, but I still make mistakes."

"We're fine, Ian," I assure him.

"I hope so because I suck at conventional norms."

"I'm glad you called."

"Me, too. Goodnight."

"Night, Ian."

We both hang up and, suddenly, sadness washes over me. It's heavy, and the loneliness in his tone knocks at my stomach. I sink into my feelings, replaying our kiss over in my mind. I liked it, though I denied it and am raddled about whether I'd like him to kiss me again. "Oh, Savannah. Get over yourself."

I push off the sofa, the pain in my head now reduced to a thrum. It's been a long day and an eventful night. Sleep is what I need.

As I enter my bedroom, I slip out of my clothes and

pull a tee shirt over my head. My soft, cushy bed is a comfort as I crawl beneath the covers. Ian speaking about his parents has made me think of my own. Mom used to say things have a way of working themselves out and, right now, that thing is Ian. I sure hope she's right.

Ian

"Ok. What do you want to talk about?" Sam asks.

His tone makes me more than self-conscious. I feel like a kid in the principal's office. Like I'm about to get into trouble for something I did. He takes a seat across the table from me, the tilt of his head in line with a half-lipped smile. I steal a glance before I talk, and then drop my gaze to the scratched tabletop. Sam's a pretty intimidating figure and could easily kick my ass. I should look at him directly—straight in the eye—but I can't. Guilt's clawing at my insides and I've had trouble doing that since my father warned me with the line, "Don't eyeball me, boy." The consequence of staring at him was a slap or a punch. Sam wouldn't do that but I feel safer when I keep my head down.

"Once I tell you what I've got to say, you might not be too happy with me."

"I'll be the judge of that," he assures.

I muster the courage to flick a glance in his direction. A faint, assuming smile bends my lips. "Trust me on this."

His new jeans swoosh against the chair as impatience makes him fidget. "I'm gonna be pissed if you don't stop pussy footin' around. Say what's on your mind, Ian. We got work to do."

I suck in a lungful of air. "I've got some things to say, Sam, and I need you to listen to me all the way through." I steal a glance and he nods. "Good. First things first; I'm no good. Never have been. Never will be. Been cursed since the day I was born. My mother loved me. My father hated me. I was collateral damage from her death as far as he was concerned." I lean forward, resting my elbows on my knees, and threading my fingers together in a tight grip. "When I was five years old, he taught me one thing; how to use a can opener. I've fended for myself ever since. Chef Boyardee™ was the dinner of choice. He washed his down with whiskey, while I drank water from the tap. He never bought milk. I got that in school. By the third grade, I got sick of drinking water. I also had trouble sleeping. I waited until my old man was asleep and drank as much as I could from his bottle while leaving just enough swigs so he thought it was him who drank it. I always put the bottle back within fingertip reach then showered and brushed my teeth before I stumbled into bed so he wouldn't smell it on me and give me a beating. I hated the taste at first but, it worked. I slept. Then the nightmares started. They stuck with me and made me anxious, so I got someone to buy me liquor, and I drank during the day. I'd get a carton of orange juice in school and put vodka in it." I look up. "I know I'm boring you but, I promise, there's a point to all this."

"I'm not bored." He leans forward on his elbows. "I know some of this but you're telling me more than I remember."

"Yeah. Probably all the shit I wish I could forget."

"We've done a lot of talking, especially when you were over in New Life Rehab, but it seems you got more to say, and I'm listening."

"See, that's it. You and me—we talk. Me and my old man never did. I learned about women through magazines he either shoved under the bed or left in the bathroom. One night I heard him making a noise, so I peeked into his bedroom. I thought he was dying. He was jerking off. I watched. I learned two things from watching my old man; how to feel something, and how to feel nothing. We never talked."

"Never? Not even about school?"

"The day they put my momma in the ground, I learned to keep my mouth shut. Driving home from her burial I felt bad for him because tears were rolling down his face. No sound. Just tears. I was just a kid—a stupid kid. I said, 'Don't cry, Daddy. Momma's with the angels.' He swiped his hand over his face, and then he punched me."

"The blow caused the back of my head to hit the window, hard. I remember seeing sparkles in front of my eyes as the coppery taste of blood ran down the back of my throat and hit my tongue. He threw his handkerchief at me. 'Your momma committed a mortal sin and she's in hell where she belongs, boy—and you damn well better not get blood on my seat!'"

"Jesus Christ." Rage contorts Sam's face, his skin flushing red as his eyes narrow.

"We spoke when my hormones started raging. My voice changed and so did I. Everything I did got on his nerves. In rehab counseling, I learned it was unconscious but intentional. When I got into trouble, I got his attention. I just wanted to get to a point where I could hurt him back and not feel a thing. One day we'd both had enough. I was bigger and stronger by then and I gave as good as I got. He never hit me again—and he never again cut me by using my mother's death as a knife."

"So, she didn't die the way you told me?"

I spit out a laugh. "She was giving Rock n Rye to a three-year-old. Sadness took my mother. I was Gigi's age when she made our 'special tea.'"

"But why lie to me about her? Did you think I'd judge her?"

I answer him with a look and he fills in the blanks. "You did."

I look away.

Disapproval shakes Sam's head as his chin drops to his chest. A few seconds later, he looks up and stakes me dead in the eye. "I got one question: why'd you try to do yourself in?"

I look into his eyes and see nothing but genuine concern. "I don't know. All I know is that my insides were hollow from scraping away the hurt."

"What hurt?"

"Dash dying, I guess. He was my friend."

"And you loved him."

"I guess. I don't know. I know that I hurt. That every day ripped through me."

"Because you loved Dash."

"Stop." I shake my head and look away.

"Say it, Ian. You loved Dash."

"Stop."

"God damn it, Ian! Dash died and left you alone. Just like your mom—"

"Oh, for fucks sake, yes! Happy? Everyone I ever loved left me. I hated them for leaving me—and I hated myself for being so goddamn self-centered that I couldn't feel sorry that they died. Asshole Ian. Only thinking of himself. Total self-centered prick." Ghoulish pain rises from a neatly stored, compartmentalized grave. "I couldn't live with myself."

"Anger's a part of grief. You loved them, Ian, and you felt abandoned. There's no shame in feeling what you felt. Grief doesn't come with instructions."

A flash of anger erupts inside of me and my gaze flies

back to him. I hated the doctors who saved me the minute I opened my eyes. By then, there was nothing left of me but bone dust and I didn't care if I lived or died. I begged a god I didn't believe in to take me to my mother or bring Dash back. I railed at God, telling him he made a mistake. Nobody warned me about death, and no one prepared me for grief. Dying is the one thing we all know is coming and the one thing we're least prepared for.

Silence falls, the heavy conversation pulling away from words leaving us both with our thoughts. I sit with my confession, knowing that we've gone far off-topic from my original purpose. I've lost everyone I've ever cared about and now, I'm about to lose Sam.

"I kissed Savannah." I vomit the words.

His eyes widen and a slinky grin instantly fills his lips. "She kiss you back?"

"What?" I rear back with shock. I'd braced myself for contempt, anger, or anything of the like but not for this reaction.

"Excuse me. Sorry to interrupt."

We both turn at the soft interruption as Savannah approaches. She comes closer, her expression puzzled. Obviously, she's overheard some of what was said, but Sam dismisses her upspoken question, looking up at the clock on the wall and then back at her. "You're here early."

"I had an appointment in town that ended earlier than I expected," she explains. "I figured I'd come in to try out a new song." She bends down and whispers in my ear. "Just so you know, Gigi was a chatterbox at Cora's this morning. It was all about fireflies."

"Fireflies?" Sam's brow quirks. "You mean, lightning bugs?"

Savannah turns to him, pursing her lips. "I didn't think you heard me, but yes. Gigi was introduced to the wonders of lightning bugs last night and she's now completely fascinated."

"Do tell ..." Sam's grin mutates to a smirk as his brows hike up. He looks between Savannah and me, pausing for a second as Savannah leaves us to go into the back room.

"It's nothing," I explain.

Sam's chuckle is low and throaty. "Uh-huh. Not to her, it's not. How'd she come to be at your place?"

"My bike broke down. Didn't you get my message? I left it here overnight. Savannah drove me home."

"So, how'd you get here today? Your truck?"

"Yeah. I hitched a trailer to it so I can haul the bike back to the ranch."

"So, she got to see your place, huh?" The smirk turns into a smug grin, accompanied by a knowing expression. He calls to Savannah, who is now behind the bar getting a soft drink. "It's a pretty place, isn't it, Savi? Ian's done got himself a jewel out there. He's done a lot of work to that house; especially how he made over that kitchen and that gigantic stone fireplace. I'll bet you liked that."

"I didn't see it. We were outside, but I did see the

pretty gardens." Her eyes soften as she turns to me and smiles so sweetly my chest swells. "Maybe next time."

CHAPTER TWENTY

Savannah

"**I** have something for you."

"For me?"

I nod but say no more. Ian's astonished look reminds me of Gigi on Christmas morning, and seeing the display in a grown man threatens to unmoor my emotions. How is it that someone who had the world at his fingertips thinks so little of himself that he's shocked by the announcement of a gift? It's a good bet that he lacks for nothing in material wealth, so maybe this is something that will speak to the part of him that hurts. That little boy inside who never felt he mattered —and he does matter, and this is the only gift I can think of that will speak to his heart.

A song.

It's the best way to reach a musician and, for all of

Ian's denying it, music is still a big part of his life. The song came to me last night in a dream, forced me awake, and ran in a loop through my head until I got up out of bed, my eyes half-lidded, and found paper and a pencil. I found it where Gigi left a hand-drawn picture of a blue guitar. She laid it on top of a magazine, its waxy crayon squiggles and swirls drawn by our personal van Gogh, in miniature. Once I had the words down, I went back to sleep, only to be awakened a few hours later by Gigi. She cuddled with me in my bed, humming a simple and sweet tune. I took it, folded the words into the notes and, in little more than an hour, wrote a song. Ian's song.

I walk away from the two men, abandoning them in favor of the stage. Heat warms my cheeks, climbing from my chest and neck. I inch back in my seat and pull the guitar close. When I glance across the room, I see Sam standing behind the bar with Ian a few feet behind him. Inhaling a deep, nerve-dispensing breath, I close my eyes for a silent moment and focus on one more deep inhale. *You've got this, Savannah.*

I lean into the microphone and softly strum, sending the song from mine and Gigi's hearts to his.

A place you should have been
A thing you should've done
Waiting in the wings
A wrong you should've right
A word you should've said

They seem like little things

Mornings fade into the night
Fireflies dancing with their light
These moments they pass
Much too fast
But you know, you know
It's the little things

I look up and Ian's eyes meet mine. A secret smile has stolen his lips, flooding warmth through me as my heart swells.

A heart that doesn't heal
A wound that doesn't fade
Is now dust in the wind
A gift you should've gave
A hand you should've held
A time when you give in
The world keeps spinning round and round
And we just tune into the sounds
'Cause you know, you know
It's the little things

I finish out the song with some quiet strumming and, suddenly, my heart gallops. It's been so long since I've written a song. The last one opened the door for Ian and me to meet but this one means so much more because Gigi's a part of it.

"Got-damn!" Sam breaks the silence, and he breaks

the silence by slapping his palm to the bar top. "That sure was pretty. I never heard that one before, Savi. That new?"

I nod. "It is."

"Well, I like it. You should keep that one in your song list." Sam turns to Ian. "What did you think?"

Ian's expression is hard to read. He nods, and smiles, but doesn't utter a word. I slide off the chair and lean the guitar against it. As I approach him, I see a look in his eyes I've not seen before and, impulsively, I reach out and touch his arm. His eyes search mine, and I can tell he's holding himself back. I'm afraid to say anything, aware that I might say something to break what I can only guess are pent-up emotions. He holds my gaze for a few seconds.

"Are you okay?" I whisper.

He nods, swallows, takes a deep breath, and takes my hand. "The song. It's beautiful."

I squeeze his fingers as relief conjures my smile. "Thank you. It's from Gigi and me; my words, her tune. You gave us something that you can't buy in a store, Ian, and this is our way of reciprocating in kind."

"No one's ever dedicated a song to me, much less written one. I don't know what to say."

"As long as you like it, there's nothing to say. Whenever I sing it, it will bring memories of last night."

"It reminds me of someone. Someone special."

His comment catches me off guard until he elaborates.

"It's my mom." Emotion catches his voice and a

groan seeps through the words. "She used to sing sweet songs like that." He pauses. "You'd think grief would lose its sting after a while, but it doesn't. The stings turn into sucker punches. It's usually something simple. A scent. A sunny day. There's no rhyme or reason. The memory takes your mind down roads you haven't traveled in a while. I guess that's the price you pay for loving someone with all that's in you; you lose them, and reliving memories of them is the most bittersweet pain your heart can bear."

I tread those same heartfelt waters and, just like Ian, can easily get caught in the undertow. "I know. I feel them too sometimes—about my mom and dad." The tugging in my chest prompts me to offer comfort and lift the veil of sadness from his eyes, but I hold back. "I'm sorry for your loss, Ian."

He nods, carefully sniffing back his feelings. "The song's beautiful and means more to me than you know. Thank you—and Gigi."

I turn away to spare him from staying too long with his memories, but he stops me by touching my arm. I'm captivated by his tender expression, his eyes glistening with unshed tears.

"My Momma used to say a song could make you feel better, and your singing always feels like a healing to me."

His words touch something deep inside and, when his hand falls away, I stay. I can't explain the depth of emotion he wears. It speaks words he cannot. I raise my hand to his cheek. The barely visible stubble is abrasive against my skin causing goosebumps to skitter up my arm. The rush hits my belly then travels to other places. I'm like a kid on a carnival ride, excited and afraid at the same time. This connection? It's something we'd do well to avoid, but it's something for which we both thirst, and I savor it, even if just for this moment. It appears he does too. We've both been scarred by love and know all too well that tender moments like this don't last.

"I hope one day you find your way back to music. You're good. Really good."

"I can't see that happening but thank you."

"Just think about it. There's something about music that washes the dust off your soul and tethers us to times and places that let our souls breathe."

He sucks in a breath and smiles as he exhales. "You're an amazing woman, Savannah Grace, you know that?"

I note the tremble in his voice and give him a sweet look. "My friends call me Savi."

A wide smile appears on his full lips, enhancing his looks. Ian is handsome yet doesn't seem to know. The cockiness with which he made his fortune with the band Boundless Hearts is gone, and in its place is a gentler look. His eyes are tender, warmer, as he holds my gaze, and the flutter in my chest explodes, releasing joy inside of me that feels like a kaleidoscope of butterflies. I can't deny my attraction to him. It resurrects feelings I harbored in my younger years but more adult and mature. Back then my hormones dictated my response and now it's the inner stature of the man that attracts me. His kindness balances equally with his body and I'm drawn to his personality just as much as the broad shoulders filling his inky black tee shirt. My thoughts drift as my gaze travels to his muscular chest and trim waist, clear evidence of the work he's put in at the ranch. The worn and faded blue jeans hug his toned legs like a second skin and I can't stop staring. This new life has been good for him, and I don't need to wonder if the near-death experience has changed him in more ways than he realizes. It has and I'm brazen, taking in this simple man with a beautiful soul.

I'm suddenly hot. The warmth I felt climbing up my neck now has me fully flushed. There's a fraction of space between us and the distance has me breathing in a musky fragrance of shampoo or cologne. I lean in just a little and breathe in a bit deeper. A quick glance around reveals that Sam's disappeared and I relish the silence. We're the only people in the room yet it feels bigger than that; more impressive. Like we're the only people in the world. The only sound breaching the bar is the buzzy, white noise, and hum from the air conditioning. He's captured me with his tender expression, one, I'm certain, most of the world has never seen.

He steps to my side, draping a relaxed arm around my shoulders as he walks me to a table. It's more a friendly gesture than a romantic one and feels completely non-threatening. When he pulls out a chair, I take a seat, and Ian crouches down in front of me, looking up at me with a tranquil expression. "Savannah—"

"Savi," I correct.

He nods, tips his chin, and takes my hand as he looks into my eyes, and I melt.

"Savi … inside and out, you're the most beautiful person I think I've ever known."

CHAPTER TWENTY-ONE

Ian

I don't know how to explain what happens to me when Savannah smiles. It's such a simple act that has such a profound effect. It almost sounds cliché to describe the feeling as if walls are crumbling. I'd been angry for so long that with each passing year, another brick was cemented around me until I was no longer defensive but numb. But this … this feeling. It's foreign and sweet. Savi smiles and suddenly I long for something I can't understand.

Most people would think that it's always the band members who take advantage of women who hang around after concerts. That we're the bad guys. The rock stars. The guys all the girls want to fuck. But there's another side to that scenario. I'd never profess to be an innocent lamb, but more times than not a gorgeous chick with a hefty rack and a full, firm ass found me long before I went looking. Even as tempting as that might sound, there are other dangers that come with that piece of ass, and I'm not just talking about disease. I'm referring to the Benjamins.

One of the things I learned by being in a band was that there are opportunists around every corner. A frisky fuck with a rockstar conjures dollar signs in some of the most beautiful eyes. Most women were thrilled to have the memory, while others wanted more. Secret babies. Tabloid headlines. Tell all stories. All it took was a little dirt, curious reporters, and a gossip-thirsty public. I never cared, but Dash did. He always thought everything through with a level head—then he'd keep me out of trouble. Or, at least, try.

I didn't know it then but there was a kid inside of me who was looking for love. Rehab required therapy, and that taught me just how jaded I'd become. I had a deep-seated belief that everybody—no exceptions—wants their fifteen minutes of fame.

Not Savannah.

She wants nothing and gives everything. The beautiful blue-eyed blonde scatters love like stardust. I've witnessed her concern and care for those she loves. That song … it was perfect.

Absolutely fucking perfect.

"HOW Y'ALL DOING TO-*NIIIIIIIGHT?*"

Savi shouts and the crowd roars. She launches into Chris Cornell's "Nearly Forgot My Broken Heart", and the crowd claps in time. It fuels her and I feel a smile nearly split my face.

I look around the room and something weird starts. Some feeling deep inside my belly. One by one more bodies hit the dance floor, while others wiggle their asses in their seats. It's not just me that's feeling something. Everyone is, and the joy inflates the room like it's filled with helium and, suddenly, it hits me too.

Shit!

Is this what being happy feels like? I feel woozy and silly, and I want to laugh because Savi's joy is coming through the music and it's fucking infectious!

I clap along with them until she finishes, and the air erupts with rounds of praise. Lots of hollered "Yeah's!" and a final round of clapping splits the crowd. She responds with a smile that curls her lips nearly to the corners of her eyes. She's practically glowing.

And my heart's nearly exploding.

"What a great crowd y'all are!"

She gets a coy look and modesty flushes her cheeks a bright pink as one by one they cease until the room is quiet. Savi bows her head as she slides into another song, and I take a step back to catch my breath. *What the fuck just happened?*

I'm dumbfounded, or maybe just dumb. Is this what they mean when they say that you're happy for someone else's happiness?

I'm almost a little panicky. Fear of the unknown, maybe? I haven't a clue.

I roll my head around my neck, cracking a few bones as I do the motion. I mentally dissect what I felt to compare it to what I know and shake some strange, unfamiliar feeling off my shoulders. I've never felt anything this intense without drugs and I feel like I'm drunk. I mean, I know the happiness I felt when Dash was happy. Even though that feeling was good, it didn't feel as good as this.

Busted flat in Baton Rouge
Waitin' for a train ...

She cuts through my thoughts with her honey-sweet voice and it's like I've taken a tranquilizer. The panicky feeling mellows, drifting slowly down, and then, I relax. This ... this feeling I know. It's the same one I get when I'm sitting around the fire pit, kicking back, and looking at stars. It's familiar. It feels like home.

And a woman did that.

Who'd thought?

I lean against the end of the bar. This whole time I've been back and forth between working and enjoying the show. Now, I'm using my break to focus on her. She sees me and, we lock eyes. My chest pinches again and I'm starting to make the correlation between it, and Savi.

* * *

A COUPLE OF HOURS PASS, and Savi closes out the night with a final song. The crowd scatters and the bar empties. Wait staff bus the tables, stack the chairs, and sweep the floors. Savi lingers, talking with a few stragglers as she walks them to the exit. It's been a long night. she's got to be running on adrenaline but doesn't show it. She's happy—nearly elated—as she walks on air over to the bar.

"You were on fire tonight," I praise.

"I feel it." She looks up at me with eyes of sparkling sapphire.

"Damn! You were good." Sam adds. "And it was a good night, too. I think it's the best night we've had since we opened." Sam pauses, then dips behind the bar. He looks out on the floor, puts two fingers to his lips, and blows. The move produces a piercing whistle, and everyone goes still. "C'mon over here."

They respond, approaching with rags and brooms in hand. One by one Sam pours a little wine into cups, about enough for a swallow or two.

"Everybody grab a glass." He slides a soda to me, taking a final glass for himself. He looks around at the faces and smiles. "I'm so damn proud of y'all. You did a good job. Not one complaint. Not one! I hope they tipped you well, but I want you to know, I appreciate you." He lifts his glass. "To Mad Dogs—every dang one of you."

"MAD DOGS!!! WOOF! WOOF! WOOF!" They bang their glasses with each barking sound, take a drink, then go back to finish so they can get out of here.

Savannah hops up on a barstool while Sam and I wash and rinse some glasses.

"How did this place come about? I mean, how did you decide on a bar?"

"He never told you?" Savi asks me, then turns to Sam. "Tell him the story, Sam. It's a good one."

"You've heard it a million times." He answers.

Savi shrugs. "So, I'll hear it a million and one. Tell him."

"It isn't much to tell. I grew up not far from here. Me, and some of my buddies, were riding through on our motorcycles. The town was more abandoned than I remembered but, we stopped, poked through the buildings to see what we could see, and then started looking up stuff—the history of the place.

These buildings have been here since the gold rush days, and they were still solid. The 'bones were good,' so to speak. The town was founded by Mad Dog men who took a chance on a dream. A crazy idea about gold. We understood them because that's exactly what we had: a crazy idea.

We came up with the insane notion that we could give the town a new life, give people in the area a place to go, and, with enough growth, give Nashville and Austin a run for their money. Good music, good eats, and a safe place to enjoy the company of friends and family. We're not where we started but this town's not near where it's going."

"You weren't afraid of the risks?" I ask.

"Yes! And no." He pauses. "Once we all started talking about it, others got interested. They liked the idea but didn't want to be involved in the day-to-day stuff, so they became investors. It's paying off. New bars are opening and young people pitch us with ideas for coffee shops, cupcake shops, and the like. We have two priorities: keep it nice, keep it safe."

The door bangs open, and we spin toward the sound.

A lone guy stands inside the entrance, a little off balance, and looking around. Then he stops, pinning Savi with his eyes.

"Savannah. I knew I'd find you." He stumbles toward her.

"We're closed." I step in front of him, blocking him with my body.

He sneers at me, sniffing back like he's smelled something bad. "Who the fuck are you?" His eyes roam over me from head to toe. "Oh, I know you. You're the guy from that band. The one who OD'd. I thought you died."

Smartass punk. My brow hitches and lips quirk as I fold my arms across my chest. "Very much alive—and we're closed."

He barrels into me. "I got business here—don't I, Savannah?"

He looks over my shoulder and I grab the neck of his shirt. "Is he bothering you, Savi?"

"Savi? *Awwwww.* That's so sweet."

His spittle hits my cheek and I walk him a few steps back. "It's after hours and you're trespassing. Past your bedtime, dickwad."

He headbutts me. I blink it off quickly and snatch the front of his shirt in my fist. "Take your drunk ass home." The words seethe through my clenched teeth. I'm about to throw him out the door, and then …

"What do you want, Drake?"

I freeze and he looks around me. His eyes narrow. His lip curls. "Well, hello, sweetheart," he cackles. "Been a long time."

He swats at my hand, but hell would freeze over before I'd unleash this asshole. His tongue darts out to lick the slobber off his lips.

"I came to see YOU!" He thrusts a bony finger at her.

"You're violating a restraining order." Her eyes meet mine. "He's not supposed to be anywhere near me."

"And what about that little girl, huh? Am I not supposed to be near her either?"

Savannah lunges from the chair. "Get the fuck out of here."

"Well, what about it, bitch; is she mine?"

Savi springs at him and the only thing between them is me.

"Savannah, No!" Sam snatches her around the waist and her cheeks turn crimson.

"I'll kill you." She says, trying to break Sam's hold.

"Get him the fuck out of here, Ian." Sam's order has me flinging Drake, hard. He hits the door frame and flings off it. His chest bumps mine. I fist his shirt once again and put my face in his. "You heard the man. Get the fuck outta here."

I throw him through the doorway and he trips, his face falling over the curb. He looks back at me as I slam the door and throw the locks.

I take a minute. My chest heaves. I turn and lock eyes with Savannah. "Say the word. I'll kick his ass."

Her body sinks. As her posture deflates, she drops her chin and shakes her head no.

* * *

JERI SIDLES up next to Savannah in a sisterly way. "Are you okay?"

Savannah nods.

"I don't mind following you home." A smile sneaks onto her lips. "I've got mace and mad ninja skills. Hiiiii-ya!" Jerri pops up, hand-chops the air, and lands in a martial arts pose which, I'm sure, isn't an actual pose.

Savannah forces a smile as Sam comes up behind her and lays his arm around her shoulder. "I got this, Jeri. I'll make sure she gets home alright."

Savannah looks up at him. "I'm good, Sam. I can drive." She then looks to Jeri. "Thank you, but I'm okay."

"Both of you don't know what kind of crazy he is, or what he's capable of," Sam warns.

"Unfortunately, I do know his kind of crazy," Jeri nods. "I'll be careful."

She and Sam exchange a look that I can't define. She holds his gaze for a moment and behind her eyes I sense that there's something more to that comment. Some story that maybe I'll hear one day.

Jeri grabs her purse, gives Savi a tender look, and squeezes her hand. "Call me if you need a friend."

Savi forces a milquetoast smile. "I will."

"I'll be right back. I'm going to walk her to her car." Sam follows Jeri to the door and, once they clear the entrance, I press for information.

"Did Drake stalk you here?"

"It looks that way," she says, sadly.

"And he's an old boyfriend?"

"He's an entitled, little prick."

"That much I figured," I weakly chuckle. I reach for Savi's chin, lifting her head with one finger. "He scares you."

"Maybe a long time ago. Now I'm just angry."

"But he tracked you? Any idea how?"

"I changed my name after I left town. I suppose I could have been more creative. My parents' murders hit national news and I wanted a fresh start, so I dropped my last name. With all the information on the internet, I guess it was easier to find me than I thought." Her shoulders pulse a quick shrug. "Also, his dad has lots of connections and resources. If Drake wanted to find me, I'm sure his dad helped him."

I swallow my rage, and give her a moment,

knowing the toxic mix of emotions that comes with being hunted. I barely have time to digest what she's told me when I hear the familiar sound of Sam's boots scuffing the floor as he approaches Savannah.

"I'm going to report him. He's not supposed to be anywhere near you." Savannah pales and he pauses. "You look like you're going to be sick."

"I'm fine," she insists. I move closer and, like Sam, note the sudden change. He's on one side of her and I take the other, concerned she might pass out.

"No, you're not, and he's the reason. He's got no business here. He should have gone to jail for what he did. How you convinced your father not to beat the living shit out of him, I'll never know. The man I knew wouldn't have let him get away with it." He runs a hand over his face before meeting her eyes again. "I'll never understand it, Savi. Never."

"He never knew." Savi's voice is barely audible.

Sam draws back. "What?" Shock lines crease his forehead. "Why?"

"Because I didn't tell him."

"Why the hell not?" Anger sharpens his tone. "Your father would ha—"

"Stop, Sam. He didn't know and I'm glad."

"But Savi … you were his pride and joy. You know he would have done something."

"And that's why I never said anything to him. I needed time to think. Drake's father has ties with some very shady people. I didn't want to take the chance that someone would hurt my dad."

"Your father could take care of himself. Are you telling me he knew nothing? I can hardly believe that."

"He did, I guess, but he gave me my space. I guess he figured I'd tell him and Mom when I was ready. I let them believe that it was just a bad breakup." Her gaze drops to the floor. "I was embarrassed."

Sam's expression withers. "Honey, you have nothing to be embarrassed about. He raped you."

"Sam!" Savi's eyes snap to him, then to me, and then she drops her face into her hands.

"Now, you look at me, Savannah." Sam pulls her hands away and closes into her personal space. She raises her eyes which are shimmering with tears.

"You told me what happened, so I'm surprised you didn't tell them—but I understand your reasons. Drake isn't nothing but a piece of shit. Any man who'd hurt a woman isn't a man, in my book. If he comes near you again, I'll be waiting for him."

"Me, too," I add.

She forces a smile and looks at her watch. "I've got to go. Gigi's waiting for me."

"I'll drive you." I pull the truck keys from my pocket.

"You don't have to do that," she says, dismissing me with a wave of her hand. "I'm fine."

"I'm not taking no for an answer. I'll drive you home tonight, then bring you back tomorrow. You can get your car then."

Exhaustion is transparent in her expression, yet there's still resistance in her eyes.

"Go with him, Savannah." Sam looks at me. "And, if you see Drake? Kick his ass."

As Savannah retrieves her purse, Sam wraps his arms around her. "I'd never let anyone hurt you, honey." His tone is soothing. Comforting.

Savi meets his eyes, forcing a sad smile. "I know."

CHAPTER TWENTY-TWO

Savannah

"Savi, that guy's a piece of shit." I look over at her. "It takes one to know one."

My gaze snaps to him. At first, I want to rebut his comment and then I remember the Ian he used to be, and a mix of doubt and curiosity beg a question. "Are you saying you've raped someone?"

"No!" Ian's head spins toward me. He takes a quick look, then turns his eyes back to the road. "I've never raped anyone. I didn't have to." He shakes his head. "There are some things in my past that I'm sure aren't a secret. Sex was something I never had to take or buy."

His transparency, and the information he offers, confirm one more time how much he's changed but, like most women, I want to know more and press for more.

"Weird question—and you don't have to answer if

you don't want to, but— didn't you worry about diseases?"

He gives a casual shrug. "You know, it's a wonder that I didn't wind up with something because I didn't worry about anything back then. I was cavalier about most things, but I always used a condom when I had sex, no matter how fucked up I was. I didn't want any 'rug rats' or 'curtain climbers', as my father would say. One Ian Stanton is already too many." He pauses. "What about you? What happened with Drake?"

A hissing sound escapes like a pin to my secret balloon. "Too much and then, not enough. Drake was charming and I was naïve. The longer we were together the more I saw through the act. The apple doesn't fall far from the tree in his family. His dad is in politics and kids of politicians have much privilege. A little too much. Lots of things they get into trouble for are swept under the rug. Once I saw that most of his charm was an act, I broke up with him. He didn't take it well."

"And, from your conversation with Sam, you never told your parents?"

I give my head a shake. "No. I'm glad I didn't." I pause for a moment of reflection as an image fills my mind. "I can't describe what it was like. To walk into your house and find your parents dead—not just dead. Murdered." My voice fades like smoke drifting away on a breeze.

"Savi, you don't have to talk about it."

"The past couple of years have tested me in ways I

never expected. Surviving rape. My parents. Being a single mom."

"You're a strong woman."

"I don't feel that way. I mean, I know those are heavy topics, but I don't feel stronger or weaker. I just feel I've grown."

"I get it, but I want you to know you can talk to me. There isn't much that shocks me and I've got time to listen anytime you want to talk." He glances at me with the sweetest sincere expression. "I'm a pretty good listener."

As I turn and gaze out the window, it's dark memories I see. Scenes like in a movie play through my head and there's one whose stain I'd like to bleach from existence and, maybe, if I bring it up, the stain will clear a little bit more.

"I didn't really know Drake until college. My father ran a large branch of a major commercial real estate business. Drake's dad owns several businesses; the biggest one is a sanitation company. Drake's an only child, isn't bad-looking, and never skimped on dates. He did much to impress me and I fell for it. When he no longer felt he had to impress me his true colors came through. He's spoiled and he has a temper. He's cruel with words and deeds. I couldn't imagine a future with someone so narcissistic."

"A guy like me. All the perks. No personality."

His words hit like a douse of cold water. "I don't believe that about you. I would think some ego goes along with the territory where you're concerned and, from what you told me, you didn't get much good as a kid. I'm sure whatever attention you got with the band felt good. I mean, did you ever set out to purposefully hurt someone?"

I pause. A slight shake tells me I've made my point.

"Drake did. I told him I didn't want to see him anymore and he insisted we talk. Foolishly, I thought that's all it would be, but he wanted to make me pay for rejecting him. And he did." I take a deep breath then look down. My knotted hands show white knuckles. "It was a mistake to let my guard down. Such a mistake …" My voice withers.

"I don't need to hear more."

His gentle tone is a hug to my wounded heart. "I want to finish. I have to stop hiding behind shame I never caused. To stop beating myself up for things I should or shouldn't have done."

He glances at me wearing a weak smile, then nods.

"Drake showed up at a restaurant where I was having dinner with friends. He made a scene, but *I* was the one embarrassed. I got him to go to the parking lot. He said he'd have a rational conversation if I got in the car. He drove and we talked. The next thing I knew we were at his condo and things got ugly. He called me a little bitch. Said I embarrassed him. Slapped me and told me we were *not* breaking up and he would decide if, and when, we were over. He pinned me …"

"Stop! Jesus." A mix of anger and disgust sour his expression.

"The look you're wearing right now is why I didn't tell my father. He would have killed Drake."

"And he would have deserved it."

The adrenaline rush that hit as the words flowed, falls, and I feel like I've hit a wall of exhaustion. "I'm glad I didn't tell my dad. Drake's father knows a lot of bad people."

"You were afraid for him?"

"I don't know. It seems kind of pointless to speculate now," I reason. Silence hangs in the air between us.

"How does Drake know about Gigi?"

The question strikes like a thunderbolt, splitting me with terror. "I don't know. He called. When he mentioned her, I hung up on him."

"He called?" Anger fills his tone as surprise jerks his gaze in my direction. "When?"

"Recently. Just like tonight, he tried to intimidate me. It isn't working. Honestly, I'm more angry than scared. I need to talk to the police. There is a restraining order. I don't know how that works across states."

Ian digests the tale I've purged in silence, which is fine because I'm weary of this trip down memory lane.

"Savi?"

"Hmm?"

"Go out with me."

"What?" I smile as the out-of-the-blue question completely wrecks my train of thought.

"Seriously. Go out with me. You need a break. I'll

take you to dinner. I'll even pay for Cora's babysitting fee."

"Why?" Befuddled, I float the question.

"Because I want to take you out."

"What's in it for you?" I laugh, still shocked.

He gives me a wry smile. "I've never been on a date before."

"Bullshit!"

"It's true. I swear. Pitiful, huh?"

"Harder to believe." The invitation has changed our moods from dark to light. Ridiculous. Downright silly even.

"Yeah, well, that was my life. Lots of sex. Nothing meaningful."

"And this? I don't want to …"

"It's dinner. What's meaningful is the company and the conversation." He shrugs. "Come to think of it, I've never dressed up for anything other than funerals. I'd like to dress up for a happier occasion. Do those things guys like to do— gentlemanly things—like open your door for you and hold your chair." His expression pinches. "Almost sounds like a pity date, doesn't it?"

"Kind of." I smile. "But it would be nice to go out somewhere other than Sam's or Cora's. I can't remember the last time I didn't go somewhere other than Mad Dog without Gigi."

"Then it's a date?"

I nod and he smiles. When he does it reaches his eyes, causing the lines and wrinkles accrued through his hard-lived life to disappear. I shake my head in disbelief.

I'm going on a date with Ian Stanton.

CHAPTER TWENTY-THREE

Ian

"Hello?" I shove the phone between my ear and shoulder while fidgeting with the buttons on my shirt.

"So, tonight's the night, huh? You're takin' my girl out?" Sam's coffee-rich voice is laced with humor.

"Looks that way. Hold on a minute. Let me put you on speaker." I hit the button on the screen to amplify the sound and then toss the phone on the bed. "Can you hear me okay?"

"Yeah. I'm glad you're getting Savi out tonight, but I don't think I need to tell you to be a gentleman. It's been a long time since Savannah's been kissed—or it was 'till you stole one from her. Then, again, other than kissing her, I guess it's been a while for you, too."

"It's dinner, Sam. I have no expectations other than

enjoying a meal with a friend." I spray cologne and rub my hand over my neck.

"Yeah, she said the same thing; 'It's just dinner, Sam." His high-pitched, sing-song voice mocks Savannah. "I say, a date's a date. Dressing up makes it special, no matter what you say. Did you get her flowers?"

"She's not expecting flowers." I did get them, but don't need to give him another reason to niggle me for details.

"Which is exactly why you should get them." He insists.

"Sam ..." I drop a gentle warning with my tone. "We're going to eat. I'm taking her home. That's it."

"And, if you're lucky, maybe a goodnight kiss."

I stop dead in my tracks. "It sure sounds like you want me to kiss her. Knowing how protective you are of her I would have thought you more resistant to the idea. I never pegged you as a romantic."

"I still have an eye for the ladies. Just never found the one I'd want to settle down with." He parades the words with pride as he humors me. My mood is light for a change. The memory of kissing Savannah filters in pleasant thoughts, though I certainly don't expect a repeat performance of the act.

"Are you still there?"

"I am. I'm almost finished getting ready."

"What are you wearing?" Curiosity steals Sam's tough-guy image and replaces it with a nosey old bitty.

A grin splits my face. "Who the fuck are you? The

fashion police? I mean, if you're taking notes, I showered, shaved, and used deodorant—*and* I'm wearing a suit. Satisfied?" I toss the blue tie around my neck and twist the fabric as I attempt a knot.

"I'm living vicariously. Don't get all uppity on me."

"What does that mean? That *you'd* like to be going out on a date with Savi?"

"Are you out of your fucking mind? She's like a daughter to me." He deflates a breath sounding like a blown-out tire. "You're a sick bastard, Ian—and, Savi, huh?"

"She told me I could call her that. Her *friends* call her that, she said." As I goad him, I make a second attempt at a knot, which is no more successful than the first.

"She must like you." He pauses. "You know I love her, but I'm glad for you, too. You spend all your time at my bar or working at your place. You go out less than she does. You both need a break."

"Come to think of it, I don't remember you ever mentioning going out with a woman."

"It's just been a long time—though, I might consider it if there's a good steak or Italian food involved," he says.

"So, you prefer the meal to the company. Got it."

"I'm just joshing you, boy. Don't be an asshole."

Boy? True, he's old enough to be my father but the way he says it, makes it sound like an endearment.

How can such a simple thing pluck at my heartstrings? For a minute—maybe even less—I got a taste of that sense of belonging. That good feeling when a dad shares an inside joke with his son or uses a familiar nickname. With a light-hearted feeling, I return the serve.

"Alright, *old man*. If you really want to know how well it's going, I'm about ready to chuck this tie out the window. I can't knot the fucking thing for love or money." I roll my neck as frustration pricks me.

"You don't know how to tie a tie?" He asks.

"The last time I wore a tie was to Dash's funeral. It was a clip-on," I confess. My throat locks up and I go still. Fear drops a chill down my back. "Maybe this is a mistake."

"What?"

"Maybe it's a sign."

"Stop with all that sign bullshit, Ian. Like you said, 'It's not a date.' Just because you can't get the tie right doesn't mean it's a sign."

"I need a tie. Then again, I'm not all that refined. I'd probably get sauce on it anyway."

"Ah, so you are going to the Italian place! Yeah, you don't need a tie for Bruno's anymore."

"No?"

"No. Wear a T-shirt and, if you wear a dark one, you'll barely see the sauce. Plenty of guys go there with T's and a jacket."

"I'm sure I can keep from spilling." Sarcasm drips in my tone. "And I'm pretty sure Savannah isn't into food fights."

I throw the tie on a chair and quickly unbutton the

crisply pressed white shirt I'm wearing and toss it aside. Fetching a black T-shirt from the bureau drawer, I slip it over my head. When I look in the mirror, I barely recognize myself. Defined muscles fill out the sleeves with full, tight material at the biceps, the bulk evidence from working on the ranch. My arms used to be spindly sticks that hung from my shoulders. I undo the belt and zipper, tucking the bottom neatly inside. "I'm going to go, Sam. I hope I can pull this off."

"You're fine; 'it's just dinner'." His high girly voice makes a comeback.

"Riiiiight," I respond, shaking my head. I look at the clock. "I really got to go. I told her I'd get her at eight."

"I've got to go too. I have a date of my own."

"What?" My curiosity piques. "Oh, you mean the bar?"

"Nope. I'm going to Cora's. She's got a meeting of her painting club 'till nine. I'm babysitting Gigi 'till she gets there. It's a good thing, too. That little one is a weasel. She'll try to negotiate her bedtime, but Cora will set her straight when she gets there."

"Have fun."

"Yeah, you too—and Ian? You don't have to be perfect. Just be yourself."

* * *

I DRIVE to Savannah's with the windows down. It's a gorgeous night. The last stretch of the sun has painted the sky with a mix of pink, orange, and blue. The breeze is easy and swirls through the open windows, nudged by my driving speed. Small talk will be okay If I can get her talking about herself. Music and song-writing are lanes we both travel. If she flips the table to talk about me, I can always talk about Dash.

The minute I think of him, a smile appears. I've got Dash's favorite Gary Clark, Jr. music playing through the speakers. In a million years, he would never have pictured me on a normal date. I think he'd be proud of me. He'd be happy for me being clean and sober, of that much, I'm sure.

"I worry about what you're doing to yourself, Ian. You're not the first to piss away money on junk. I don't want you to wind up in the twenty-seven club."

"I'm fine."

"Are you, though? There's four of us. We're really picking up momentum. We could ride this gig for the next thirty years. Hell, look at Jagger. I'm no psychic, but if you keep wrecking yourself like this, you might not make your twenty-eighth birthday."

He was right. I almost didn't make it. But here I am, straight and going out with a beautiful woman.

I press the phone button on the steering wheel. "Call Dash Barrows."

The mechanical voice repeats my command. ***"Calling Dash Barrows."***

It instantly goes to voice mail. ***"This is Dash. You know what to do."***

Do I?

A lump in my throat emerges and I swallow. It

happens every time I hear his voice. Skylar never shut down his account and, I'm certain, there are times she feels the same need I do. I wait for the—*beep.*

"I'm going on a date." The words rush out with a snicker. "Well, it's not supposed to be a date, but it's a fucking date. A real one, Dash. And I don't mean just me banging some random chick. This is a good woman … I like her. I think you'd like her, too. She's the chick who wrote 'Heal Me' and won your contest. I'm not sure if you orchestrated this from where you are but, if you did, stop me if you see me doing anything stupid. Make me choke on a roll or something but, for god's sake, stop me."

CHAPTER TWENTY-FOUR

Savannah

I open the shower door and a rush of steam escapes, fogging up the mirrors. The instant temperature change from hot to cold makes goose-bumps appear and the chill puckers my nipples. I wrap a towel around me, the plush material feels soft against my sensitive skin.

I'd left the bathroom door open so I can see Gigi through the crack. She's been watching Bluey in my bed since I stepped into the bathroom. I can see her through the drifting fog escaping through the widened space. Nearly disappearing in the middle of my King-sized bed, she's adorned with old costume jewelry I've given her. Resplendent in the many-colored rhine-stones, the light catches the jewels. Gigi sparkles and finishes off her regal appearance by wearing the tiara Candace gave to me on my twenty-fifth birthday.

I have mixed feelings about dinner tonight with Ian. He remembers nothing of our night together. For him, that time is caught up in the overdose and the events that followed. It's one of several reasons I've unlocked my heart.

I turn back to the task at hand, massaging moisturizer into my legs, arms, and the rest of my body. The cream feels good on my skin, while the pressure loosens tight muscles.

I turn to the mirror and grab my makeup bag from beneath the sink, satisfied by the sound the contents make as they clack inside the leather bag. A swipe at the condensation clears the mirror and I study my reflection. I haven't dated since I learned about Gigi. She was just a little bean in a picture, but the connection was strong. Her existence was a caress in my chaos, and she's lifted my heart like it was helium-filled with her mewing cries and full-belly giggles. Everything I do is for her. This dinner is the first adult thing I've done for myself.

"Hi, Momma." My little munchkin skips into the bathroom and comes to stand beside me. With her pointer finger, she traces and studies the faint silvery evidence that's proof on my skin of her growing inside me. "Do dems hurt, Momma?"

"Nope. They don't hurt at all."

"I think dems pretty," she whispers as she places a sweet kiss on a spot.

Though fleeting, a thought arises, and I wonder how Ian would react to the sight. No doubt he's seen countless women naked, all pumped up and perky with various plastic procedures.

"Where's you goin' Momma?"

"Out with Ian."

"Oh, I like hims, Momma."

"You do? Why, baby? What do you like about him?"

Her expression morphs, reminding me of an old-time Kewpie doll my mom used to have. Her eyes go big and blue like the sky on a fresh spring morning. She braces her head with an "L" formed by her thumb and index finger as she ponders the question.

"Ummmmmmm. He likes buggies and wormies, and lots of stars, and dogs, and me, and you, and Sam!" She bobs her head up and down. "I like him, Momma, 'cause E-ban's a good person."

Her simple criteria makes me smile. "I guess he is."

"He is, Momma. You gotta trust the process."

My head spins from the mirror to her as my brows pinch. "Where did you hear that?" I laugh.

"I dunno. I just did." She shrugs.

Ian isn't just a nice man. His connection to Gigi has haunted my nightmares and fed my dreams. I never thought to give him space in our lives as anything more than an acquaintance but, seeing him through the eyes of a child has shown him in a different light. He loves Gigi. Of that, I'm certain.

I close my eyes, affording myself a moment of pleasure to revisit images of Ian and Gigi together. Her smile. His hugs. Her high-pitched squeals. They're friends of the heart.

And it happened right in front of my eyes.

I'm not sure how that makes me feel. I'm possessive and extremely protective of people I love. There are so few of them and so many bad people who drift unnoticed in a world where violence finds good people. *But Ian's not one of them.*

The thought wraps around my heart. Ian's been misjudged by those who've not walked in his shoes, including me. I'm one of many who've not felt his pain or wrestled with his demons and, yet, stood in judgment. It was shallow of me.

I return my gaze to the mirror and my stretch marks. I'm more than my physical appearance just as Ian is more than his past. More important than that, I want to set a good example for my daughter. I've not lived in his skin, nor he in mine, but I never want Gigi to see me as one of the high and mighty who judge without heart. I don't want to be that person. Maybe children should be our teachers instead of the other way around. They love without reservation or judgment and are surely the sweetness in the world.

As I wrap my hair around the brush bristles and run the blow dryer, the quiet humming sound coaxes me into a more serene state. I'm looking forward to tonight. Dinner with Ian is an opportunity to know him better, but also one to know myself better.

As I SLIP into the black dress, the fabric cools as it slides over my skin. It's a simple one with a modest neckline but is sexy in a Carolina Herrera way. It's been in my closet forever, hidden in the back since I moved here, the tags still dangling from the sleeve. It zips up the side; the teeth disappearing into the fabric and resting against my skin.

"You looks so pretty, Momma." Gigi's breathless compliment makes me feel all warm inside.

"Thank you, baby." I smile and hold my hand out in an invitation for hers. "We have to get your things. Sam's going to pick you up and take you to Cora's."

"Yay!" She takes my hand, and we walk out of the bedroom. My hips sway as femininity takes control and with each step, Gigi copies my strut, the long beads hanging down her front bouncing from side to side.

"We is pwetty like princesses!"

"Yes, we are, sweet girl." I scoop her up in my arms and twirl us around, Gigi squealing with laughter. We're having a giggle fest when my phone rings.

"Hello?"

"Savannah." Ian's tone is deep and as serious as the grave.

My smile fades. "What's wrong?"

He pauses, then lets out a long sigh. "I think this might be a mistake."

CHAPTER TWENTY-FIVE

Ian

I go silent after the comment knowing the reason for my hesitation is coming from fear rather than disinterest, yet not knowing how to voice it without sounding like a pussy.

"Tell me why," Savannah says softly.

My first reaction is surprise that she isn't pissed off. My second is uncertainty. Her request is a simple one but opening up to her, knowing I'd make myself vulnerable is something unfamiliar because I've played life so close to the vest since getting straight. But, if ever there was a time to test this friendship, it's now. "What if I fuck this up?"

"What if you do?" she quickly responds. "It's only—"

"Dinner. I know. But we're good now, Savi, you and me, and that little girl who puts a spark in my life I didn't know I was missing. If I fuck up ..." I choke thinking of the ramifications, struggling to put my thoughts to words. "Savannah, this … this life I've got … this peace I've found … I can't los—" The tremble in my voice nearly exposes me, so I stop talking.

"This life you've fashioned for yourself is safe, Ian. It isn't going to slip away." She assures.

I clear my throat and strengthen my tone. "Listen, you're a reasonable woman. You followed the band. You've read the things they printed about me. There's a reason they called me asshole Ian."

"Were the reasons valid? Were you an asshole?" The questions are sincere.

I huff out a laugh. "Well, yeah. I guess I was."

"And now? Are you an asshole now?"

My posture deflates, and I wipe my hand over my face, thankful she can't see me right now. "I don't know. I'm not sure how I can judge my own character. I mean, that first night at Sam's, I was kind of a prick to you."

"And I was to you." She pauses. "I'll tell you what; show up. That's all you have to do. Show up for our dinner and honor your commitment to take me out. Don't think about what's happened in the past. Don't worry about what will be in the future. Show up. Stay present. What happens, happens. Do you think you can do that?"

"Yeah, but—"

"No buts," Savi interrupts. "Dinner with me. A friend. A simple commitment. I'm holding you to your word and I'll leave the door unlocked so I can fluff up my hair and finish getting ready."

Leaving me no room for thought, she disconnects.

* * *

I TWIST THE DOORKNOB. It's unlocked, just as she said.

"Savannah?"

"Be there in a minute," she calls, the sound of her voice trailing down from upstairs.

I walk around the living room, meandering to take in her style, and pause to look at photos on the mantle above the fireplace and strategically placed on top of a piano. Most are of Gigi at different stages of her life, and I can't help but smile. She's a cutie and these photos catch her in the silliest poses. I don't know much about babies, but she wasn't all wrinkly and squishy-faced, but more round and rosy-cheeked. She's got a sparkle that doesn't fade from picture to picture, and I find myself smiling as I look at each one.

On the other end of the mantle, beyond the central photos of Gigi, are images of Savannah and a man and woman, whom I'm guessing are her parents. The resemblance between the two women is uncanny. Their smile in the photo shoots a pang of envy through my heart. The affection reflected in the images is almost palpable, and most definitely something I've never felt. I shove my hands in my pockets and nod. I'm happy for her. She's lucky to have this collection to hold onto. I guess I am too. I have one photo of my mother: none of my old man.

As I move about the room draped in creamy colors, I find myself relaxing. Even the mountain of Gigi's toys in the corner is nice and neatly stacked next to a large wooden box with her name painted in pink script lettering.

"Hi."

I turn at the sound of her voice, and the vision causes my breath to catch. If I thought Savi was pretty before, she's even more so now. Confidence fills her every step as she crosses the room like a queen with a demure smile filling her red lips. Black stilettos dangle from her fingers. With her back straight and chin held high, I can't think of a more perfect example of elegance and grace.

"I was admiring your taste. It looks nice in here."

"Thanks," she says glancing left and right. "It's a challenge to keep it this way. The minute Gigi wakes up, the toys come out. She's got more in the family room which is typically more an obstacle course than living space." She pauses, looking at the flowers in my hand. "They're pretty."

"Oh. Yeah." I lift the blooms, filling the space between us. "These are for you."

She drops her shoes on the carpet and takes the flowers from my hand. "Thank you. I'll put these in some water. Be right back."

I watch as she disappears into another room then just as quickly is back. Holding onto my arm she slips her feet inside her heels. Instantly she gains a few inches putting her at eye level with me. The simple black dress and sun-colored hair are all she needs. Clearly, I'm out of my league.

"You look beautiful," I say, my voice exposing a bit more awe than I intend.

She smiles, a hint of a blush creeping onto her cheeks. "Thank you." Tipping her head toward her shoulder, she gives me a coy look. "You're not too bad yourself."

"Thanks." I pause to enjoy this moment. I've been around hundreds of women—maybe thousands—but none compares to the woman standing before me. Those eyes and that smile are like a kick in the chest. This is so new to me, and the emotions so clear and fresh, I have a new appreciation for my sobriety. Pleasure and pride sink into me in a new way, and I feel the effect all the way to my marrow. I believed there was nothing left of me after Dash died, but the effect of Savi's nearness is proof you can breathe new life into bone dust.

"Speaking of Gigi ..." I scan the room. "Where is she?"

"Sam picked her up a few minutes ago. He took her to Cora's for me."

"I didn't realize he'd been here already. I was hoping to see her."

Curiosity tips her head. "You sound disappointed."

"I am, I guess."

"You'll see her soon," she assures. "Tonight's for the adults."

I look around. "Adults?" I tease. "You say that as if there's more than one in the room."

She rolls her eyes, tucks a small, beaded purse under her arm, and issues a look. "Well, this adult is famished. Ready?"

I capture her arm, and she looks down at the spot.

"Something wrong?" she says as she looks up and meets my eyes with her beautiful blues.

"One minute."

Her brows pinch.

"Just, thank you. You talked me down off a ledg—"

"Dinner. Remember? No pressure."

Her eyes twinkle and I lose myself in her gaze. I breathe in a deep, fresh supply of oxygen clearing away troublesome thoughts, savoring this moment and the way she makes me feel like a million bucks. The pink hue in her cheeks warms in intensity and the sight causes a tightening in my chest. Looking into her eyes, I bear the sweet squeeze with ease.

THE DRIVE to the restaurant is quiet and easy, both of us content to listen to the soft jazz filling the space. When we arrive, I park, and she reaches for the door.

"Stop." I place my hand atop hers. "Let me, please."

She pauses, clearly understanding my intent as she nods and waits patiently. I come around the car, open her door, and offer her my hand. As we approach the entry door, she stops while I hold that door open as well, then slips her arm through mine as we approach the hostess. "Reservation for Barrows."

"Of course, Mr. Barrows." The woman looks down at a seating list on the dark oak stand as she retrieves two menus. "Follow me, please."

We do, trailing behind her to a beautiful, shaded courtyard. It's a joined outdoor space in the rear of four buildings. In each corner, they've mounted large fans, cooling off the Nevada heat. The buildings are old, but the age adds character to an otherwise bland space. In the middle is a huge, three-tiered fountain. Water trickles down the sides, providing a tranquil setting. We follow our hostess to a table for two, topped with a crisp, white tablecloth and a low-sitting floral arrangement with a candle lit within a globe in the center. Soft, lush, creamy blush-colored roses are framed with bunches of smaller blooms, so slight they seem to float around the bigger flower heads. I look over at Savannah who's soaking it all in. We steal a quick glance at each other as I hold the chair out for her and then take my seat.

"Your waiter will be with you in a moment," the hostess chimes as she hands us menus.

Savannah gives me a look then follows the woman with her eyes. Once the hostess is out of hearing range, she leans toward me with a hiked brow. "Barrows? As in Dash?"

"Yeah." I shrug it off. "It's probably not an issue

these days, but I didn't want my name to trigger any camera-happy sleaze bags."

She nods, indicating she understands, and we turn our attention to the menus, making small talk about what sounds tasty. When our waiter arrives, he interrupts the chatter. After reciting the specials of the day, he takes our order for drinks, then disappears as soft Italian songs play in the background.

"I've never been here before, but Cora says the food's delicious," Savannah says, breaking the silence.

"It's definitely a change from Mad Dog."

"I like it," she says, wrinkling her nose. Her eyes light with delight as she glances around the room. "It's cozy."

I agree with a nod. Over her shoulder I see the waiter approach with our drinks. He offers me a sample of the wine and I hand it to Savi.

"I think the lady is a better judge of what she'd like." The man defers to Savi.

"It's delicious," she says, approving. He pours more into the glass, takes our order, and leaves.

"So, what do you like to do in your free time?"

"Free time?" Amusement sparkles in her eyes, the effect highlighted by the flickering candle. "There's little of that in my life. I'd say, when Gigi's asleep, normal house chores are done, and when it gets quiet, I like to read," she answers. "But I also love being outside. Gigi and I go for hikes or walks. I like getting her out of the house to appreciate nature. She loved your ranch, what she could see of it."

The sound of Savi's voice is something I could listen to all day. It's soft and sweet, and I find myself taking mental note of her interests.

"What about you?" she asks, turning the tables.

"I like working on my ranch. It beats going to the gym." I shrug indifferently.

"What I could see of it is beautiful. It was a little hard to tell in the dark."

"You and Gigi are welcome anytime. You should come out during the day. I think she'd like the chickens. I have a few different breeds, so I get some pretty colored eggs. I also have a horse. She's a rescue and really sweet. It's almost as if she appreciates her new home. I haven't named her yet. Maybe Gigi could help me pick a name."

"Oh, she'd love that! She loves animals." Savannah's radiant smile lights up the room and it fists my heart. I could look at her all night and never grow tired of the sight. The gentle slope of her nose. The delicate curve of her lips. The twinkle in her eyes when she talks about Gigi. I take in every aspect, committing them to memory.

Our conversation continues to flow easily as we wait for our food, and I find myself relaxed in Savannah's company. She has a way of putting me at ease, and I feel as if we've known each other for years instead of months.

"Ian, I know some about your time with the band and I know Sam's your sponsor, but would I be imposing if I asked more about ..."

"You want to know what led me to the straight and narrow path?"

"Well, yeah, I guess. You always hear stories about rock stars and their excesses."

I pause, pressing my lips together as I inhale a deep breath.

"No. Forget I asked." She waves me off, quickly dismissing her request. "I'm a little too curious for my own good."

"No, I've got nothing to hide. Everybody's got a story and, honestly, so much misinformation's been written, I'd rather tell you mine in my own words. The tabloids fed the public whatever would make them the most money because that's how it works."

"I don't want to make you uncomfortable."

"Not possible. The truth is it goes way back. My problems started when I was a kid, but then, therapists always ask about your childhood.

When I was a kid—not much older than Gigi—I feared the boogeyman. My room was dark. The white walls picked up shadows from the window and those were scary as shit when I was alone in bed, but not when I was with my momma. With her, I felt safe. We were alone a lot because my dad traveled for work. I was her friend. Her confidante. She talked to me like I was a grown-up. Most of the time I didn't understand what she was telling me about her relationship with my father. She confused me more than anything. One minute she was mad at Daddy for going away, and then, in the next, she would praise him for being such a hardworking man. There were fits of anger. She'd throw things and break them against the wall, yelling and screaming she didn't need him. She scared the hell out of me when she got like that. I'd hide under the bed. Eventually, she'd pull me out and we'd get down on our knees and pray that God would keep Daddy safe. That's what led to mine and Momma's 'tea parties'.

She'd chatter while the water boiled, telling me about how she met Daddy at a coffee shop and how he promised to take her to Paris. I'd listen while the tea steeped in the pot. Then she and I would sip from Mamaw's China teacups. It was a special brew, Momma said, one that would help us sleep and have good dreams." I look down at my hands as the memory engulfs me, then release a long exhale before looking up at Savi. "I didn't realize until therapy that it was Rock n Rye. The tea was sweet, like the rock candy she bought me on my birthday, but the brew burned as it went down my throat to my belly. I thought it was the temperature, but it was the alcohol. She'd make me drink two cups every time. Then we'd go back to bed. I'd fall asleep, escaping the boogeyman, as she pet my head. "Goodnight, Peaches," she'd say so soft and sweet that it lulled me into a dreamless sleep."

Suddenly I realize my focus drifted and I turn my attention back to Savi. "That's what started me escaping my pain and I didn't stop chasing the numbness until I overdosed." I lean back in the chair, taking in the shocked expression she tries to hide. "Anyway, that's enough of my history. Dinner's here."

She says nothing as the waiter approaches and sets the plates on the table, once he's gone, she reaches for my hand.

"I'm sorry for what you've been through, and I appreciate you sharing it with me."

"It is what it is. Ancient history." I nod and we both look down. I have a massive mound of spaghetti and meatballs in front of me, and she ordered a dish of manicotti. She closes her eyes, inhaling a whiff of the meal.

"Mmmm. This smells delicious." She takes a sip of wine, then pushes away from the table. "Excuse me for a minute. I want to wash my hands."

As she stands, the chair legs catch on the ground and Savannah misjudges the distance. She bumps the table, hard. The water and wine glass topple, and the plate of steaming spaghetti slides from the table and lands right in my lap.

CHAPTER TWENTY-SIX

Savannah

"Holy shit!" Ian grabs the edge of the table and pushes away from the scalding inferno that's burning his crotch. He jumps back and the steaming hot food falls onto the bricks below. "That's fucking hot!"

I cringe as thick, red marinara clings to his pants. "I'm so sorry!" Mortified and stunned, I'm momentarily rooted to the spot. Two waiters rush to offer help, using napkins to brush the lingering food to the ground. It seems to make the situation worse, and Ian takes a backward step, pushing their hands away. "Stop!" He grabs one man's arm. "Stop!"

The man instantly pulls back. The hostess, seeing the commotion as she seats two more customers, rushes over. "Oh my gosh. Are you okay, sir?" She gives the two men a hard look. "Did one of you drop the plate?"

"No," Ian stops her. "They were trying to help," he says.

I look around. Several customers are snapping pictures with their cell phones. I move close to him to block their view.

"I'm so, so sorry. What can I do to help?"

He takes his eyes off me and the mess and he, too, sees the picture happy customers. "I'm going to the bathroom. Can you tell them to box up our food?"

I nod. "Of course." I follow him to the double doors leading to the inside of the restaurant to thwart further attempts of amateur photographers. The hostess follows me, while the waiters clean the table. Once Ian's inside, I turn to her. "Could you please box up our meals?"

"Yes. I'm so sorry this happened."

"It's not your fault. I bumped into the table. If you can get the food ready to go, I'll grab my credit card."

"No, ma'am." She puts up a hand. "There's no charge."

"Thank you." I rush to the table and grab my purse. When I look up, I spy the voyeurs. It's a handful of people and suddenly, my anger spikes. They know who he is, and they know what they're doing.

I give them a hard look.

I bite back bitter words. Knowing these few people could turn opportunists in a heartbeat and could make Ian's life hell and sabotage the peaceful, quiet life he craves, I reach into my bag, turn to the hostess, and give her a one-hundred-dollar bill. Her eyes widen.

"Please have everything ready at the front door and help us make a quiet exit."

"I thought that was Ian Stanton," she whispers, staring at the door separating us from Ian. It's a brief move then she puts her eyes on me. "Yes, ma'am. I'll take care of everything."

* * *

IN THE CAR, I fear his silence speaks volumes. Not one word did he utter during the drive to his house. Once we arrive, I'm shocked when he comes around to my side of the car and opens the door.

I stare at his outstretched hand, then take it. The instant our eyes meet, I drop my gaze to the ground as he helps me out of the car. My stomach is still bottomed out over what happened. "I don't mind staying here while you change."

He opens the back door, grabs the bag and bottle from the restaurant, and holds it up. "Aren't you going to eat?"

Momentarily caught off guard at his blasé tone, my sight hops from him to the bag, and back again, catching the calm tone. "You aren't upset? I thought you'd be pissed."

His brown hikes. "You think too much."

He smiles and I'm stunned. A brief moment passes,

and I smile back, relieved that he doesn't seem irritated. Drake would have completely flipped out.

"Pot, meet kettle?" I scrunch up my nose.

He rolls his eyes then turns to the house. "I don't think too much," he throws over his shoulder.

"Ha! No? You're the most introspective person I know. You torture yourself," I say as I follow him.

"I do not, and that's all there is to it." He refutes, closing the subject as he approaches the door. "I'll change, then we'll eat. I tried the gentlemanly thing. It didn't work out, so my kitchen will have to do."

The screen door creaks as he pulls it open. He presses a code into the keypad mounted on the inside door. It beeps and he turns the knob, then he steps inside and flips the light switch. I follow.

"Make yourself at home. I'll be down in a minute. I'm going to change."

I step tentatively through the kitchen as he disappears up a set of stairs. I don't travel far, but just far enough to see into the family room. I glance quickly at the stairs then rush back to the kitchen table. The bag is sitting there, though I don't recall him setting it down. No matter.

My heels clip-clop on the hardwood floor, even though I'm nearly running on tiptoe.

"You might want to take those off," he calls from upstairs. "The floors are pine, which is a soft wood. It was a bitch to refinish. Your heel tips will leave divots —and feel free to wander around."

I slip off my heels and place them by the back door.

As I straighten up, I wipe my hands down the front of my dress to stave off wrinkles as I go back to the family room doorway.

The first thing I notice is an enormous stone fireplace and a sigh escapes. I love the smell and warmth of a good fire.

My shoulders relax and my stomach knot unravels as I roam the room. I drag my finger over a pile of books on an end table and cock my head to read the titles. *Marketing and self-improvement books, huh?* I press my lips together as I move on.

Ian's furnishings are eclectic. Not what I'd expect from someone who I would have imagined hiring a decorator. What I see reminds me of Ian's former Bohemian stage style. The chairs and sofa look plush and comfortable, well-worn leather with a few dark, forest green pillows on each. The place is rustic and relaxed. Like him.

"Not what you pictured?"

I jump. His silent, barefoot approach startles me. I turn. He's shirtless in sweats and my jaw nearly drops. Muscles that were hidden beneath his clothes ripple from shoulders to waist. He looks absolutely delicious.

"You're reading my mind." I cross my arms over my chest and take a step or two toward him. "The floors are beautiful." I glance down then up, meeting his eyes. "Sorry if I scratched them."

He shrugs, moving past a pair of open windows dressed in plain, straight curtains in the same hue and texture as the pillows.

"I'm sure they're fine. A few dings will add character." He goes to a cupboard and pulls open a door. "Doesn't exactly scream 'rockstar,' does it?"

"I like it. It's you."

"I'll take that as a compliment." A smile tugs the corner of his mouth. Ian looks so much younger when he smiles, and much more handsome.

My heart skips.

"Follow me. I'll heat up our dinner." He sets the plates down and snatches the bag. When he flips another switch, a longer, darker part of the kitchen lights up. My eyes widen. It's a stunning, high-end, complete chef's kitchen.

"Alexa. Play soft jazz."

Music emerges from speakers that blend in with the crown molding and my head moves to count how many. There are four; one in each corner and the music fits the vibe of the room. I watch as he pushes a button beneath the polished stone-topped island.

"I've never seen a stove like that."

"La Cornue Chateau 150." He rattles off the information then takes his eyes away from plating the meal to look up at my wide-eyed expression. "It's from France." He smiles.

I'm flabbergasted, disbelieving what I just heard him say.

"What?" He chuckles.

"You cook?"

"Don't you?" His brow playfully quirks.

"Touché." I agree with a tip of my head then look

around. "I just never heard a guy rattle off the details of his stove."

"Ah, but is it just a stove?" He jokes.

Is it? I have no idea but it's a massive piece and the focal point of the room. He's giving me the impression this room might be his favorite. Soft green paint covers the walls, with a white hue overhead on the ceiling. One entire wall is covered with pegboard, which is filled with all sorts of pots and pans. I look over at him as he reaches into the bag and empties the containers of food onto the plates. I look around the corner of the island just in time to see the plates disappear into an under-mounted microwave. He holds up the re-corked bottle of wine.

"Yes?"

I nod and he goes to another cabinet and retrieves a long-stemmed wine glass. I walk to his side as he uncorks and pours.

"Can I do anything to help?"

"I think I can handle it." He juts his chin and looks over toward a cozy, semicircle nook. There, an oval table sits in front of a pillow-backed window seat. On the other side is an old church bench with a tufted cushion matching the one at the window. "Go. Sit. Take your wine. This'll only be a minute."

I follow his instructions, taking a seat at the window side of the table. The moon isn't full tonight but its glow shines over a small garden.

"Are those herbs you're growing out there?"

I turn as he places a tall glass of ice and a Coca-Cola directly across from where I'm sitting. "It is."

"So, you do like to cook!"

"Never said I didn't." He returns to the beeping microwave and pulls out the plates. Once he's approached the table, he sets the plates down and takes a seat across from me on the bench. "I used to eat so much fast food on the road." He shakes his head. "Cooking gave me something to explore and, a man's got to eat, right? Besides, when we get the occasional rain and the windows are open, it's the best smell." He picks up a fork and smiles. "Dig in."

I do. I haven't eaten all day. Apparently, neither has he, and we fill our stomachs in silence.

I watch Ian eat and he glances up, meeting my eyes. The corners of his eyes crinkle but his expression softens. His smile graces his lips more than he knows and the look reminds me of the tenderness inside a man who's endured so much. The lines etched in his tanned skin aren't just from time spent working in the sun, but of a hard life.

Funny how everyone sees the privilege and not the pain.

"C'mon, Savannah. Eat." He juts his fork toward my plate.

There it is.

That relaxed man I saw chasing fireflies with my daughter. Sometime between the night he overdosed and now, he's found peace. I wonder how foreign a feeling it must be to someone navigating the newness of a quiet and uneventful life— especially given how chaotic his life used to be.

His stare intensifies and my gaze drops to my plate. I cut the manicotti with the edge of my fork.

"Tell me about Gigi."

I lift my eyes. "What do you want to know?"

He pushes his chair back a few inches from the table. "I don't know. Whatever you want to tell me. She's quite the little spitfire." His shoulders pulse. "What was it like holding her in your arms that first time?"

I swallow my food as a dreamy feeling settles over me and set my fork on the edge of the plate. I tent my arms, resting my elbows on the table and interlacing my fingers. I think for a second as the memory of holding her after she took her first breath settles in my mind's eye. "It was incredible. Like time stood still and everything and everyone else faded away." I begin, my voice soft and full of emotion. I catch his gaze. "It was magic."

"Was she a hard birth?" He quizzes.

"I don't know how to answer that. I'd gone through hours of labor. The doctors were talking c-section because my blood pressure was erratic. Before we could decide, my labor suddenly became fast and hard. Gigi was calling the shots." I lean back and sip the wine as he patiently waits for more.

"She was early—four weeks. She had to go to the neonatal intensive care unit immediately following her entrance to the world but, before they took her away, they placed her in my arms." A small smile tugs at my lips. "I've never been the same since."

"Sounds surreal."

"It was insta-love. I breathed her in. Felt the softness of her hair against my cheek. When I kissed her, my heart exploded." A duet of tears tumbles down my cheeks. "Like I said, magic."

"Guiliana is the *best kind of magic*."

Out of nowhere, fear stabs me, and I suck in a breath. Ian instantly notes the change.

Ian's brow pinches. "What's wrong?"

I say nothing, imprisoned by irrational thought.

"You're pale. Tell me." Concerned, he reaches for my hand and our eyes meet. "I promise; it's okay."

Feeling awkward and embarrassed, I look away from him. "It's stupid. It's just with Drake showing up …" A picture flashes through my mind. "It was a dream," I explain, shaking my head. "I guess I'm just still shaken up a bit."

"Want to talk about it?"

"I don't know."

All of a sudden, my appetite wanes. Not really paying attention to what I'm doing, I push away the plate. A silent lull drops. A few awkward moments later, Ian speaks.

"How worried are you about that guy?"

"I don't know, but maybe I should be."

"Why's that?"

"Because he's unpredictable and it isn't just me I have to be concerned about."

"You're worried about him hurting Gigi?"

"Or Sam. Or Cora. Or you. Or anyone else I love and care about. Anyone he sees as a threat." I'm rambling and, when I look at Ian, he's grinning. I'm confused. "Why are you smiling?"

He gives my hand a gentle squeeze. "No reason." He looks me dead in the eye. "Nothing's gonna happen, Savi. Promise." He peers at my plate. "Now, c'mon. Eat your dinner."

I pick up my fork and, though I'm perplexed, he stares as I take a forkful. The look is intense in his beautiful eyes, sending a shiver down my back. I don't know what it is but there's a secret hiding there.

CHAPTER TWENTY-SEVEN

Ian

What Savi doesn't know is that I'd do anything to protect her and Gigi, and Drake is the least of my worries.

"What do you remember about your overdose?"

"Wow." The sharp sense of surprise snaps my eyes wider, hiking up my brows as I dab at my mouth with the napkin. "That came out of nowhere. Are we doing a 'best day' story to 'worst day' conversation?"

Savannah tips her head as a shadow of regret falls over her expression. "I'm making it awkward. I shouldn't have asked."

I dismiss the hint of remorse in her voice. "I don't care. It's just a topic as far away from sweet babies as you can get." I dab my mouth with the napkin. "I've got nothing to hide from you, Savannah."

A sweet smile fills her lips.

"Long story short, I was drunk and high—but that was nothing new. We were going on stage in half an hour. I'd tried making small talk with the guys, but they didn't want to have anything to do with me. Nobody knew what to expect when I got on the stage.

I was depressed that day. I got hit with a sucker punch of grief and their shunning made it harder. Every step in front of an audience reminded me of what used to be. They accepted Dash's death and were moving forward. I wasn't. I couldn't. To sing I had to be numb. I was screwing up. Messing up songs. Stumbling as I tripped over my own feet. I fucked up nearly every performance. If I ever had any real friendship with the guys, I tanked it. We lost the camaraderie we had when Dash was with us. I couldn't hold a decent conversation with any of them unless I was high. All that did was piss them off.

"It sounds horrible," she says, barely above a whisper.

"It was, but I deserved it. You feel it when you're the outcast. It doesn't take a genius to figure it out. I thought by joking around it would ease the tension and they wouldn't feel so bad about Dash. All I did was irritate them." I shrug. "Everybody deals with death their own way. All I could see was my own pain, but I could feel theirs. It was unbearable. I needed an escape."

"What happened that night? What was different?"

"I fucked up. Like, big time, fucked up. The show. The meet and greet. After it was over, the guys let me know how they felt. It wasn't so much what they said, but the passive-aggressive shit hit hard as a brick."

"They didn't see your pain." Her blue eyes blind me with their charity. The tenderness I see there reminds me of her soft heart.

"I didn't see theirs." I pause. "After the meet and greet, we would grab dinner together. That night they left me out. I went to my room, my insides all twisted, knowing I'd no one left. I let them down. I let myself down. I didn't want to be here anymore. I was having stomach pains, so I went to the vending machines."

I push the chair back and take my plate to the sink. Savi does the same. She places her hand on my back. "You got any coffee?"

"Yeah. I'll make some."

Savi goes back to the window seat as I pull some beans from the freezer. As I measure, grind, and fill the machine with coffee and water, I digest the crux of the story. It's crazy that it feels good to tell this story to her. Like confession must feel in a church.

I go back to my chair while the coffee brews and find Savi sitting quietly with her legs pulled up on the cushion.

"Is that all you remember?"

I'm shocked she wants to hear more. "No. I remember the vending machines; I couldn't even get that shit right. The machine kept spitting out my money. I was about ready to toss it all and—I know this sounds crazy—an angel came and helped me. It was just like momma told me: *Your guardian angel is always with you and will protect you and come to you when you need them.*

She was more beautiful than I could have imagined and everything my mother described to me. Her voice was a melody and she led me to a box. At first, I thought she was taking me to heaven. The light was so bright. Then there was darkness. I thought we might be on the way to hell." I throw up my hands. "Now I know it was an elevator." I look up into Savannah's eyes and clear my throat of sudden emotion.

"She loved me. Then she left me. Just like my mother."

"What?" Her eyes widen. "Why would you think that?" Savannah asks.

"It felt real enough but I'm pretty sure I'm more suited for the company of demons. Not angels."

Savi's lips purse. "All this talk about angels and demons." She goes to the beeping coffee pot and moves one of the cups I placed on the counter. "It's nonsense. You're a good person, Ian Stan—*Oww!*"

In an instant I'm at the counter, grabbing her hand, and placing it under cold water.

"I wasn't paying attention."

"It's fine. Let the water run over your fingers for a minute."

She obeys and moves close. After a few minutes, she pulls her hand back. I watch as she examines her fingers. Confident there's no blistering, she slides her cold hand into mine.

I look down and meet her eyes. She goes up on

tiptoe, her lips so close to mine I can feel her breath. Desire catches fire inside of me, but I have to stop, reminding myself that this is *just dinner*.

"Savi, you've had a bit to drink."

"Shh. I've had one glass and I know what I'm doing."

"Do you?" The deep tone of my voice is strained.

"Yes. I do." Face to face. Eye to eye. She presses her lips to mine and parts them with a flick of her tongue. It's a sultry invitation, and I accept. Nothing feels as good as the velvety feel of our mingling lips and twisted tongues. This is our second kiss and it is so much sweeter than our first.

I feel drunk.

I hook my arm around her waist and pull her into me. A soft moan as her breasts hit my chest sends a rush of blood to my cock. This is new. I've never been sober when with a woman, other than our kiss that firefly night. She pulls back, breathless.

"I …" Her gaze darts away then comes back to meet mine. "Ian."

"Maybe we should stop." I take a step, but she pulls me back.

"No." The heavy whisper is sweet in my ears.

Her head falls back. I kiss her throat and inhale her scent.

"Woman," the word rumbles against her throat. "What you do to me …"

"Shh." She pulls up, the sound teasing my ear, and then runs her tongue along the shell. A sound deep and guttural steals my voice.

Her fingers play at my waist, then she slides a hand down inside my sweatpants. My thoughts go askew, and I suck in a breath. Does she realize I'm basically a virgin? That I've never experienced a woman's touch without being fucked up or drunk? How could she? Why would she? This? This isn't sex to me. It's a whole new fucking experience.

There's an intense but playful look in her eyes. I don't expect it. Pretense isn't her style. She doesn't have to act at being slutty or sexy. She's simply having fun.

She looks up at me with thick, dark lashes fluttering over sky-blue eyes and takes my cock in her hand. There's no fabric to dodge between my pants and my cock. No boxers, tighty-whities, or other such bullshit. I don't wear anything more than I need and prefer nothing between me and my balls.

"I want you to fu—"

"I won't. Don't even say the word." She pulls back, rejection making her blush, but I refuse to let her escape. "I want you; I do. But what I want to do doesn't resemble the definition of fucking. For me, fucking has always been quick and dirty. I've had that. I want more with you."

"But you said—"

"I know what I said but you're the first woman who means something to me. I want my first, sober, meaningful sexual experience to be with you. I don't want to fuck you, Savi. I want to make love to you."

"Tenderness softens her expression, and her posture

slackens. She melts in my arms as I hook an arm around her back and the other beneath her knees and lift her. There's so much testosterone surging through my body she feels as light as a feather.

I press my lips to hers, needing more of the taste that she'd awakened as I carry her into the bedroom.

CHAPTER TWENTY-EIGHT

Savannah

I feel young, and I feel old. The girlish crush I had on Ian has been replaced by something more. Something I could never have anticipated. I don't know where this will lead, and I don't want to analyze it because, for tonight, I simply want to love him.

He sets me down on my feet and my toes curl into the plush carpet.

"Let me see you." The words carry a hint of begging as his voice drops to a husky depth.

His tone caresses me with the coffee-rich sound and elicits a thrill that sends a shiver down my back and raises goosebumps on my skin. I pluck the zipper beneath my arm with shaky fingers as I move to remove my dress. The plastic teeth separate easily. I cross my arms and pinch the fabric at my hips, inching it upward until I've clutched the hem. Ever so slowly I pull the garment over my head and in burlesque queen fashion I hold it out to the side of me then drop it to the floor.

He sucks in a breath as my breasts come free. The tips instantly stiffen from the slight change in temperature. Goosebumps surface immediately and skate freely over my skin. Though the Nevada nights hold a chill, warmth flushes my face as I stand bare before him except for the minute covering of a lacy, black thong.

Ian takes a step forward as he reaches out and cups a breast. He awakens a need as he runs his thumb over the puckered tip, but that isn't his focus. Instead, his eyes bore into mine, infusing me with desire.

"Do you know how fucking beautiful you are, Savannah?"

A flood rushes to my core as his words caress my soul. His words are a bouquet that blooms inside of me, filling me with a rush of emotion that closes my throat and steals my words.

Ian takes my hand and leads me to the bed, and I drift down at the edge. He drops to one knee and leans in, his face mere inches away from mine. Tingles wash over me as he looks deeply into my eyes, and I see things in their depths that he doesn't let anyone see. He bares his heart and soul, allowing me a ticket to see inside to the man he hides from the world.

Pressing his lips to my forehead, my eyes drift closed as he moves down and places kisses on my temples, cheeks, and the valley at the base of my neck. The touch is light and chaste as he worships at the temple of my body and I respond without will, my spine bowing, arching toward him as my flesh begs for more.

Placing his hands at my waist, he places a kiss to my belly, then pulls back and takes my hand. Pressing his lips to my knuckles he makes me feel royal, like a princess, and it momentarily catches me off guard. It's such a tender move and the waterfall of emotion it induces threatens to drown me.

I don't know what I expected. If anything at all I presumed the fervor of a man starved for sex, but I see something in Ian that arouses me and races my pulse. In this new version of him, I better understand his need to love and be loved, and that sweet pain swells my heart.

He stands, then moves to lay on the bed. I put my feet up and push back with my heels until I'm lying beside him.

We're eye to eye for a moment, then I trace down his body with eager fingers. Shoulder to rib, rib to chest, then down as my hand sails on waves of muscle. I tease along the trail until I reach his hips, then graze with light touches over that delicious V that all women find so damn sexy. A rumbling sound ascends from low in his throat and escapes with a gasp as I slip my fingers inside his sweatpants. He lifts to assist me as I tug at the fabric, then pulls them down over his hips. I push the garment down until it reaches his knees and my efforts halt as he kicks it away in one, swift motion.

My eyes feast on Ian's body, raking up and down to take in this new version of him. My breath hitches as I discover he's worked his body into the form of an ancient god; his former thin-railed rockstar shape now completely gone.

I look down and the sight of his cock excites me. He's stiff as a brick and I enjoy a potent rush of power. It sings through me as I note that it's me who made him hard as stone. I want to give Ian this experience. I want to tease and taunt him in every way possible, making this time with me something that burns into his heart and mind like a bright red brand.

A devilish feeling comes over me and I'm suddenly more vixen and vamp. I lick my red-stained lips as I move down and close to the swollen crown and exhale a hot breath across his skin. He shudders as the air brushes his most sensitive part and the move sends a jolt that makes his cock jump and further thickens his already rock-hard shaft. I peer up at him, feeling a seductive grin curl onto my lips. The look I give promises him sweet violence and when he touches my shoulder and swallows a gulp of anticipation, I pause for a moment to drink it in.

I feel powerful, like I can save him from himself and the self-deprecation he's hidden for so long. I'd been such a child that night of the concert, taking what I wanted when we were together. I was selfish. Self-absorbed. Solipsistic. I was hurt because I wanted the notice of a rockstar. Now, all I want is the man.

Memories of how I drove him to the edge that night, then abandoned him, convict me. I want this night to be moonlight and madness. Penance for the sin I committed long ago. That night I took something that wasn't mine to take and, in return, had been given a most precious gift. He thought me the angel who'd save him from himself. But I took from him when he was most vulnerable, and every action has a reaction. Life changed that night for us both. I'm no more angel than the man in the moon but I can give him wings. I'll make him soar on a different kind of ecstasy than the one that nearly took him that night. One of pleasure, not pain, helping him soar high enough to see mistakes don't make a person. It's how you rise.

CHAPTER TWENTY-NINE

Ian

She licks her lips before taking me into her mouth, the hot burn of her tongue marking me. It's a silly sense of belonging to someone, but one which makes my younger self happy.

She touches a part of me that makes my head fall back, as a moan travels from my cock to my lips. It's exhilarating. I feel the weight of responsibility fall and I reconnect with a touch of the depravity I've buried inside. It's temporary, I know, but I'm determined to enjoy every moment of this time with Savi.

I jolt as she nips my skin and tugs my sac just a slight bit hard. She wraps her polished, petite fingers around the base of my dick and squeezes the shaft just a little too tight. I relish the potent mix of pleasure with pain and suck in a breath as she takes me all the way down her throat.

"Oh, god …"

I throw my arm over my eyes as I smother a smile, and she continues the sweet assault. She's relishing the effect she has on me and presses her tongue against a most sensitive area around the rim. Without any substance to mask what I feel, the move induces involuntary twitches from my cock as it rubs against the back of her throat.

"Holy fuck, Savannah …"

My words trail off as she runs her tongue from base to tip and moans the most beautiful sound causing a reverberating effect that leaves me breathless.

She pulls back and we each steal a glance, both of us breathless. The corners of my mouth curl into a grin as she fists my cock. Stroking slowly, I watch her eyes fasten on my every move. I let her have her way for far longer than I should and, when I think I can't barely take another stroke, she leans in, and swirls her tongue around the engorged tip, then eases me agonizingly slow all the way down from tip to base. She swallows, and the contraction makes my balls draw up tight.

"Woman …" It's a beastly growl more than a word. "You're so fucking beautiful."

Our eyes meet. I can't take anymore. I need to be inside of her.

I sit up and grip the top of her arms. In one, swift move I drag her over every electrified muscle. Sparks ignite when our eyes once again lock, and I catch my breath as I fall into the sky-blue heaven. "Do you have any idea what you do to me?"

She nods and sinks a bite into her bottom lip as she smiles a coy smile, and I crash my mouth against hers. I drive my tongue past her lips, assaulting her mouth while capturing her tongue. As I plunder the sweet space, the taste of her berry-flavored lip stain passes my lips. A surge of desire rushes through me. I feel like I'm going to explode from wanting her. This tasting and touching is a tease and one I find deliciously addictive. Lust bathes my sex-starved brain, and the sensory experience escalates an appetite stronger than any previous craving.

The feel of her skin.

The sound of her moans.

The taste of her lips.

I want more.

She falls to my side. I slide my fingers over the contour of her jaw, down her throat, and to her breast. I move so I can taste her, and she moans as I lick the hardened, stiff peak.

The warmth of her heat against me is intoxicating, and my cock throbs with need as I pull her closer still. She gasps and, despite my best efforts to take this slow, a sudden, desperate longing amplifies. It's fiercer than I've ever experienced, and it's been too long. I want to feel her body pulse around me, God help me. Fill her because I need and want her much more than I dreamed.

I pull away the thong that's nothing more than a scrap of lace and throw it over my shoulder as I bury my face near her sex. "I'm clean."

"Me, too—and I'm on the pill."

She shudders and her thighs fall apart. My heart pounds quick beats as I move on top of her. As I press the swollen tip against her entrance, desire burns hot in my core. Her sex weeps as she wraps her legs around me. She digs her heels into my backside, pulling me close as I breach her entrance. The feeling of her is bliss and I want to plunge inside of her, but I'm determined to make this moment last. I move painfully slow, grinding my cock into her inch by inch, and enjoying every inflection in her sounds and each change of expression until I'm seated deep inside of her.

It's a painful, beautiful, passionate Nirvana.

She writhes beneath my touch and a rush of wetness welcomes me. Lust permeates the room with desire so thick it's almost palpable. I cage her breasts, imprisoning them with my fingers as I drag my dick back out painfully slow. With calloused fingers I slide my hands to her waist, gripping as I piston inside her in one, full thrust.

Savannah pulls me down to her. Her fingers tangle in my hair as my mouth takes hers, but I'm relentless as I continue the thrusting, sweet torture. She shudders as I release her mouth, her breaths growing ragged, and pleasure shimmies down my spine.

I pull back and reach down between us, seeking her hidden gem with eager fingers. She groans with pleasure as my knuckles scrape against the sensitive bundle of nerves. The smooth, velvety feel of her is a sharp contrast against my rock-hard length. Heat radiates between us, and an electrifying rush runs through me as I buck back and again thrust deep. Her sex tightens, gripping me with a newborn spasm and the clench ripples pleasure through me.

It's insanity at its best, and one to which I gladly succumb. This woman means more to me than even I've admitted to myself.

She grips my shoulders, and I roll so she's sitting on top, impaled on my dick and digging her nails into my tanned flesh. I'll gladly bear the scars as I've never thought or felt this way about a woman before. Fully present, I lock eyes with her. A blush colors her cheeks as she begins to undulate her hips and her breasts lightly bounce upon her chest.

The intensity between us grows as we move one against the other, the unison like a well-crafted song. As she rocks her hips into mine, I feel my balls tighten with an impending orgasm and the friction is making me crazy. Each stroke drives me wild as pleasure reaches every inch of flesh rabid for release.

The pace increases and the flames inside me roar into an inferno and I drive into her as she struggles for breath, her release fanning the blaze for us both. We welcome the violence as blissful sensations take over, and we ride like we're feral.

Beasts with one goal.

She bites her lip and a drop of blood surfaces as ripples of pleasure rock us both and my climax surfaces full throttle. My dick shudders, then screams, as raw sounds of need tear from my throat and waves upon wave of pleasure crash over me. The tsunami saturates my veins as I roar, shattering as I drive, and my release empties inside of her until I'm spent.

CHAPTER THIRTY

Savannah

The ride home is initially quiet. I'm lost in my thoughts and, although I glance over at Ian several times, he says nothing, content with listening to the mellow sounds of Miles Davis playing through the radio. His expression is relaxed as he drives through the serene darkness.

I never thought I'd want more from Ian. In fact, I never thought I'd see him again after our one night, but here I am wanting him. But, like him, I also have that fear of impending doom. That if I love someone, if I let myself get too close or comfortable, something will go wrong. It's that part of me that's always waiting for the other shoe to drop. Because of my parent's death, and my relationship with Drake, fear always hid in the shadow of my thoughts. Though a future as a family would fulfill a dream, I wonder if it's possible for me to lay my anxious thoughts to rest and see promise in the days ahead.

"How are you doing over there?" I ask as I glance over at Ian and am met with a smile so tender it feels like a hug.

"I could ask you the same question." His lips quirk with unspoken words, and a sly tone.

I blush. "I'm fine." I reach for his hand. "Despite the rocky start, tonight was perfect."

He nods. "I learned something tonight."

"What's that?"

"When eating spaghetti with you and Gigi, bring a change of clothes."

Seeing a lighthearted Ian brings me joy. I laugh and he squeezes my hand.

A shrill, high-pitched wail cuts through the quiet, capturing our attention. Ian looks in the rear-view mirror while I simultaneously turn to look behind us.

Flashing red and white lights adorn a massive firetruck as it sails in our direction. Ian pulls over allowing them access and, once they pass, he eases back into the drive. We've barely gone a short distance when, yet another firetruck careens down the highway, its howling squeal splitting the air.

"Must be some fire," I say as Ian once again moves to the side of the road.

"I hope wherever they're headed that they get there before it gets out of control." I give voice to inner thoughts, sharing a small thing that gives me comfort. "I say a quick prayer whenever I see or hear emergency vehicles. I don't think I'll ever forget the sounds of sirens approaching my house." I no sooner say the words when a third squeal caterwauls behind us. This time it's an ambulance. As it passes, we exchange puzzled glances.

"I can't remember seeing so much activity in Rock Hills, but the ranch is further away from the fire station than you are, so I don't hear much."

He pulls out. The emergency vehicles are quick and many car lengths ahead, but I notice we're all traveling the same route. When Ian looks over at me, his somber expression speaks volumes.

"Ian, I don't have a good feeling." Fear skitters over me, and my scalp prickles. As Ian closes in on my neighborhood, I see that my street is blocked. "Oh, my god." My voice trails off as a policeman stops us. Undeterred, Ian rolls down the window.

"Can't let you through," he places his hand at the base of the open window.

"She lives here." Ian's flat, serious tone doesn't move the man.

"Sorry. I can't let you through."

"Bullshit." It's a statement of fact and Ian throws the car in reverse, backs up, and pulls into the closest driveway. He quickly parks then both of us act, springing the doors open a second or two before we fly out of the truck. He grabs my hand and we run.

"Hey!" The officer calls out, but we ignore him. We sprint toward my house. I gasp. It isn't my house that's on fire. It's Cora's.

I scream.

"Gigi! Gigi!" The thick scent of smoke hangs in the air, stinging my eyes and nose. I race toward the house, only to be stopped by both a policeman and a fireman. "Let me go!" I struggle against their hold, as desperation tears my voice like threadbare rags.

"Get the fuck off her." Ian shoves them as he shackles my waist. I fight him, adrenaline exploding through my limbs.

"Savi, stop!"

His plea is met with tears. "I need to get Gigi!"

"You can't go in there, Miss. It's not safe," one of the men says.

I ignore him, spotting a man in black pants and a white shirt who is standing back from the second firetruck. I point Ian toward him, and we rush in his direction, navigating an obstacle course littered with thick, ropey hoses and puddles of water. As I see the man issuing orders to a few others I pull, and I trip as my hand slips from Ian's. "Ow!"

He stops, but I quickly right myself.

"Are you hurt?" He holds me at arm's length, attempting to assess if I'm injured.

"I'm fine." I hiss, dismissing his concern as I shake off the pain. "I need to get to Gigi." Ian nods and we continue.

"Hey!" He calls out and the man approaches. When the distance evaporates between us, I grab a fistful of his sleeve.

"My little girl. She's three." Despair shreds my voice

as the mix of smoke and threatening tears burns my eyes. "She's wearing pajamas, pink with silly flamingos." A sob wracks my body and a vision of my baby punches me hard in the gut. "She has blonde hair and big blue eyes. Her name is Gigi." I choke on a sob as tears freely flow. "She was in that house." Ian's arms surround me, catching me as my knees start to fold. "Please. *Please!* I need to find my little girl."

Ian holds me tight, and I manage to turn, burying my face in his chest. I'm shaking, though his arms lock me tightly against him. I can hear the officer speaking into the walkie-talkie as he nestles my head beneath his chin.

"They're doing everything they can." His attempt to comfort me gives me little consolation.

"I can't lose her, Ian. I can't lose Gigi."

"I know, Savi. I can't lose her either."

I pull back and look up at his face. His eyes are shimmering with tears, but he looks away, as if ashamed of his transparent emotions.

"Ian …"

"I can't, Savi. Not after everything. Not after all I've been through."

His heartbreaking confession rips open old wounds. I know what it feels like to lose the people who matter the most, but his is a different kind of pain. I've always known love before loss, but Ian hasn't, and the potency of his feelings for Gigi bleeds through his words and, like me, the thought of something happening to her stabs us with a steely knife. I wrap my arms tighter around him, letting him rest his cheek on my head.

"We've got to let them do their job."

"What if it's too late?" Heartbreak clings to my words.

"Shh. Don't even think like that. They'll find Gigi and Cora."

He attempts to reassure me with soft, whispered words while sharing my fears. An impending headache surfaces as I suffocate my anxiety and suffer my racing heart and the pounding beat in my head in silence.

"What's your little girl's name again?" The fireman asks.

My head snaps up. "Gigi." Her name tumbles from my lips like a breathless prayer.

He smiles. "Follow me. I'll take you to her."

I wipe my face with the back of my hand and look up at Ian as we quickly stride behind him. "Thank you for holding me up while I was falling apart." I dab at my eyes, knowing, if Gigi sees me like this, she might get scared.

"Ditto," he says, giving my hand a reassuring squeeze.

CHAPTER THIRTY-ONE

Ian

As we closely follow the man leading us to Gigi, we can't escape the bitter, acrid air. Savannah and I turn the corner of the house, and the fireman points to an ambulance. "Just want you to know we got everyone out. See, right there? Pink PJ's. At the EMT vehicle?"

Through the smokey haze, we turn. A flash of candy pink color snatches our eyes. There, in the dark, chaotic scene, we see Gigi. We rush toward her. Her pout cuts me, and her cry is a faint whimper that rings louder in my ears as we get closer.

"Gigi?" Savannah calls out and Gigi's chin pops up. Previously huddled on a stretcher just inside the yellow and red door, now her head darts side to side. My heart races as we get a better look at her. She's pulled herself into a ball with her arms tightly bound around knees pulled close to her chest, but it's the shaky, puckered bottom lip that destroys my heart.

"Gigi! Gigi!" Savannah runs toward her.

"MOMMA!"

As soon as Gigi spots her mother, she scrambles away from the technician and off the stretcher. Like an expert escape artist, she flies.

"Hey!"

The technician calls but Gigi doesn't stop. The next instant finds her catapulting into Savannah as she snatches the little girl into her arms.

Their reunion unchains deeply buried emotions that hit me like a wrecking ball. Gigi sobs, her face buried in Savi's neck, and I choke back a sob as she gives her baby a million kisses. Cheeks, eyes, chin; she leaves nothing untouched. I wait a moment, then take a place beside Savannah and Gigi reaches out for me, arms outstretched and fingers grabbing at the air. I take her hand and swallow a lump of emotion as she squeezes my hand over and over but doesn't let go. I close my arms around them both and note Savannah's trembling body. I tighten my hold, lending my support as adrenaline takes its toll.

* * *

SAVANNAH IS STANDING a few feet away from a sleeping Gigi when I enter the room. What I see in her is the definition of self-soothing. With her arms wrapped around her waist, it's as if she's giving herself a hug. She hears me, and her head turns.

"I just spoke with the doctor. They're going to keep Cora overnight. Her blood oxygen isn't at a level they're comfortable with, so, she's staying."

"That's probably for the best," she nods.

Savi takes a seat as I peer over at Gigi, who's sound asleep in a hospital crib. "How is she?"

"Sleeping. Finally. She's exhausted. Her pediatrician was here for another patient and the ER staff notified her. I'm glad she came to check Gigi. She thinks twenty-four hours of observation is needed as well." She pauses. "Did you talk to Cora?"

I nod. "Yes."

"Does she know how the fire started?" There's a plea in her eyes.

"She's very upset." I take a seat across from her. "She said the fire chief questioned her. Cora has a little space heater in the kitchen. She told me she uses it in the morning because she gets up early and sometimes there's still a chilly bite in the air."

"I know she does. I've seen it."

"Then you know it wasn't that old, the cord wasn't frayed ... she said she always pulls the plug before she goes to bed, and she didn't use it today, so she's sure it wasn't plugged in. Well, apparently, from what they can tell, the cord was split. That's what caused the fire, but she doesn't know how."

A pained expression tightens her face, and she groans.

"Cora said she ran into the kitchen the minute she smelled something. The smell was pungent and burned her nose. She was about to get Gigi and run out, then call the Fire Department, but Gigi ran past her to get a baby doll she left on the chair. By then, the smoke was thicker. Cora grabbed her and the doll but slapped a dishtowel over Gigi's nose and mouth. The neighbor behind her was taking out his trash and saw the blaze. He called the Fire Department, then ran to Gigi and Cora. He walked them across the street to another neighbor's porch. The fire trucks were ahead of us, but not by much. That's why we couldn't find them right away. Too much chaos."

Savi tosses a look to the ceiling. Her body stiffens as she shakes her head. "I shouldn't have gone out tonight."

"Don't do that, Savi. You can't play that game with yourself."

Still gazing off into the distance, sadness and guilt corrupt her face. "I shouldn't have. I rarely leave her except for work."

"Then, you deserve a little time to yourself, don't you think? It was an accident. That heater and Gigi are at Cora's almost every day. It could have happened anytime."

Her gaze lowers to me. "Well, that's fodder for my anxiety." Sarcasm kicks the comment as surely as the thought kicked her ass.

"Sorry. It's the truth," I say as a matter of fact.

Her gaze darkens and intensifies. "I could have lost her, Ian. I could have lost them both."

CHAPTER THIRTY-TWO

Savannah

"But you didn't. That's all that matters." Ian leans forward and takes my hand in his and pats the back of it. "C'mon. Let's get something to drink. I saw some vending machines down the hall."

Vending machines.

Inside I snicker. That's where all of this started; me and Ian. One crazy concert, two drunk people, and a night that would change both our lives.

I've convinced myself that keeping Gigi's parentage a secret was a badge of honor for me.

Single mom.

Don't need anyone.

I can do this myself.

Those were the justifying statements with which I lied to myself. The truth is that keeping the identity of

Gigi's father a secret was because I was afraid. I could tell myself another lie and say that I didn't know without a DNA test who her dad was, but that thought was laid to rest the moment I saw them together. They look too much alike and I know Sam saw it the night of the spaghetti incident—well, the first spaghetti incident.

I shouldn't let it but that thought tickles me inside. I feel an instant pang of guilt because this is not the time for amusement. Truth is Gigi is as much like me with her bit of temper, as she is like Ian in her looks. If Ian hadn't arrived when he did that night, Sam would have called me out on it. The only reason he didn't was because he wanted a private interrogation. That's when Ian showed up.

One good thing came out of that night with Ian. The best thing.

Though I've kept her all to myself, maybe I've done an injustice. Knowing now what happened to Ian that night, it makes what I'm about to do easier. Both of us had a terrible thing happen at a nearly identical time. While I realize that Gigi was my saving grace, Ian had no such sweet miracle to help him heal. He's done it alone. I need to change that.

"Ian, I need to tell you something."

How do I say words that will alter him forever?

He says nothing until we're standing in front of the machines.

"I'm listening. What do you want? Soda? Water?"

"Doesn't matter," I say dismissively. There are a few

tables with chairs. A myriad of scenarios jumble through my thoughts like a traveling carnival. Like acrobats, they roll and tumble, each one trying to take center stage. But nothing about this is funny, and I struggle to compose my thoughts.

The canteen area is small and the weight of what I'm about to do suffocates me. As I walk over to a small table and take a seat, my knees are shaking. Ian is close behind me. He slips his leg over the chair directly across from me, sits, and pops the top of two soda cans. He slides one across the table to me.

"Drink it. The caffeine will help your headache." He grins and butterflies flutter inside me. "So, what do you want to tell me?"

Tears sting my eyes, and I suck in a breath. Despite my best efforts to blink them back, twin tears race over my cheeks. Exasperation hits me, and my head falls back. Disgusted with myself, I wipe them away, then drop my chin and face him. He reaches for my hand, but I pull it back.

"There's so much I want to say, but don't know where to start."

"The beginning. That's always a good place," he states flatly. As I hesitate, concern lines form on his face.

I try to steady my nerves as I gather the courage to speak. "There's no easy way to say this." I slowly raise my eyes until they're locked with his. "Gigi's your daughter."

The news stuns him with its slap and his eyes widen with shock. "What?"

"She's yours."

His brow knits and his eyes bore into me. A second later his gaze falls to the can he's holding, his fingers digging into the metal. "Bullshit." He shakes his head as he looks away. "How?"

I reach across the table and curl my hand around his fingers. "Gigi was conceived the night we met. The night of the concert."

His eyes meet mine. "That's impossible," he insists.

"I wouldn't joke about something like this." My stomach twists into angst-filled knots. I can't read what's going on inside his head and I've never had a fondness for the unknown.

"How the hell?" He looks away as he wipes a hand over his face, then collapses back into the chair, giving me his full attention. "Explain."

I swallow hard. Anxiety builds as I shuffle words to lay out a palatable explanation. Interlacing my fingers, I place my hands on the table in front of me like a child sitting properly in school.

"My friend, Candace, rented a room for my birthday. We wanted to drink and party it up that night. It was her present to me. When I won the contest, I received two VIP passes, and she was my 'plus one.' We didn't know the band was staying at the same hotel.

After I met you, I was really down." I force a weak smile. "I had a huge crush on you at the time, and the Meet and Greet was a disaster."

His brows perk. "I can only imagine."

"Candace and me … we drank so much that night. So much." I close my eyes, slightly shaking my head in subtle disapproval at the memory. "I drank so much I was dehydrated. We were already drunk; we'd had more than our share at the concert. When we got back to the hotel room we had even more. Candace passed out, but not me. I couldn't sleep. We'd already downed the waters in the room, so I went in search of the vending machines. You were there." I look up at him.

"And?" He presses.

"It wasn't until you came to town, and I saw you two together that I couldn't deny it anymore. Drake was over, and I was regular like clockwork. I knew." I pause for a breath. "I'm sorry. I'm so sorry. I never expected to see you again. Was terrified someone would have seen us on the elevator and would pull me in for questioning. I was already going through so much because of my parents and, when Gigi came, she was …"

Perfect. The word falls from his lips like a whispered prayer.

Remorse hits me with tsunami strength. "I should have said something. I was so immature. I was scared. You'd overdosed and I thought there might be footage from hotel security that showed you with me. All I could think was that I wanted to talk to my mom. I needed to talk to her and tell her what happened. I knew she'd be furious, but I thought I could possibly be in big trouble, so what was a little more? Even though I knew she'd be pissed, I also knew she'd know the right thing to do. Knowing I was probably the last person to see you that night was terrifying. I didn't know if I should go to the police or wait and see if they contacted me—I just didn't know."

"Were you questioned?"

"No." I shake my head, wishing away the memories that followed.

"And you never got to talk to your mom, did you?"

Ian waits patiently for an answer as I struggle to stay composed. Finding a speck of courage, I look deeply into his eyes, seeking compassion and understanding as I try to make this right.

"I thought I was afraid when I left the hotel but nothing about that night seemed important once I got home. I don't know when the police got there but they were all over my house. They might have asked a question or two because they asked where I was, but I remember little. The questions I do remember were more like what I was doing before I came home and found my parents ..."

"Murdered? Holy shit." He gives me an incredulous look.

"Yes." My voice becomes whisper soft as my thoughts walk over their graves. Silence looms as we struggle with our thoughts.

"Gigi's my daughter." He whispers.

"Yes," I reply softly.

"And there's no chance Drake—"

I cut him off. "I'm sure. Drake always used a

condom. Even if it had broken when he raped me, the timing would be off. Besides, you have a birthmark on your hip. I saw it tonight. Gigi has the same mark. If we did a test—"

"Stop." The word escapes his lips like a blast of wind through a tangle of branches, his fingers combing through his hair like a desperate attempt to hold onto the truth. "And you've known this since she was born?"

"Subconsciously, I didn't want to think she belonged to anyone but me. I didn't need or want financial help, and I'd just lost my family." I shrug. "I don't know … Gigi was my lifeboat."

"And you didn't want me to sink it."

"Yes—well …"

"And you never thought to come to me?"

"How? Why? Every television station and major network was hunting you down and I didn't know I was pregnant until seven weeks after. I was grieving. I thought my period was off because of shock. Once I realized what was happening, Sam told me my parents had a hefty life insurance policy and I had set up a trust for me. And why would I look for you? You were an addict in rehab. Who knew how long you'd stay clean? Once Gigi made her entrance, she was my world. I didn't want you in it. Besides, if I approached you for DNA confirmation, the press would have made my life, your life, and Gigi's, a miserable hell. At the time, I didn't care what you did with your life, but I wasn't going to let you screw up hers. I was damned and determined to give her the best one possible—and you've heard that cliché about momma bears and cubs? I never thought myself capable of violence, but I would do anything to keep her safe. Anything."

He studies my face for a moment. "That's why you acted like a bitch the night I came to Mad Dog."

"Yes, and I won't apologize because I was in a completely different headspace at that time. I didn't want you here. I didn't know your connection to Sam. There was a small thought—both from excitement and fear—that you somehow remembered me. My imagination ran wild. Then, when you didn't recall me or the song ... well, let's just say my pride made me livid." I steady my thoughts, trying to carefully choose my words. "It's obvious I don't feel that way anymore. Ian, I don't expect anything from you. Gigi and I are—"

"My family," he interjects. "So, stop before you say something stupid."

"Are you angry?"

"Damn right. You could've told me."

I throw my head back as a quiet, mocking laugh erupts. "Right. Like you would've believed me."

"Maybe. Maybe not," he shrugs. "I might have insisted on a paternity test, given the stories I've heard about guys in other bands, but I had a right to know."

Instantly, my mood changes. "Rights? You didn't have any rights," I angrily insist. "You were a junkie in rehab. You weren't 'father' material. I didn't want anything from you, and I didn't want any of that mess around my baby."

"I could have sent money."

"I didn't—and don't— need your money. Gigi and I are fine." I look away and take a few cleansing breaths to abate the tension between us. "Look, the fact is, you weren't good for us then. You weren't even good for yourself. But there's a world of difference now. I've seen it. More than that, I believe it. I wouldn't have told you if I thought otherwise. Gigi is the most precious thing in the world to me." I pause. "Speaking of Gigi, I need to go check on her."

"I'm going to call Sam. I'm sure he'll see this on the news, and I want him to know everything's okay." He pauses. "Does he know I'm Gigi's father?"

"I never came out and said so but, when he came to help me after the murder, I went on a crying jag. I blurted out everything. It was like I was emptying my soul. I'm sure something came out about me sleeping with you. In the purge I said things about Drake, the concert, and everything that happened that night … like I said, I was hysterical, and I don't know what did or didn't make sense to him, but Sam's pretty good at piecing things together." I press my lips together, my posture quickly deflating. "This isn't how I wanted to tell you."

He looks at me through tired eyes, yet I see no animosity there. "It's a lot to take in but we'll figure it out."

I push myself away from the table and exit the room, leaving Ian alone to process all that I've told him. We're so different than we were that night. I have no clue what happens next but all we've been through has made us the people we are today, and I like who we are. That's what I hang my hopes on.

I travel down the hall to check on Gigi, lost in my thoughts. When I reach her room, I see an empty crib. Puzzled, I turn and walk to the nurse's station.

"Excuse me." A nurse behind the counter looks up. "My daughter, Guiliana, isn't in her room."

"Let me check with her nurse." The woman pushes away from the desk and disappears through a doorway. A few minutes later she returns with another nurse, one I recognize from earlier when she came in to check on Gigi. She approaches me with a puzzled expression.

"Ms. Grace, Gigi's father said he was taking her to the playroom."

My heart seizes as terror strikes me like a lightning bolt. I run down the hallway, barely hearing the two women running after me. There's a pounding rush in my ears as I race toward the playroom doorway, barely catching myself as I skid to a stop and capture the attention of stunned children and parents. I don't see Gigi.

"Did any of you see a little girl with blonde curls come in here?"

One answers "no" while the others shake their heads. I turn to the nurse who followed me, panic evident in my raised voice.

"How could you let something like this happen? I thought you had strict identification protocols."

"We do, Ms. Grace," she says, confused. "Her father

was wearing a badge. He said he'd just come from the airport."

"Whoever he is, he's not her father!" I shriek.

"Oh, my god. I'll call security." She rushes down the hall.

I search for the door to the stairway, spot it, then run to it. Without thought I sail down the flights of stairs and through the lobby. Seeing no signs of Gigi, I sprint through the automatic doors, my lungs screaming for air as adrenaline rushes through my veins for a second time tonight. I sprint to the end of the crescent-shaped driveway and find myself lost in a sea of cars in the main parking lot. A black Mercedes slows beside me. A dark, tinted window lowers enough so I see Gigi lying unconscious in the back seat. A scream rattles my insides and, just as it's about to unleash, the front passenger window sinks enough for me to see Drake's haughty sneer. Suddenly, the unvoiced scream strangles me. I'm living a nightmare.

"Get in the car, Savannah."

CHAPTER THIRTY-THREE

Ian

"What do you mean, she's gone?" Disbelief washes over me as torment twists my gut.

I listen as the nurse explains and learn that a man she believed to be Gigi's father has taken her.

"Do you know where Gigi's mother is?"

"I don't," she answers. "The last I saw her she was entering the stairwell."

Though every muscle in my body aches with fury, my soul trembles.

"Did you call security?"

"Yes, sir. They're aware."

I rake my hand through my hair as I absorb the scale of what's happened, and it's the not knowing that's gutting me. Regardless of what the security team discovers, this incident will remain inexplicable to me.

Disbelief mingles with anger and my heart races. I haven't had time to fully comprehend that I have a daughter, yet I feel the gut punch of loss. That sweet little girl—*MY* sweet little girl—and her mother deserve better than me, but I will find them. I don't know where my relationship with Savannah is headed but I don't want to lose them.

Desperate thoughts take hold as revenge stokes a fire within. With each tortured thought my inner rage intensifies. I have an appetite for payback. Someone has stolen something of mine. Something I never dreamed to have.

Though I can't compare what I'm feeling to that instantaneous love I've heard of when a mother first gazes upon her baby's face, what I'm feeling is equally as powerful. I love Gigi. I think I've loved her from when we first met. She's independent and strong but, seeing things through her eyes gives me a new appreciation for life. I can only hope for more such opportunities.

Horrific possibilities corrupt my thoughts as I pace from one side of the hall to the other. There's a purpose behind Savi and I reconnecting, I'm sure of it. I've done nothing to deserve grace in this life but, if there is a god, Momma said he loves little children. I can only hope that's true.

I look around and feel the need to act. The first thing that comes to mind is to call Sam. He answers with his usual, teasing tone.

"Hey, Amigo. What's shakin?"

"Gigi's missing."

"What the fuck?" His tone instantly changes as I blurt out the news. "How?"

"She was taken from the hospital. Savannah's missing, too."

"Where are you?" He demands.

"I'm still at the hospital but the nurse said Gigi's father took her."

"What more do you know?"

"Hold on a minute." I approach the nurse and put the phone on speaker. "Can you describe the man who took Guiliana?" The nurse trembles nervously and her chin quivers. Her eyes are red-rimmed and it's obvious she's distraught. I must hold back my anger and frustration. No matter my personal feelings, I can't lose my shit. Making this woman feel any worse than she does won't serve any good purpose.

She lowers her eyes. "I spotted an ID badge on him, but the image of his driver's license was blurred. Tall, but not too tall; maybe five-foot-ten. Nice suit. Dark hair. Dark eyes. Darker skin than Ms. Grace."

Her body trembles with nervous energy and she gives me a sorrowful look. Her bottom lip shakes. "I'm sorry I don't remember more. He had a badge ... He gave her a stuffed animal." Her helpless tone fades away.

The woman beside her, who is also a nurse, makes a protective move and wraps an arm around her. Gigi's nurse turns her face into the woman's shoulder and the woman gives me a stern, tight-lipped stare.

"Sir, we've notified the security team. They're doing everything they can." She tips her head as her brow pinches. "Aren't you Ian Stanton?"

I trudge away, unwilling to answer questions. All I can think about is Savi and Gigi. I'm determined not to lose any more people I love.

Love?

I freeze. *Do I dare love anyone?*

My mistakes haunt me, and I fight with myself on the days I want to give up, but the idea of losing Savannah and Gigi makes clear the realization that I love them. Although I know it's irrational, I have this fear if I love anyone, I'll jinx it.

My mind races with doubts. Negativity creeps in with thoughts like 'good things don't happen to people like me'. Old habits are hard to break, and old mindsets even harder. I shove the thoughts away. This is no time for a pity party. My immediate concern is protecting my two blue-eyed girls.

* * *

As I wait for Sam my hands clench into fists. My knuckles burn with the strain and my fingernails dig into my palms. My thoughts race as I think about the bastard responsible for this. As I piece everything together my bones ache and every breath I take burns with revenge. It's Drake who's responsible for this, I'm sure of it. If I get to him before the cops do, it's almost a certainty I'll go to jail.

Another code rings out through the speakers. Everything seems surreal and I'm impatient. It's like I'm moving through quicksand. I don't know what to do with the rage inside of me and once the elevator doors close, I punch the metal door. *Goddammit!*

I pull my hand back for examination and see bloodied flesh. Dismissing the minor ache, I wipe a few weeping knuckles against the side of my jeans. I've never felt so helpless and when the elevator door opens at the lobby, I feel a pinch of relief as I spot Sam.

He comes towards me. His eyes travel from my face to my fist, and a sober nod silently tells me he understands.

"C'mon." He turns and I trail him to an exit door where an officer stands as a sentry. "Hank, let us through. He's with me."

"Sure thing, Sir." The policeman moves aside.

Sir? The man addresses him with a reverence I've not heard before. My brain squirms for information and a question claws forth as I follow behind him. "Who the fuck are you?"

Sam shakes his head. "Not now, Ian."

Everything blurs as we sprint across the parking lot in silence toward Sam's truck. Once we're inside we quickly fasten our seatbelts. My cell rings and, when I pull it from my back pocket, Savannah's name comes up on the screen. I punch the speaker button.

"Where are you?" My tone is low and grave, then I hear her voice.

"*—made a big mistake doing this. People will be looking for us.*"

"*Shut up.*"

"*Where are you taking us? Why are we headed toward Discord?*"

"*I said shut up!*"

I hit the mute button. Somehow, Savannah connected the call undetected and is now attempting to give clues.

"*Why is my daughter unconscious? What did you do to her? She's shivering.*" A pause. "*If anything happens to my baby, I'll—*"

"*Whose baby?*"

It's Drake, and his ominous tone bristles the hair on the back of my neck. Urgency rises inside of me. I've gone from Rock Hills to Discord Flats and remember where the highway turns to back roads. The uptick in home sales that Rock Hills is having doesn't reach that far out, so I concentrate on sounds that might lead us to them faster. So far, all I hear is humming tires, indicating a smooth road. That tells me they're still on the highway.

"*Drake, I need you to listen to me. This is a mistake. We can turn around and head back. I'll figure out a way to help you.*"

I look over at Sam. His face is so tight it's a wonder his jaw doesn't snap. In the silence, we exchange a look as we detect the graduating sounds of a smooth road to gravel.

"*You're such a stupid bitch. I don't need your help to stay out of jail, Savannah. My father knows people—but that isn't what this is about. Even you, with all your fancy words, can't act as mediator between me and The Brethren. The kid is part of an exchange."*

He pauses, then chuckles.

"What? You didn't think I knew about your kid? There's a market for blue-eyed blondes. I don't care about you, and I don't give a shit about that kid. You said it yourself; I'm a monster. Right now, you two are currency, and I've got a debt to pay."

The phone goes dead.

Sam's brow furrows as his eyes shift between me and the road. "He's been on the move for an hour. Discord isn't a mining town anymore, but a 'disposal'. Lots of empty holes in the earth and it's where The Brethren store guns before they run them. I never heard of them trafficking humans, just guns and drugs, but nobody just strolls in and out of Discord. There are consequences for trespassing. You got to know where you're going. Some old mines are shut up or caved in, but some are filled with product." He pauses to give me a grave look. "Let's just say nobody goes there after dark with good intentions."

"Jesus Christ." I shake a horrific mental picture from my mind and stare out the window. "I went there once to get the bike fixed. I didn't know."

"Yeah. They have legitimate businesses for cover. Gun runners and drug dealers will use just about anywhere, but the mines are just as good a place as any to hide shit you don't want found. Discord's the perfect place. Kind of hidden. Kind of out in the open. The Brethren know what they're doing. His voice drops as he gives me a quick glance. "And so does the ATF."

"What kind of shit do you think Drake is into that he's using people to pay a debt?"

"I don't know but, I doubt it involves The Brethren. They're some seriously tough motherfuckers, but they don't use kids for currency."

"How do you know about all this?"

He doesn't answer, just keeps his eyes on the road.

Fatigue and frustration overwhelm me. It combines with anger and impatience and the toxic mix swirls in my blood like a cesspool. My chest tightens as the idea of something happening to Savi and Gigi makes it hard to breathe. There's a rage inside me and the unfamiliar emotion spins thoughts of death and destruction.

"I don't give a shit what happens to me, Sam. I'm going to find them, and I'm going to kill him; I swear it." The bitter words are ashes in my mouth.

Sam's expression is hard as stone. His tone is as deep and calm as the depth of the ocean, and just as deadly. "We'll find them, and we'll be cautious. Not for him, but for them."

He's right. For their protection, it's important to have a plan. Hasty actions could seriously jeopardize their safety but of this, I'm sure; I'd gladly trade my life for theirs.

We approach Discord's outskirts and Sam kills the headlights and parks the truck behind an abandoned building. He hands me a gun.

"You know how to shoot?"

I nod. "Yeah, but I don't know how much I trust my shots. I went to the range twice with Dash. I won't hesitate to shoot. I'm sure I can hit the mark but can't guarantee exactly where."

"Don't matter, as long as we get the girls."

CHAPTER THIRTY-FOUR

Savannah

The old tunnel is narrow and dark. Gigi woke in the car and is now on my hip. Drake is behind me and holds a small flashlight providing the only light. My bearings are off in this carved-out grave and the atmosphere is eerie and haunting.

"Where are we going?" I ask, trying to keep my voice steady. Gigi's cries fill the space.

"Shut her up and keep walking." Drake orders. His voice is a raspy hiss.

She cowers and I rage inside. My daughter has never had a reason to fear anything, and I swear on my life I'll make him pay for introducing her to the concept.

"I don't have much of a choice, now, do I? Not with that thing pointed at me." I give him smart-mouthed words to take his attention off Gigi. I refuse to allow

288

tears to choke me, and I refuse to say the word 'gun'. Gigi's scared enough. "People will be looking for us."

"Who? The asinine babysitter or that old man? Maybe you think that junkie who works at the bar will save you." He laughs. "No one will find you, Savannah —or maybe they will. Either way, I don't care." He shrugs, cold and indifferent.

Gigi shivers and huddles against me for warmth. Her whole body is vibrating. She's still in a hospital gown and it isn't doing much to keep her warm. The pull up diaper she's wearing is wet and isn't helping. These dirt walls are pitch dark and it's cold in here, like a tomb.

"You won't get away with this. You overestimate your privilege."

His lips twist into a malicious smirk. "They haven't caught me yet."

"I haven't been gone long enough."

He stares at me like I'm an idiot and shakes his head. "Naïve doesn't even describe you. Your stupidity astounds me."

"You're violating a restraining order. I think it's you who lack smarts."

"Seriously? Do you think anyone cares about a fucking restraining order these days?" He shakes his head in disbelief. "The apple doesn't fall far from the idiot tree in your family, does it?"

"Momma, I wanna go home." The desperation in Gigi's plea forms a lump in my throat.

"*Momma, I wanna go home,*" he mocks. His cruel

and contemptuous words sting. I throw him a glare, but it's Gigi's tone that pierces the darkness inside of me.

"Shh. Soon, baby." I croon softly in her ear.

"Lying to her like you lied to me?" His tone sends shivers down my spine.

"What are you talking about?"

"Doesn't matter. Soon, you'll be gone, and I won't even keep you as a memory."

A scuffle behind me sets my nerves on high alert. I think it's a rat, but a beam of light reveals two men. Not rats at all—or are they?

"This what you got?" The more menacing-looking of the two men inspects me. The other man is shorter and emotionless, observing us with cold, reptilian eyes. My gaze shifts between the two as I attempt to mark details to memory when the man of lesser height bares two dark stained teeth in a lecherous smile. Instantly my blood chills and my skin crawls. He rocks back on his heels and leers at me.

"You did good, Drake."

"Told you I would," he shrugs and then looks away, an air of confidence breathing new life into him.

Gigi sniffs back tears. The child who's never known fear now trembles with it. I hold her tighter.

"So, what now?"

"Payment." He looks me over like I'm merchandise and I narrow my eyes.

"Whatever he's promised you, I can meet and beat."

He ignores my offer and approaches us, licking his

lips. He then wipes his arm across his mouth in a revolting gesture. As he reaches for Gigi, I scream.

Jumping back, I bare my teeth. Any mercy I might have possessed is suddenly gone and I turn savage. "Don't touch her!"

His laugh is sinister as he pulls back his filthy hand.

"Girl, you got a mouth on you, but I like a little fight," he scoffs. "Drake here got himself in a bind and needed cash. Too much blow and not enough money. It's not the first time he's fucked up and had to do something illegal to pay off a debt."

The other man pauses, lowers his chin, and looks at me with threatening eyes. "Too bad you didn't go home after that concert, girlie. I could've gotten a better price for you before you had that kid, or, I could have kept you myself and sold her, but he came up with the cash. Who would've guessed your father kept that much money in his house? But Drake knew. It was enough to settle the score." He pauses to sneer. "At least, it was enough that time."

His sinister words hang in the air, suspended by omens and danger. My eyes travel from him to Drake. "What's he talking about?" I don't wait for an answer as I snap my head around and confront the despicable man. "Was it you? Are you the bastard who killed my parents?"

Murder coats my words and Gigi whimpers. I jerk her back up onto my hip, my arms around her with a death grip.

"Me? Hell no," he laughs. "I don't do shit like that.

That was all him. He doesn't mind getting his hands dirty." A devious nod in Drake's direction sends shivers up my spine. "And he never got caught. Got away scot-free. Go figure."

"Go to hell!" I scream. "If I don't kill you first, you'll go to jail for the rest of your miserable life." I level the threat and believe I'll make it come true.

"You think you're getting out of here?" The three of them laugh. "Who's going to save you, girlie? Ian Stanton? He owes me big time, too."

Deep confusion pinches my brows together as I try to make sense of his words. "What's Ian got to do with it?"

His slimy smirk freezes me in place as he slowly reveals a truth so hideous it makes me sick. "You're a smart girl. I'm a businessman. Ian had enough blow to last him that night, but I brought him more. I saw you leave his room. He was too wasted to pay me, and I told him I'd get it the next day. You know what happened but he's still alive, ain't he? Ian owes me. Drake owed me." He pauses, sniffs, and sneers. "You see where this is going, right?"

His words twist a knife in my stomach. I know who's responsible for my parent's death, and I understand I'm about to pay a debt I don't owe. I scream. "We don't have anything to do with this. Let us go."

He cackles, my words falling on deaf ears. Gigi clings to me as if her life depends on it. Little does she realize it does. Her pull-up diaper is soaked and sagging around the back of her thighs. The smell of urine is thick and mixes with the putrid stench of packed soil and rusty metal. She holds me tighter, her small hands gripping my shirt. It's rage rather than fear that courses through me and I taste bile in my throat. Angry tears sting my eyes and blur my vision until all I see is the same shade of red that painted the area beneath my parents' dead bodies, and I scream a primal scream inside my head. Every fiber of my being vibrates with wrath. Drake has no idea what I'm capable of because the woman I've become since he last saw me is now a mother. That same anxious girl who obeyed him died that terrible morning. He might have brought out the fear in me but the girl in my arms made me a warrior.

CHAPTER THIRTY-FIVE

Ian

"*D*id you hear that?" I freeze and look over my shoulder. Though darkness swallows my every step the sound of a scream chills me. My heart thunders in my chest, the beat keeping pace with my racing thoughts. I take another step, though a sense of urgency makes me want to run.

"It came from over there." Sam's low voice barely registers above the pounding rhythm in my ears. With a gun in one hand, the other one balls into a fist. A switch flips inside my head. I have no plan and am unconcerned for my safety as an adrenaline rush puts wings to my feet.

"Ian, stop." I ignore the desperation in Sam's voice and keep going, no matter the consequences. Getting to Savi and Gigi is all that's on my mind and the impulse is one I can't comprehend. Despite the risk, I move, driven by a force I can't explain. I'll be damned if I waste one more breath moving at a snail's pace to get to my little girl and her mother.

"God damn it!" I hear Sam behind me, but he isn't alone. I catch a glimpse of other men when I glance over my shoulder.

I run to a pile of old tires and the shadowy figures keep their distance as Sam comes near.

"Who the fuck are they?" I spit in a hoarse, desperate whisper.

"Discord help," Sam answers equally as low. "Don't blast off like that again. You're going to get somebody killed."

I don't know what the hell to think. The locals are territorial and don't welcome outsiders, but I'll take any help we can get at this point. Though The Brethren have a reputation as black-hearted bastards, it only takes a shred of decency to make a man protect a child.

I count on that thought, halting my steps as murmuring voices become my compass.

"Get behind me," Sam orders.

I follow his lead, inching slowly as we navigate the darkness, and the other men do the same. Sam puts his hand up and we stop as a beam of light bounces off the walls of an abandoned mineshaft.

Crickets, whose sounds have been stunned into silence, start once again with their fiddler's song. I can't make out how many people we're up against, but I'll take any cover that the night sounds give.

A man comes ahead of Sam. "I know this hole like the back of my hand. Let me take the lead."

"I got your six," Sam answers low.

As we wait, hoot owls signal to each other. Nature buzzes all around and my skin prickles when I feel a touch on my shoulder.

"Stay close," Sam says, and I nod. The other man puts a set of something like binoculars to his eyes and I'm guessing they're made for night vision.

He comes near enough for us to see him and points. I follow with my eyes, struggling as the pitch darkness nearly renders me night-blind. We inch forward together, our silent footsteps fueled by determination. Just as the moon peeks from behind the clouds, the man juts his head forward, then moves slowly with expert precision. We follow with caution, keeping out of sight as much as possible. My head is filled with questions—who he is and who does he work for—but I squelch them, careening my thoughts back to what's going on inside that mine.

The entrance looms a ghostly shimmer of light from within a mineshaft and I feel a refresh of adrenaline course through my veins.

"You're a smart girl. I'm a businessman. Ian owes me. Drake owed me. Without them, I wouldn't need you. You see where this is going, right?"

My head jerks up at the sound of my name and the same question Savannah asked was now mine as well. *What do I have to do with this?*

I jolt forward, ready to rush in, but Sam locks me

down with a vise grip on my shoulder. "One more minute."

He bores an intense look straight into my eyes, conveying strength and courage. It convinces me we can do this if I trust his timing. I'm still beneath his stare, and he loosens his hold. Jerking his head toward the hole in the wall, Sam silently nods and lifts one finger. I understand his message and wait as sound trickles from the opening.

Sam lifts his hand, and moves his finger in a circle. The chills that creeps into my bones feels like a warning. It's a reminder that we're playing a deadly game and the stakes are high. Two men—no, three—come around. There are five of us standing in a tight semicircle, barely breathing, like lions in wait. My finger is poised on the trigger, preparing to pounce at any moment, as we all stand ready for the next command.

"Come near us again and I'll fucking kill you!"

My ears perk. Savi's angry.

"What are you going to do with them—"

"You're a sick little fuck, Drake. You know you don't give a shit; you just want to know if I'm going to fuck her before I sell her—or is it the kid? Don't tell me you want her first.

The psycho laughs and my vision tunnels. I'm suddenly no longer in control. Everything around me fades away as a feral growl rips from my chest and I detach from reality and go wild.

CHAPTER THIRTY-SIX

Savannah

A savage cry rips through the space, and the air thickens with adrenaline. Like roaches, Drake and the other men scatter as a relieved sob escapes me. A flock of men rush into the old mine, and weapons glint in the pale light. I see a flash of metal in one's hand, and a knife in another's. Fearing the danger of a stray bullet, I run, anxious to get Gigi as far from here as I can.

A sliver of pale moonlight hits the mouth of the mine and I rush to the bright ochre color. It's almost close enough that I can touch it, but before I get there, someone snatches my hair and yanks me back.

"Where do you think you're going, bitch!" Drake's voice ravages my ears.

He pulls my hair again, and then, just as quickly,

releases me. I fall forward, stumbling as Gigi screams. I drop to the ground, pulling her face to my chest, as Ian issues a blow to Drake's head with the butt of the gun. As he falls, Ian rushes to me, grabs my arm, and pulls me and Gigi up from the dirt floor.

"Come on! We got to get out of here."

We take off running but before we can escape, a shot fires, and Ian stumbles.

"Ian!" I scream as blood emerges from his shoulder. Gigi throws her arms around my neck, squealing and crying as she squeezes me in a stranglehold. Tears rush down my face as I swallow a sob.

"Fuck!" He pulls at the neck of his T-shirt for a rapid look. "It burns but it just grazed my sholder." He turns to Gigi. "It's okay, kiddo." Sucking in a breath, fury flashes in his eyes. "Get her out of here. Now." He issues the order through gritted teeth. As I begin to move, I catch a glimpse of something out of the corner of my eye.

Drake looms in the background, moving toward me and Gigi. My heart pounds as I run from the mine and burst out of the entrance and into the night air. It's chilly and she's wet but I keep running, bouncing Gigi on my hip as I heave for air. I keep running until I can no longer hear anything or anyone, just Gigi's terrified sobs.

I pull her close, soothing her as I rub her arms to warm her skin. "I wanna go home." She nestles against me, her cries now joining with hiccups.

"I know, baby. It's okay."

"Momma!" Gigi screams and points as men approach. I grab her up and take a step back.

"Don't come any closer!"

"We won't hurt you. Where'd they go?" The man's gruff voice chills me as, confused, I point to the mine.

The group goes past us, but one pauses to peel off his jacket. "Here. Put this around her."

In a stupor, I nod, at a loss for words. I take the leather and wrap it around my little one. I don't know where I am and there's nowhere to go, so I drop to the ground as Gigi hooks her legs around my waist and rests her head against my chest.

* * *

MINUTES TICK BY. The clouds have disappeared, and we sit in the moonlight, waiting as time passes painfully slow. Gigi's passed out against me. Both of us shiver. It could be fear, the cold, or a combination of both. My nerves are still on edge and, when I hear a noise, I spring to my feet so I can grab her and run.

"Savannah!"

I recognize Ian's voice, and a cry explodes from my chest. Relief washes over me as he comes near. When we lock eyes, he gives me a look with an intensity I've never seen. It cuts straight to my heart and takes my breath away. He lifts Gigi from my arms, and I fall into him as he presses a kiss to her head. Sam's behind him.

"Are you okay?" he asks.

I nod.

He glances at Gigi. "She okay?"

"She's wet and cold."

She lifts her head from Ian's shoulder. "I wanna go home," she whimpers, breaking my heart.

"You are chickadee." Sam forces a smile that quickly flatlines. "You're shivering."

"I's wet." Her voice is hoarse and gruff, like an old woman who's spent years in a smoky bar.

Sam's eyes fill with concern. "Let's get her warm before the cold sets in her bones." He turns to the man beside him and extends his hand. "Jameson."

It's the man who gave me the jacket. He's tall and looks like Sam. His hair isn't as silver but is just as thick. With broad shoulders and thick, ropey arms the two look nearly identical.

"I've got to get back." He tips his head toward the mine. "You go. We got this." His voice is comforting, like warm honey.

Sam nods to the man, the lines around his eyes soft. "Send anyone asking questions to me. I'll take care of it."

The man, Jameson, nods. "It's good to see you."

Sam presses his lips together and nods. Jameson looks over at me. "Keep the jacket on her, ma'am. I'll collect it sometime."

Is he friend? Is he foe? Should I be grateful or afraid? I don't have time to think about it.

"What's going to happen to them?" I ask, my voice hoarse.

"I don't know, and I don't care." I can feel the anger radiating from his body. "Whatever happens to them, they deserve worse." He keeps me close, the embrace offering security and protection as he tightens his arm around me. "C'mon. Let's go home."

CHAPTER THIRTY-SEVEN

Ian

*T*hree months later ...

Jeri takes the microphone. The stage lights bathe her in a warm glow. "I want to thank you all for coming out tonight. Mad Dog Run is celebrating its fifth birthday and all of us want to recognize Sam Weston for being a Rock Hills trailblazer!" She pauses as applause erupts from the crowd. "We have some special guests tonight. First, some of you might recognize Ian Stanton standing over there by Sam, but did you know it's the same Ian Stanton from Boundless Hearts?"

As the audience turns to look at me, I promise myself that, whatever this is, I'm going to get Jeri back. I wave and speak to Sam out of the side of my mouth. "What the hell's she up to?"

"Not sure."

I can tell by the humor in his tone he's lying.

"As a surprise to Ian, I'd like to introduce Mr. Charlie Paul and Mr. Tommy Henry *also* of Boundless Hearts. Surprise, Ian!"

Shock ripples through me as Charlie and Tom pass me by.

"Hey, Ian." Charlie slaps me on the shoulder.

"Lookin' good, asshole." Tom punches my arm.

Neither linger long enough for me to ask questions, and they cut through the crowd bumping fists and slapping hands. I'm stunned to see them and, yet here they are. I can't help but smile that they're here. Charlie takes the microphone and exchanges a look with Jeri that makes her blush.

I've never seen Jeri blush.

"Ian, that woman of yours got us here. We're glad to see you, brother." Emotion chokes me as Savannah joins them on the stage.

"Thanks, Charlie." The crowd goes wild seeing Savannah. She hasn't performed since that night in Discord Flatts. Instead, she's spent most of her time with Gigi, doing her best to rebuild her sense of security. For my part, I hired security. It was necessary after the local press discovered I was in town. Savannah and Gigi have spent more time at the ranch and Gigi understands that Marcus now lives at the ranch to keep us all safe. Most nights she sleeps between Savannah and me, and I find myself watching them both as they sleep. I ask myself *"How did I get so lucky?"* every single day.

Savannah quiets the audience down. "I know you're wondering what all of this is about, Ian but, as much as it looks like we're playing hot potato with this microphone, I'm going to pass it to one more person; Skylar Barrows."

Skylar stops on her way to the stage. "I love you, Ian." She hugs me around the neck as I stand flabbergasted. "It's good to see you."

Speechless, I watch as she joins Savi onstage. The two men move back as the two women embrace. Savi hands Sky the microphone and the applause of the crowd simmers down.

Skylar, ever the epitome of serenity and grace, looks over the room full of people.

"It's been a while, hasn't it?" She smiles as the audience chuckles. "I believe each time we evoke the name of someone who's passed on, it lets them live again. Dash was a man who loved life and he truly loved the guys in the band. They'd been together since they were kids, and he believed music was the common ground on which everyone walked. I share that sentiment. With Sam Weston's help, and without Ian's notice, I've learned much about Rock Hills. Over the past few weeks, Sam's shared its history and the vision for future expansion. Today, it's my honor to announce the formation of The Barrows Foundation for the Arts."

The room fills with applause once again. Skylar patiently waits for quiet before she continues.

"The Barrows Foundation is a three-fold venture. It will provide grant money to entrepreneurs who desire to repurpose buildings for music venues, and stipends for those using their talents in music and architecture. To finish off this trio we'll build a music venue where national acts will perform while on tour and, with your help, Dash's memory will live on."

Everyone in the room is now standing, and hoots and hollers ring out.

"A long time ago, Savannah Grace won a song-writing contest and Boundless Hearts recorded the song 'Heal Me'. That song gained them their first platinum record. Today, we have three or the original four here to play it for you." She waves me up to the stage. "C'mon, Ian."

It feels surreal as I cross the room and step on the stage, and I sweep a look over the room. There's electricity in the air; a collective anticipation of what will happen next.

Skylar steps off the stage. Savi follows but stops.

"Are you okay?" She asks.

I shake my head as I pick up the guitar. "Baby. I can't believe you pulled all of this off."

She shrugs it off. "It was just a few phone calls," she says as she looks up at me with those big blue eyes that sparkle like sapphires. She's never looked more beautiful to me. Her long, blonde hair cascades down her back in soft waves. Her sweet expression adds to her delicate features giving her a radiant glow. I lean down to give her a tender kiss. "You're an amazing woman."

"And you're a wonderful man." She tips her head toward Charlie and Tom who are up on the stage and ready to perform. "Have fun."

I roll my shoulders, releasing the tension that collected there. Mic cords and speaker cables run around the stage. It all takes me back.

I don't think I've stepped on Mad Dog's stage since I've been here. I adjust the mic and stand so it's just the right height and angle. Taking a breath, I look out at the faces of the people.

"Savannah wrote 'Heal Me', but she didn't intend for it to be played the way we recorded it. I look to Charlie and Tom. "I'd like to do it her way, guys. Follow me, okay?"

Near the back of the room, Savi sits at a table with Sam, Cora, Gigi, and Marcus. Her eyes are fixed on me, and I'm overcome with a sudden wave of emotion.

"Baby, come up here and sing this with me."

She nods, smiling, and kisses Gigi, then passes her to Cora before coming up to the stage.

"You know, I'm a lucky bastard," I say into the mic. "I got a second chance—you all know the story. I'm not sure I deserve it, but I'll take it." I point and look up. "This one's for you, brother."

I clear my throat of emotion and begin to play the intro. I've sung these words a hundred times, but I finally get the message. I feel the words the way Savannah meant them, only this time instead of falling off my lips, they're coming from deep down inside.

They say making mistakes is a part of life

And I say that's good livin'
Sin'll stain your mortal soul
And some things ain't forgiven ...

She picks up the second part and I feel the heart and soul of the song. It's like I got a new life, and it feels damn good to be here.

Ian

My two girls.

I look over at Savi and Gigi—*my* Gigi. The part of my soul that'll live long after my physical body ceases to exist even though, at one time, I thought it would be in the best interest of humanity that my bloodline end with me.

Not when I look at her.

She's perfect.

"It's going to be a gorgeous night." I look over at the woman by my side. The sky behind her is ablaze with swatches of orange, pink, and purple, promising a beautiful sunset. She holds my hand as we walk to the barn, admiring the flowers.

"I see you planted bleeding hearts. They're one of my favorites but I'm not sure they'll make it out here. It's too hot."

"They will. I'll find a way."

She bumps against my side and looks at me, wrinkling her nose, as I pull her close and Gigi runs to the corral. I let the rescue horse roam while the three of us had supper. She's getting used to the place. Just like Savi and Gigi.

I've heard it said that having a kid changes everything. The time I've spent with Gigi proves that statement. I feel like there are two chapters in my life story: one of death and destruction, and one of rebirth. The only love I'd ever known was what I learned from my mother's brief existence and the love of a friend. Now, I have so much love I have a new thirst for life. I spend my days seeing the world through Gigi's eyes. Everything seems fresh and new. At night, I have the love of a good woman—a woman who's promised to be my wife.

I watch as Gigi goes to the fence to feed the horse an apple.

"When are you going to give your horse a name?" I ask.

"I did aw'ready but it's a secret." She props a hand on her hip. I'm happy to see she's getting back that sassy little way she's got about her.

"Well, you never told me."

"It's a secret."

"A secret, huh? You didn't name her one of those bad words I say sometimes, did you?"

"No, silly. A boo-tiful angel who loves you gived it to me—and angels don't use bad words." She turns to the horse and pets her with a now slobber-covered hand. "He's so silly."

"An angel loves me, huh?" I look to Savannah. "You know anything about angels? Other than what I told you about my momma?"

She returns the question in my eyes with a blank stare, shrugs, and puts up her hands. "Don't look at me. I don't know anything about it."

We enjoy a few silent moments, breathing in the approaching night air as the sky transforms, shifting and blending like a slow-moving kaleidoscope.

A whoosh of wind sends a high-pitched whistle through the trees, swirling dirt that dances in the air.

"Feels like a storm's coming," I call out to Gigi. "C'mon kiddo. It's time to go inside for the night. I'll come back out and put your no-name horse in the barn."

"Okay."

"Listen to that singsong, sweet voice she uses with you. It's like she loves you or something," Savannah says.

"*Or something*, most likely," I tease.

We turn toward the house as Gigi slaps her hands together to knock off a mixture of slobber, horse hair, and dirt. No doubt Savannah will have her in the bath as soon as we go inside.

"I just love her!" Gigi gushes as she runs to join us, and she slips her grubby hand in mine. She nearly trips over her feet as she walks and turns to steal one more glance at her horse.

"Good night, Peaches! I love you."

The End

WANT to know more about ROCK HILLS? Next up is Borrowed Time: Rock Hills Book 2. Turn the page for Chapter One.

THANK YOU!

Thank you for reading!

DD

xoxo

CHAPTER 1

Lily

I used to wake up ready to chase the world. Today, I just want out of its reach.

The city wakes up like it always does, loud, unyielding, and already in motion before my feet touch the floor. Horns echo off high-rises, sirens wail somewhere in the distance, and footsteps pound the pavement with purpose. It's a place that thrives on noise, hustle, and the next thing. But inside of me, something else is happening. A quiet unraveling. Not a dramatic one, and definitely not visible. It feels like a slow undoing that hums beneath the surface that's as soft as breath, sharp as loss. Somehow, the city doesn't notice when people need a break. Maybe it never did.

Soft morning light spills through the floor-to-ceiling windows of my Manhattan condo, stretching in lazy gold slices across polished concrete floors.

Outside, the world rises fast. The early hour commandeers espresso machines to serve the masses. I'm familiar with the hiss in the café below. Taxis blare their impatience while a man on his phone barks orders like the sidewalk is his stage. I hear his muffled voice. Every day, the sounds blend together, orchestrated by the demands of the business world. It's the same city song that once set my pulse racing. Today, it just makes me tired.

Glancing across the room, I see my suitcase waiting by the door. It's a hard-shell, cobalt blue vintage one I found tucked in the back corner of a consignment shop in SoHo. I got a rush of excitement the second I saw it, and something in me paused. That deep, unapologetic cobalt was a bold hue I used to wear, and the piece called to me. My mother once said the old Samsonite was "Hepburn chic," and she was right. A little classic. A little rebellious. A little me.

I packed it two days ago, folding my clothes into rolls like Elena taught me on our post-college trip through Europe. Back then, organizing calmed me. It made the world feel smaller, simpler, a bit more under my control. This time, I packed slowly. Not just clothes, but pieces of solace. My softest cardigan. Worn jeans. The scarf my mother knitted for me when I moved to the city. And of course, my favorite coffee mug. I even took time to queue a playlist for the ride, filled with acoustic tracks and cello instrumentals; Brandi Carlile, Fleetwood Mac, the classic, timeless songs of the Beatles. These are the tunes that once steadied me. Each note hits like a memory I didn't know I needed, wielding a soundtrack for an ending I can't yet name.

My apartment is silent. Too silent but not sound-proof. It's designed to perfection. Everything is arranged just so, including the art books and throw pillows in intentional colors. My kitchen counter gleams like it's never been used. Once, that felt like control. Now, it feels like a showroom for someone else's life. It also explains why I said yes when my parents asked if I wanted to co-own the cottage.

Brighton Wharf has always been our vacation spot. Every summer, we return like pilgrims. The same creaky dock. The same sea-salted mornings. The same traditions that tether us to the place. When the cottage came up for sale, my parents said they didn't need my money—but they wanted my name on the deed. My heart is, and always has been, in that place, and I said yes before they could finish the sentence. Now I'm driving there. No assignments. No deadlines. Just me, my suitcase, and the kind of homesick ache I can't explain.

The elevator hums as I descend, and I catch my reflection in the mirrored walls. I'm wearing no makeup. There's no Zoom meetings and no profes-sional appearance today. Just Lily. The woman whose name is under the headlines. It took me a while, but I've become the one who no longer believes my worth is measured by what I accomplish before breakfast.

I hit the West Side Highway, and the city exhales

behind me. That's when I engage the playlist, and the unknotting begins. My muscles loosen. My mind quiets. I let it. As soon as I hit the back roads, I roll down the window and breathe.

An hour into the ride, my phone buzzes. I press the button on the steering wheel.

"Hey, Mom."

"Hi, sweetheart. Are you on your way?" Her voice is soft, but something in it perks up my ears. She sounds like she's been waiting to share good news.

"I am," I say. "Just passed Stamford."

She hums that maternal sound that says everything without saying a word. "Lily, everything is so pretty. I hope you love it. The curtains are up. The guest room's finished, and you wouldn't believe the butterflies this morning! Monarchs, swallowtails, even one I didn't recognize. I watched them from bed for almost half an hour. It felt like they were dancing just for me."

She's so happy, and I love the joy in her voice. My mom is the best, and she deserves this dream. I blink fast against sudden tears. "Sounds like we need to name the place the Butterfly Bypass."

She laughs. "I love that! Let's do it."

"What's Dad doing?"

"Your father's working on the crossword. He won't admit it, but he loves this place already."

That lands. My dad isn't a man of easy sentiment, but if he's found peace here after a lifetime of working, then I know I will.

"Want me to grab a pizza?"

"Perfect. He's starting a fire. I saved that bottle of red."

When the call ends, I don't turn the music back on. I let the silence wrap around me like something sacred.

Somewhere near New Haven, I cry. Not because anything is wrong but because the release feels holy. There's something about getting away from work, the city, and all the things on a to-do list. At some point, the pressure loosens. It's as if my body remembers I've been holding too tightly for too long and is finally telling me to let go.

As the road narrows, the signs change, and the trees bend toward each other. They look like they're whispering secrets, their leaves filtering the sunlight until a soft golden glow falls across the pavement. The air shifts, and Brighton Wharf doesn't feel like a destination. It feels like a memory come to life.

I spot the cottage as I turn onto the street, and it's everything we ever hoped for. Weathered gray shingles. White trim. Massive blue, pink, and purple hydrangeas spilling over. When you've loved a place for so long, it paints a picture in your mind. Now, that picture belongs to the three of us.

When I pull into the driveway, the front door opens before I can cut the engine. My mother steps out in her slippers, arms already outstretched, her expression pure joy. My father lingers on the porch behind her, his hands braced on the railing.

"You're here!" Mom wraps me up before I can even close the door.

"Yes. Finally," I whisper.

We meander to the door, arm in arm. Dad moves aside as she pulls me into the house, where the air smells like lavender and sea salt. A fire glows in the hearth, and above it, the mantle is decorated with the unusual shells we've collected over the years on our morning beach walks. The walls are painted a soft, watery blue. Everything is peaceful and simple but nothing feels small. I stand in the doorway, breath catching.

"It's beautiful. I don't know how you got it all done so fast, not to mention, without that horrible paint smell."

"That wasn't me, Lily. I hired painters and asked them to add something to cut the scent, but thank you. I worked hard this week to put a few touches on it to make it feel like ours. I know you'll want to add your own too. I just wanted it to feel like a sanctuary."

"It does, Mom. It really does."

Her eyes soften as she leans in and rests her head against mine.

* * *

BORROWED TIME: Rock Hills Book 3

WANT to know what DD's up to? Sign up for her newsletter at www.ddlorenzo.com.

Turn the page to read the acknowledgments.

ACKNOWLEDGMENTS

No one writes a book alone and these past years have been about rebuilding and restructuring. I have some special people in my corner, and I'd like to acknowledge these folks for their friendship, love, and support.

Rhonda, if not for your prodding, Ian's story would never have been told. Thank you for prompting me to give him his narrative.

Nickiann and Cheryl, thank you for your friendship and your input. You both help me to make my stories better.

Samantha, you are an amazing woman, and I'm so blessed by your talent and our friendship. You've been an anchor for me through some very tough times. I love you, and am forever grateful to know you.

Willow, your friendship is truly a blessing, as are you. You are as beautiful inside as you are on the outside, and your example as a leader in the industry is an encouragement to many, including me. I love your positivity. It's effervescent! I love you, sweet friend.

Lydia, I absolutely love and adore you. Your laughter fills any space you occupy, and your professionalism in this business is inspirational. Your chicken soup is as magical and healing as your tender heart. You are, truly, one of a kind—the good kind.

Ellie, thank you for your ability to reduce any geek issue to a level I understand. You're a remarkable woman, and our friendship is a joy.

Michelle, your smile is as sweet as your heart, and I'm so proud of you for so many reasons. Pushing through and moving forward in any situation isn't easy, and you've done it with an amazing display of grace. I'm looking forward to our growing friendship.

Heather, thank you for all you've brought to the writing world, and to me. I'm in awe and inspired by your innovative spirit and your friendship.

Mimi, you, your light heart, and your boisterous laugh jolt me from my seriousness. It may seem like nothing to you to make someone belly laugh, but I assure you, it's a gift, and your kindness touches my heart.

Ivone, I adore you. I always say, "Women have the power to lift each other up, or rip each other up. It's a choice." Thank you for always, *always*, being a lifter.

Alyssa, little did I know when you went above and beyond to pull this story out of me that I would gain a friend. You've encouraged *my* voice and have renewed my confidence in my fashion of storytelling. Thank you for your hard work and your belief in me and my books.

Renita, your constant encouragement and expertise in this industry have made me a better storyteller. I'm grateful for your friendship and the work you put into my stories. Onward and upward, lady!

Jon, thank you for continuing to believe in me even when you thought I'd stopped believing in you, and for reminding me to look everyday for the sparkles.

Sandy, Bernie, Debbie, Carol, and Chrissy, you know what you mean to me and how much I love each one of you. If you have any doubts (or want to hear me repeat myself) I'll be happy to revisit the topic with you anytime over lunch/dinner/cocktails, LOL!

Rich and Paul, the neighborhood "Breakfast Club." Who would have thought that the worst of circumstances would bring into my life the best cheerleaders? Thank you for your encouragement, your love and friendship, and our lunch and coffee dates. Whenever I venture out of the writing cave you guys always keep me smiling. Your friendship is a gift, and I love you both.

Matt, you're one of a kind for so many reasons. I love you. Thanks for being there whenever I need you.

Rick, I'm so glad God gave me you for a brother. I'm not sure I can articulate how much I love you. Tough times have made us closer, but, no matter what, I always know you're there for me. Your support means the world to me, as does your love and understanding. Thank you for encouraging this chapter of my life and emboldening me to chase my dreams.

Mom, I love you. You sometimes drive me crazy, but that's the nature of mothers and daughters. If not for you

I would have given up writing a long time ago. I thought I'd done so when, at fourteen, you said you were going to send something of mine to a publisher. I got so anxious about it I tossed a box of manuscripts into the trash. After you recovered from your shock (anger) over my actions, you encouraged (nagged) me to write again (and publish). Thank you. It was the encouraging push (shove) I needed.

Dom and Lane, you are my reasons. You are my joy. You are everything good in my little world. If you asked me for the moon I'd try my hardest to give it to you. Forever, and always, I love you a bushel and a peck.

Amy and Megan, you are my heart. You're brilliant, beautiful, and kind. There isn't *ANYTHING* you can't do. You both possess a sweet inner strength that carries you through the days. You're equal parts fierce and tender, and I love you beyond measure. Thank you for encouraging me to allow my characters to speak without censure and to put their thoughts, hopes, dreams, and disappointments on the page, no holds barred. I hope to be an example to you that there's no dream too far you can't reach, and you're never too old to dream them. I love you both a bushel and a peck.

And, finally, Jimmy D. You may not see it, but what a remarkable man you are. You love everyone. You make everyone laugh and smile. Your friendship is a gift to so many. You patiently picked up the pieces of my broken heart, and being the sweet friend you are to everyone, found something to interest me and make me smile. Words. Through crossword puzzles and jokes that I never seemed to get, you joined the legions of friends and family who were helping me glue myself back together. Then friendship became love. A very different kind of love than the one I so painfully lost. I wasn't looking for anything of the sort when your love found me. The countless tears you wiped away eventually morphed from sad ones to happy, and all the while you encouraged me to just be myself. With each day that passes you remind me that I'm not where I want to be, but I'm not where I used to be. You are a born encourager and an amazing man. You blessed a part of my life I thought I'd tucked away forever. No matter how dark things might be, you make me see the bright side, and with it my days have become easier and my heart has found peace. I love you, and I thank you for loving me.

OTHER TITLES BY DD LORENZO

The IMPERFECTION Series

No Perfect Man

No Perfect Time

No Perfect Couple

No Perfect Secret

No Perfect Woman

No Perfect Beginning: An IMPERFECTION Series Prequel

The ROCK HILLS Series

Boundless Hearts: A ROCK HILLS Origin Story

Bone Dust: Rock Hills Book 2

Borrowed Time: Rock Hills Book 3

Standalones

Indiscretion

(An Aleatha Romig's Infidelity World Novella)

Heels, Rhymes, & Nursery Crimes

(A multi-author series)

Twinkle, Twinkle Little Star: Fragile Flower to Femme Fatale

ABOUT DD LORENZO

DD Lorenzo is an award-winning author of Women's Fiction and Romantic Suspense novels. She loves coffee, long lunches with good friends, and fresh flowers to balance her obsession with anti-heroes. You can find her most days plotting and planning her character's lives from her beach house on the Delaware shore.

To stay updated with DD's books, please visit her website at www.ddlorenzobooks.com and sign up for her newsletter. Want the inside scoop? Join DD's reader group, DD's Diamonds, at www.facebook.com/groups/ddsdiamonds

Stay connected with DD:

facebook.com/ddlorenzo.author

x.com/ddlorenzobooks

instagram.com/ddlorenzobooks

pinterest.com/ddlorenzo

bookbub.com/authors/d-d-lorenzo

goodreads.com/D_D_Lorenzo